CAROL FINCH

'Carol Finch is known for her lightning-fast, roller-coaster-
ride adventure romances that are brimming over with a large

one of the best historical Westerns I've read—ever!'
—*Romance Reader at Heart*

Carol Finch, who received her BS degree from Oklahoma State University and taught writing at Oklahoma Community College, Redlands Community College and Oklahoma University's School of Writing, is a member of Romance Writers of America® and has been inducted into the Oklahoma Professional Writers' Hall of Fame. She has received nineteen nominations and nine career achievement awards from *RT Book Reviews* for Historical Love and Laughter, Historical Adventure, Best Contemporary Romance and Storyteller of the Year, and has won the RomCon award for Best Romantic Suspense. Carol Finch has been a published author for more than twenty years.

Elizabeth Lane has lived and travelled in many parts of the world, including Europe, Latin America and the Far East, but her heart remains in the American West, where she was born and raised. Her idea of heaven is hiking a mountain trail on a clear autumn day. She also enjoys music, animals and dancing. You can learn more about Elizabeth by visiting her website at www.elizabethlaneauthor.com

Pam Crooks grew up in the heartland of Nebraska's sandhills, where the code of the Old West still runs strong. She read her first romance novel way back in the '70s, and she's still reading them today. Even better, she loves to write them, too. Since 2001 she has had over ten historical Western romances hit the shelves. She is one of the founders of the popular website Petticoats & Pistols, a ten-author blog dedicated to promoting Western romance: www.petticoatsandpistols.com Pam still resides in Nebraska, with her husband (who is not a cowboy) and their growing family—four daughters, two sons-in-law and three grandchildren. Contact Pam via e-mail from her website, www.pamcrooks.com, or snail mail at PO Box 540122, Omaha, NE 68154, USA.

COWBOY CHRISTMAS

BY

CAROL FINCH
ELIZABETH LANE
PAM CROOKS

First published in Great Britain 2010
by Mills & Boon, an imprint of Harlequin (UK) Limited.
Large Print edition 2011
Harlequin (UK) Limited, Eton House,
18-24 Paradise Road, Richmond, Surrey TW9 1SR

© Harlequin Books S.A. 2009

ISBN: 978 0 263 22405 4

The publisher acknowledges the copyright holders of the
individual works as follows:

A HUSBAND FOR CHRISTMAS
© Connie Feddersen 2009

THE HOMECOMING
© Elizabeth Lane 2009

THE CATTLEMAN'S CHRISTMAS BRIDE
© Pam Crooks 2009

Harlequin (UK) policy is to use papers that are natural,
renewable and recyclable products and made from wood grown in
sustainable forests. The logging and manufacturing process conform
to the legal environmental regulations of the country of origin.

Printed and bound in Great Britain
by CPI Antony Rowe, Chippenham, Wiltshire

CONTENTS

A HUSBAND FOR CHRISTMAS

Carol Finch

This story is dedicated to my husband, Ed, and our children, Jill, Jon, Christie, Durk, Shawnna and Kurt. And to our grandchildren, Kennedy, Blake, Dillon, Livia, Brooklynn and Harleigh. Hugs and kisses!

Chapter One

Lone Ridge, Texas 1880s

Victoria Thurston paced back and forth across her neatly organized office at the rear of the bakery she had owned and operated for the past eighteen months. She paused to inhale a fortifying breath as she stared—for the forty-eleventh time—at the disturbing letter she had received from her mother.

You have become a successful businesswoman, she reassured herself. You should have enough self-confidence to approach Marshal Daniels with your request.

Only she hadn't worked up enough *nerve* yet. Victoria huffed out her breath, hoping to relieve the knot coiling in her stomach. Every time the vision of Marshal Logan Daniels popped to mind, she broke into a sweat. Yet, the city marshal was

the only man alive who could resolve her problem
and place her in good standing with her parents.

"Otherwise, I'll have to conveniently dispose of
the city marshal," she mumbled to herself. "That
might alleviate my immediate problem, but it will
spoil the festive holiday season."

"What am I saying!" she scowled at herself. "Just
get this over with so you'll know if you have to
resort to drastic measures."

Before her firm resolve fizzled out Victoria wheeled toward the door. She locked up the
bakery, drew herself up to the full extent of her
five-foot-six-inch stature and pelted toward the
marshal's office. Still a bundle of twitching nerves,
she halted outside the door to drag in a calming
breath. Not that it helped. She was a nervous wreck
and she had yet to utter one word of her unusual
proposition.

Although she had been practicing what she intended to say for the past half hour, her mind went
blank when a deep, commanding voice boomed
like a cannon from the other side of the door.

"Stop that racket and sit down right now!"

Victoria's confidence shattered when the city
marshal whipped open the door and nearly mowed

her over on his way out. The scowl on his bronzed face evaporated as he stared down at her. She felt dwarfed by his muscular six-foot-three-inch frame and her resolve crumbled in one second flat. She squelched the impulse to turn tail and run back to the bakery.

The powerfully built marshal, who was even more physically appealing at close range, stared at her quizzically. She gathered her bravado and tilted her head back to meet his dark-eyed gaze.

"Marshal, I'd like a word with you, but if I have come at a bad time, I can return later," she said over the racket ricocheting off the cells at the rear of the office.

Logan Daniels tipped his hat politely then gestured for her to come inside. "Now is fine, ma'am. My prisoner can chew on his fingernails to stave off hunger until his breakfast arrives."

"I could bring him some pastries from my bakery—"

"No need," he interrupted as he gestured for her to take a seat. "I'm sure Henry Porter will be here shortly. I was going to check on him but we'll wait him out." He glanced curiously at her. "What can I do for you, ma'am?"

Victoria plunked into the chair, but nervousness put her back on her feet as the marshal sank into his seat behind his desk—which was as well organized as hers. She glanced toward the cells where a male prisoner was scraping his tin cup against the metal bars and demanding to be served breakfast immediately. When she refocused on the ruggedly handsome marshal, her courage faltered once again.

"Pipe down, Tanner, or you'll skip breakfast altogether," the marshal thundered ominously.

Victoria wrung her hands, fiddled with the pleats of her green dress then drew in a determined breath. "You probably don't know me, Marshal, but—"

"You're Victoria Thurston," he interrupted, watching her curiously, while she paced back and forth across the office.

She halted then blinked. She was surprised he knew her. Although they hadn't been formally introduced, she had admired him from afar since she opened for business.

"Please call me Tori," she requested.

He smiled slightly then inclined his raven head. "Very well, Tori. How can I help?"

The moment of reckoning had come. She bolstered her courage and blurted out, "I have a proposition for you."

"Really? I usually arrest women who proposition me."

She hadn't expected a teasing sense of humor from a man who was in the very serious business of dealing with murderers and thieves. Since he was having fun at her expense, she was not particularly amused. She was far too nervous and apprehensive for that.

"Let me rephrase that, Marshal—"

"Logan," he corrected with a smile. Then he glared over his shoulder when Tanner commenced scraping his cup against the bars again. "I told you to clam up!"

His loud voice made her flinch. She shifted uneasily from one foot to the other, ready to get this over with. "I would like to hire you for the holidays. I will pay you exceptionally well for your assistance, Marshal."

Both dark brows shot up his forehead. *"Hire me?"* he parroted. "To do what?"

Tori felt the flush of embarrassment suffuse her face and neck. In all her twenty-three years, she had never felt so awkward. Logan must have noticed her discomfort because one black brow climbed a mite higher and his sensuous lips twitched as he studied her astutely.

She gathered every smidgen of courage she had left and said, "If you aren't otherwise engaged and can get away from your duties in town, I would like to hire you to be my husband for the holidays."

His onyx eyes nearly popped from their sockets and his unshaven jaw scraped his chest. He stared at her as if she were a strange and curious creature from another galaxy far, far away. *"Marry you?"* he chirped.

"Pretend to," she amended hastily, and then went back to her pacing.

When Tanner struck up another racket to complain about his delayed breakfast, Tori whirled toward the door leading to the cells. She glared at the scraggly haired, unkempt prisoner who stopped making a commotion to stare owlishly at her.

"Sir," she said tersely. "I am having a serious conversation with the marshal. Where I come from it is considered very rude to interrupt. I will gladly furnish you with a variety of pastries from my bakery if you will allow me to conduct my business here."

Tanner kerplunked onto the cot and stared curiously at her. "What flavors you got, bakery lady?"

"Apple, peach and vanilla-filled tarts that will make your mouth water," she tempted him.

He nodded his greasy brown head agreeably and flashed a smile that called attention to his two oversize front teeth that reminded her of a horse. A moment later, Henry Porter arrived with a tray from his restaurant.

Tanner glanced from the stocky, bald-headed café proprietor to Tori. "I still get the pastries, too. Right?"

"Certainly. My treat. And happy holidays to you, Tanner," she said cheerily.

"Not gonna be happy days if I have to spend them in the calaboose," Tanner grumbled. "I'm innocent."

"No, you aren't," Logan scoffed in contraction as Tori stepped aside to let Porter slide the tray of food under the bars.

Logan appraised the strikingly attractive bakery owner pensively as she came toward him. He was still reeling after her unexpected request. He couldn't fathom why this shapely brunette, who had discouraged potential suitors since her arrival in town, wanted him to marry her. *Pretend to marry her*, he corrected silently.

What was the catch? There had to be a catch. There was always a catch. Logan was a man who dealt in—and dispensed—consequences. Plus, in thirty-two years of hardscrabble existence, he'd learned that nothing was what it seemed.

Call him a cynic, but he'd suffered through enough life experiences to know that nothing was simple. Especially this attractive female with her startling Christmas request.

His appreciative gaze swept up and down Tori's alluring physique for the tenth time as she approached him. Her curly, mahogany-colored hair glistened in the light. Her luminous evergreen eyes, rimmed with long, sooty lashes, focused directly on him. Her face was still flushed and the scooped neck of her gown indicated that her flush extended farther south.

Logan wondered just how far south her blush went.

This wasn't the first time he'd visualized Tori naked, he was ashamed to say. But she had rejected so many eager suitors the past eighteen months that he had kept his distance. People had been trying to gun him down for years. He didn't need to be gunned down—in a manner of speaking—by a woman. Even the one who had caught his eye the moment she arrived in town.

"Now then, Marshal—"

"Logan," he corrected again.

"Yes, of course, Logan. I realize this is highly unusual."

"You can say that again," he mumbled. "Why do you need to hire a husband?"

"Not just any husband," she inserted quickly. "Just you in particular."

Logan supposed he should be flattered, but he was too cautious by nature and profession not to expect the other boot to drop. "Explain," he requested.

Tori opened her mouth to do just that, but she clamped her lips together when Henry Porter breezed into the main office.

"Sorry for the delay, Marshal," said Henry. "We had an excessive number of customers show up at the same time this morning. The town council is having breakfast while reviewing the last-minute details for the town's holiday festivities."

"Not a problem for me, but Tanner is a bit on the impatient side. Which is why he tried to take money from the bank before he made a deposit," Logan said wryly.

Henry snickered as he nodded his shiny head. Then he smiled at Tori and doubled at the waist in a respectful bow. "Always a pleasure to see you, Miss Thurston. I trust you will furnish us with a few of your delicious pies this afternoon. The usual half dozen, I hope?"

"Of course. I'll get started after I finish my conversation with the marshal," she assured him.

Logan bit back a grin when Henry exited and Tori wrung her hands while she paced.

"I made a critical mistake," she admitted. "However, I did prevent my father from forcing me to close down my business and return home to Fort Worth." She whirled around to pace in the opposite direction. "Six months ago, when my parents insisted that I come home to marry the 'nice young man' they had earmarked for me, I informed them that I had married the marshal of Lone Ridge so they needn't fret over my safety here in West Texas."

Logan barked a laugh then compressed his lips when Tori halted to narrow her eyes at him. "So we have been married for six months already, have we? You do know where people go for lying, don't you?" he teased mischievously.

She planted her hands on his desk and leaned forward. His gaze dropped to the enticing hint of cleavage she unknowingly displayed. Logan had the wildest urge to reach out to drag her across his desk and kiss those lush pink lips right off of her. He was grateful that he was sitting behind his desk. Otherwise, she would know exactly how—and to what extent—she was affecting him.

"It was a white lie," she insisted self-righteously.

"How do those compare to the black ones?" he couldn't help but taunt. "How much are you willing to pay for the white lie that involves *me*?"

She pushed away from the desk and stood erect. "As much as you make in two months," she tempted him.

He whistled, impressed, then said, "Plus my bounties and rewards? Your bakery must be doing well."

"*Plus* bounties *and* rewards?" She scowled at him. "I never expected highway robbery from a well-respected law enforcement officer."

He shrugged and grinned. "White lies don't come cheap, you know. You have to pay here and now or in the Hereafter. Your choice."

When she flashed him an agitated glance, he bit back another grin. Teasing Victoria Thurston was the most fun he'd had in a long time. She added an intriguing spark in his otherwise difficult life of dealing with thugs and scalawags who refused to call a moratorium, just because it was the Christmas holidays.

"Very well then, I'll pay the equivalent of two month's salary *plus* bounties, *if* you agree to accompany me to Fort Worth for the holidays." She stared hopefully at him. "You can get away for a few days, can't you? Deputy Horton can fill in, can't he?"

"If I ask him nicely, I suppose."

Gabe Horton, like Logan, had no family to visit during the holiday season. Ordinarily Logan and Gabe worked the holidays together and shared Christmas dinner over the desk in the office. Hell, Logan had no idea what it was like to share the holidays with family. It would be a new experience for him. Maybe afterward he'd fully understand the jokes he'd heard about dealing with in-laws.

Tori half collapsed in relief. "Thank you," she gushed. "I backed myself into this corner when I informed my parents that I was married. If you hadn't agreed to come with me, I was going to have to concoct a tale of your extraordinary bravery and your unfortunate demise in the line of duty."

Logan chuckled when he discovered this spirited female had planned to dispose of him—figuratively speaking—if he didn't agree to her holiday charade. This was an entirely new twist from criminals who actually *had been* trying to kill him for years, in hopes of escaping the long arm of the law.

"Mind if I ask why you didn't inform your parents that I had to be on duty during the holidays and we couldn't get away? That's a reasonable explanation."

Tori went back to her restless pacing. Not that he minded. It gave him the opportunity to admire her feminine physique without staring rudely at her enticing curves and swells.

"My older sister, Priscilla, her husband and her five-year-old son are coming from Boston for the holidays. It's her yearly visit to Texas," she elaborated. "Since I was busy establishing my business last year, I stayed here for the holidays. My parents sent out the royal command that you and I must put in an appearance because no one has met you. Therefore, I'm forced to produce you for their inspection or dispose of you and arrive in widow's digs, lamenting my lost love."

"You wouldn't have had to kill me off," he suggested. "You could have hired an imposter since none of your family has met me. Edgar Scott from the general store has a terrible crush on you, you know. He might have taken the job for nothing."

She paused to glare over her shoulder at him.

Then she wrinkled her nose, shook her mahogany-colored head and said, "Edgar isn't my type."

"And I am?" he teased devilishly. "What is your type, Tori?"

"You are having entirely too much fun at my expense," she grumbled. "If I wasn't at your mercy, I would have plenty to say about it, I promise you that."

Logan didn't doubt it. From what he'd seen of Tori, she was a strong-minded, independent woman who could speak for herself. Still, knowing that about her, he couldn't curtail the exotic speculations of what it might be like to have Tori at his mercy and wrapped up in his arms. Her hypnotic green eyes and kissable lips were inspiring all sorts of fantasies that he had trouble controlling.

Logan gave himself a mental slap for what he was thinking and tried to distract himself by asking, "When do we leave for our holiday trip, *dear*?"

"In two days, *darling*," she replied, beaming with delight. "If you don't have formal clothing for the Christmas Eve ball my parents host annually then—"

"Whoa, hold your horses, honeybunch," he hooted in interruption. "This pretend marriage is becoming more complicated by the minute. This is going to cost extra if I have to purchase formal clothing. Plus, I can't dance."

She flicked her wrist dismissively. "Not to worry. I'll teach you. Just pack your party manners and a stylish new suit and I'll pay for the extra trouble. Even if this trip is going to be more expensive than I anticipated it will be well worth it to satisfy my family's curiosity about our marriage."

Logan didn't have any party manners and he was beginning to feel uncertain about pulling off the charade. He'd grown up in poverty in a border town in southern Texas. With only a few years of formal education under his belt he'd been forced to support himself by herding cattle, battling outlaws, renegade Indians and inclement weather.

He had the sneaking suspicion that Tori Thurston came from money and that he was not her type at all. He was simply part of her white lie and she planned to tolerate his presence to save face with her stuffy family.

Maybe being without family wasn't so bad after all.

He was on the verge of telling her the deal was off, no matter what she was paying for a hired husband. However, the moment he stared into those intriguing green eyes he sensed there was much more to the story. Something that drove her to swallow her pride and embarrassment and approach him with her unusual proposition.

Unfortunately Logan didn't have the chance to ask prying questions about the circumstances of this holiday get-together because Tanner commenced scraping his cup against the bars, demanding a drink of water and the mouthwatering pastries Tori had promised him.

"Thank you, Logan. I'm indebted to you," Tori murmured as she spun toward the door. "I'll do my best to make this holiday with my family as painless as possible for you. Tell Tanner I'm on my way to fetch his confections."

She whizzed off like a whirlwind that had breezed in to disrupt his life then left his mind spinning with wary apprehension. His lack of proper upbringing would likely be glaringly apparent to the Thurstons of Fort Worth. He had earned respect in this town because he was handy with his fists and a variety of weapons and very little frightened him these days. But suddenly uncertainty and self-doubt hounded him. Feeling uneasy, he strode off to inform his prisoner that his bakery treats were on their way.

* * *

Tori expelled a gigantic sigh of relief as she returned to the bakery. She anticipated several obstacles along the way, but she hoped to get through the holidays with her well-meaning but maddening family. With a little coaching for Logan, she felt certain she could fool her sister and parents into thinking she was happily married. That would complete the image of her successful career in this outpost community in West Texas that had become a thriving crossroads for travelers and supply wagons moving back and forth between army garrisons and trading posts.

Her footsteps faltered when she looked beyond resolving the immediate problem of hiring a husband and speculated on the inevitability of visits to Fort Worth for future holidays.

"Well, I'll worry about that when the time comes," she told herself dismissively. "Once I've produced a husband for their inspection, I can use the excuse that Logan has to remain in Lone Ridge to keep the peace while his deputy takes well deserved time off."

She had no idea what she'd do if her parents came to visit *her*. That was another bridge she'd cross later.

After Tori unlocked the door to the bakery, several customers arrived. She set aside Tanner's treats and the custard pie she planned to offer Logan for agreeing to play her charade. While she waited on her customers, it occurred to her that she didn't know anything about Logan's likes and dislikes, his taste in food, his leisure activities or anything else.

All she knew was that the brawny lawman appealed to her physically and that pretending to be smitten with him in front of her family wouldn't require a great deal of acting. All she had to do was venture close enough to inhale Logan's masculine scent—just as she had done this morning when she leaned across his desk to get right in his handsome face. She'd stared at his sensuous lips and wondered what it would be like to kiss him. Then she'd become lost in those fathomless midnight-colored eyes that were surrounded by thick lashes.

She knew absolutely nothing about his background but she speculated that his ancestry was a combination of white, Indian and Spanish. Whatever the exact combination, his dark complexion, dark eyes, thick raven hair and muscular physique was enough to make even the most self-disciplined and pragmatic woman—of which she prided herself in being—swoon.

After the steady stream of customers made their purchases then trotted off, Tori gathered the pie and pastries to deliver to the jail. The prisoner licked his lips in eager anticipation when Tori crouched down to scoot the plate beneath the bars. He snatched up an apple tart, drizzled with icing, and bit into it. Then he leered at her and said, "Damn this tastes as good as you look, sugar."

"Watch your mouth, Tanner, or you can forget about your tasty treats."

When Logan's deep voice rumbled close behind her, Tori nearly slammed face-forward into the barred door. She hadn't heard him enter the back room. She pivoted in her crouched position to peer at Logan who loomed over the prisoner like a thundercloud. My, he can be extremely intimidating when he wants, she noted.

Tanner, who was only two inches taller than Tori, snatched up all the treats and curled up on the cot before Logan did as he threatened. He shoved the pastries in his mouth with both hands. Disgusted by his table manners, Tori came to her feet and strode away. With Logan a step behind her, she halted beside the pie she had placed atop the over-size safe that graced the corner of the office.

"This custard pie is my way of saying thank-you for your cooperation. If you don't care for it, I'll exchange it for one that I'm baking for Henry at the restaurant."

"Custard is fine." Then he said unexpectedly, "I think we should go to dinner this evening. If we are pretending to be married, we need to get to know each other better before we arrive in Fort Worth."

"Of course, I was thinking the same thing myself." She offered him a smile. "Shall I meet you at Porter's Café after you're off duty?"

He shook his dark head. "I'll pick you up at your house."

She arched a quizzical brow. "You know where I live?"

He grinned wryly. "I *am* the city marshal, ya know. I make it my business to know everyone in town. It goes with the job of protecting the public. Last summer I followed you home one night after dark."

Her brow rose even higher and he added, "A drifter was trailing after you and I wanted to make sure he didn't do something I was going to make him regret."

Tori inclined her head slightly. "Thank you for that. I guess I'll see you this evening..."

Her voice trailed off when the deputy entered the office. Although Gabe Horton's complexion, his height and muscular stature were similar to Logan's, it was the marshal who drew Tori's gaze and inspired her speculative thoughts.

Not that Gabe wasn't appealing in his own right, she amended.

He just wasn't Logan Daniels.

The auburn-haired deputy, who looked to be one or two years younger than Logan, glanced between them, and then stared at the pie sitting atop the safe. His brows rose in wry amusement as he turned his attention back to Logan. "What did you do to earn a special-delivery pie?"

Logan ignored the teasing question and focused on Tori. "I'll be there at seven."

"Be where at seven?" Gabe asked interestedly as he watched Tori's hasty departure. "Did I miss something?"

"Yep." Logan scooped up a slice of pie then took a bite. His taste buds went into full-scale riot and the delicious dessert melted on his tongue. "Damn, that woman can cook like nobody's business," he said around the mouthful of food.

"Not to mention that she looks good doing it." Gabe helped himself to a slice. "I'll ask again, Logan. What did you do to deserve this pie?"

"I married her."

Gabe choked on his pie. Logan reached over to whack him between the shoulder blades until he caught his breath.

"You *what?*" Gabe croaked, frog-eyed.

"I'm going to Fort Worth with her in two days to become her holiday husband."

His longtime friend stared incredulously at him while Logan savored another bite of the tasty pie. Then Gabe said, "I don't get it."

"You don't have to get it. You just have to hold down the fort while I'm gone," Logan said between mouthwatering bites of the best crust and flavorful filling he'd ever wrapped his gums around.

"What's going to happen tonight at seven?" Gabe wanted to know as he waggled his brows suggestively.

All sorts of tantalizing visions danced in his head. None of them had anything whatsoever to do with holiday sugarplums or hasty pudding. They were erotic and arousing. Ruthlessly Logan squelched his provocative fantasies and said, "I'm taking Tori to supper so we can get to know each other better."

"*Tori?*" Gabe taunted wickedly. "You're already calling her by a pet name? Didn't know you'd worked past a first-name basis so quickly. Didn't know you were such a ladies' man, either."

Logan frowned darkly. "You know I'm not."

"Then why *you* instead of *me?*" Gabe wanted to know. "*I* can pretend to marry her and *you* can stay here for the holidays."

"She asked me first." Logan took another heavenly bite of pie. "If she keeps bringing delicious pies, I'll do anything else she asks, too."

A devilish grin pursed Gabe's lips. "Damn, Logan, you've been as tough as nails for as long as I can remember. Never figured you for such a pushover."

"A man can change," he contended as he brushed the flakes of piecrust off his shirt.

"Right before my very eyes, too, it seems." Gabe finished off his slice of pie. "Should've known your sweet tooth would become your downfall." He wheeled toward the door then said over his shoulder, "I'll be here at six o'clock to relieve you,

Romeo. You'll have time to swing by the boarding-house to get spruced up before you pick up Tori."

"Thanks, I owe you."

"Damn right you do, friend," Gabe said then left.

Logan sat there for a long moment, telling himself that he had to keep his hands off the green-eyed beauty who was his pretend wife. In addition, he shouldn't have that second piece of pie that was calling to him from atop the safe.

"You can have one but not the other," Logan bargained with himself.

Then he got up and walked over to slice off a second helping of better-than-paradise pie.

Chapter Two

The moment Tori and Logan entered Porter's Café, heads turned in synchronized rhythm. Whispered voices serenaded them as they crossed the dining room.

"This is worse than the debutante ball my parents forced me to attend after my graduation from Miss Peabody's Finishing School in Houston," Tori mumbled.

Logan nodded several greetings to acquaintances as he guided Tori to the corner table then seated himself with his back to the wall.

"I see that you and Wild Bill Hickok follow the same policy," she observed as she sat down next to Logan so she had a partial view of the customers in the restaurant.

"It's better to see trouble coming than to let it sneak up behind you. You know what happened to Hickok the one time he dispensed with caution."

She nodded grimly then changed the subject. "Where did you attend school? It's important that we know each other's background in case my parents fire questions."

"I lived with my mother until she contracted diphtheria and died."

"What of your father?" she asked. "Did you stay with him afterward?"

Logan removed his Stetson then combed his hand through his thick raven hair. Tori's fingers itched to do the same but she kept her hands clasped in her lap. It amazed her that she experienced the impulsive urge to reach out and touch Logan when other male acquaintances didn't stir such unprecedented feelings inside her.

"I wouldn't know my father if I saw him." Logan leaned forward to rest his elbows on the scarred table. "He must have been half Indian and half Mexican, I suppose… What about you?"

"Mostly English ancestry. The prim and proper variety." She smiled faintly. "I was the misfit who broke tradition and struck off to make my own life."

When Logan chuckled in amusement, a warm sensation flooded through her. For a moment, she forgot all eyes were on them, speculating about the extent of this budding friendship between them.

"Your parents certainly can't deny that you've made a success of your business." He leaned away from her when Henry Porter set two cups of steaming coffee in front of them.

When Henry strode off, promising to serve the house special, Tori shrugged. "I haven't met my parents' expectations, which is why you were dragged into these holiday festivities. You are keeping me from looking like the pathetic spinster compared to my bright, shining star of a sister."

Logan arched a dark brow. "Building your own business doesn't count?"

"No." Tori took a cautious sip of hot coffee. "The Thurstons measure success for their women by another yardstick. I was the ugly duckling who lived in my sister's shadow. I couldn't compete with her when it came to meeting my family's expectations and carrying on tradition."

Logan barked a laugh. "You aren't an ugly duckling. One glance in the mirror confirms that you're attractive."

His compliment pleased her. "Late bloomer. But Priscilla is dainty, petite, blonde and blue-eyed like our mother. Men stumble all over themselves to stare at her."

She cast him a warning glance. "You will have to restrain yourself from doing the same. I am paying you well and you need to behave as if you only have eyes for me. It will be difficult, I promise you, when you clap eyes on Cilla."

Logan sat down his cup and regarded her pensively. "You don't sound envious of your sister."

Tori blinked. "Why heavens no. However, there were times growing up when I resented my parents' lack of consideration toward me. That had nothing to do with Cilla. She's kind, gentle and deserving of the attention bestowed on her. It isn't *her* fault that I didn't fit the family mold and she never once tried to make me feel inferior."

When Henry delivered two juicy steaks, a heaped stack of potatoes and hot rolls, Logan's stomach growled in hungry anticipation. He made a point to emulate Tori's table manners for practice so he wouldn't embarrass her when they arrived at her family's home.

Personally he couldn't imagine how her parents could have ignored her in favor of their older daughter. Furthermore, he was curious to see if Priscilla was everything Tori claimed she was.

And the blonde snip had better not look down her nose at Tori, Logan mused as he took a bite of steak. No one was going to overlook or criticize his wife when she went home for the holidays.

Good Lord, what was he saying? He was playing a role that Tori designed for him. He had no reason to be possessive or emotionally involved. She was *paying* him for this temporary charade and he better not let himself forget it. Unfortunately appearing together in public in Lone Ridge had prompted local speculation and gossip to run rampant. Logan wondered how Tori planned to explain their lack of contact when they returned from Fort Worth and went their own way again.

"Tell me about your friend Gabe," Tori requested. "Have you known each other long?"

"Since I was fifteen and I went to work at a large cattle ranch in southwest Texas."

"Fifteen? When did you lose your mother?" she asked.

"Three years earlier. When I moved into the bunkhouse on Socorro Ranch, Gabe was there with his uncle who raised him," Logan elaborated. "His uncle died in a stampede during a storm so Gabe and I became brothers of sorts. We are inter-

changeable and we take turns being each other's
deputy when we move from one town to the next."

Her long lashes swept up and Logan nearly
drowned in the sea of her deep green eyes. "When
will that be?"

Logan shrugged casually then bit into his roll.
"Whenever the mood strikes us. We've been one
place and then another for as long as I can remember. The boardinghouse in town where I hang my
hat is one of many places we've lived."

"I've always wondered what it's like to go where
the wind takes you," she murmured as she touched
the napkin to the edge of her mouth. "But my
father owns and operates a newspaper. My pater-
nal grandfather settled in Fort Worth and my father
wasn't inclined to pull up sticks. Mother is from
Boston but she's entrenched in Fort Worth society
now."

"What about your sister?"

Tori smiled fondly. "Cilla is the Chosen One.
She was groomed to become the perfect hostess
for social engagements. When she married Randolph Spradlin, as our parents requested, my ma-
ternal grandfather urged them to move to Boston
so Randolph could work his way up management
at Grandpapa's manufacturing firm. Plus, Cilla

has Timothy, the heir apparent, to raise. According to Mother's letter, Cilla divides her time between child rearing and various charities that Grandpapa wants her to support. She has wealth, connections and the perfect life my parents wished for her."

"Sounds like a fairy-tale life," Logan commented. "Maybe you should reconsider and have me shot down in a standoff before you venture to Fort Worth. Maybe the gentleman your parents earmarked for you can provide more luxuries and comforts than a marshal in a town that sits in the shadow of Lone Ridge."

Tori scoffed. "This quaint town, nestled in this box canyon, suits me fine, thank you very much. I own my own business and I set my own hours. Perfect is in the eyes of the beholder, after all." She grinned mischievously. "Besides, I have a capable, reliable husband who has a reputation of handling trouble quickly and effectively. What would I want with a stuffy, hidebound gent who bears my parents' stamp of approval?"

Logan leaned toward her. "All teasing aside, Tori. I don't have refined looks or a blue-blooded pedigree. The last thing I want is to embarrass you in front of your—"

She reached across the table to press her index

finger to his lips to shush him. "You're perfect," she insisted. "Follow my lead in conversations and let me teach you a few dance steps to get us through the Christmas soiree and we'll be fine."

Logan folded her hand in his and said, "You're forgetting one small detail."

"I am? What's that?"

"In order to behave as if we share the affectionate bond of matrimony we are going to have to appear to be intimately involved. How do you plan to handle that?"

Tori swallowed hard and silently admitted that she hadn't factored that into the Christmas equation. She had focused on persuading Logan to agree to her scheme and convince her parents that the marriage was real.

"I can tell by your expression that you haven't considered that. I don't think that will be as easy as minding my manners and learning dance steps."

She could feel her face pulsing with embarrassment. "Good Gad, are you suggesting—?"

He nodded and grinned wickedly. "Yes, I am. We're going to have to practice touching and kissing…at the very least…if you expect to pull this off convincingly."

Well, at least he hadn't suggested what she

thought he meant. The prospect of hopping into bed with him held deliciously wicked appeal, but she was hesitant to surrender to her whims. She hadn't even kissed very many men in her life—and that was counting pecks on the cheek—so she wouldn't know how or where to begin being intimate.

She stared at Logan's sensuous mouth and wondered if he would savor or devour a woman when he kissed her.

"What are you thinking?" he asked as he watched her watch him intently.

Tori's face went up in flames again. She wormed her hand from his, stared at the buttons on his shirt and said, "You do not want to know."

"Yes, I do," he contradicted. *Tell me.*

She grabbed her fork and stabbed at her potatoes. "I feel like one of the prisoners you've interrogated."

"Sorry, prying information is part of my profession." He continued to stare intently at her. "Tell me."

She didn't meet his gaze. She was too self-conscious. "I was wondering what it would be like to kiss you…Am I going to have to be this honest with you the whole blasted time we're pretending to be married?"

When he chuckled, she glanced up to see his dark eyes glistening with amusement. His smile affected every line and feature on his rugged face and Tori felt a corner of her heart cave in. *Oh great,* she thought. *The last thing I want for Christmas is to wind up with a broken heart.*

"How was your meal?" the balding proprietor questioned as he came to stand by the table.

Tori flinched. She'd been so distracted that she hadn't noticed Henry. "It was delicious, as always."

Henry winked and grinned. "Wait until you taste dessert. The pies we serve are exceptional."

"None for me," Logan remarked. "I ate the pie Tori brought by this morning."

She gaped at him, amazed. "The entire pie?"

"No, I let Gabe have one piece."

Tori slumped back in her chair. She wasn't sure if Logan had a voracious appetite or if he really liked the taste of her pie. She shifted her attention to his empty plate. Not a scrap of food left on it. Must be his hearty appetite, she decided, a mite disappointed.

A few minutes later, after they exited the restaurant—with all eyes still on them—Tori paused to stare up at Lone Ridge. The full moon beamed on the craggy precipice like a spotlight. The community was nestled against the towering rock walls of the box canyon and it fairly glowed in contrast to the dark of night. Despite the December chill in the air, the prospect of kissing Logan sometime between now and midnight warmed her from inside out. Not to mention that her body tingled with erotic anticipation as he assisted her into the buggy.

"Miss Thurston?"

She glanced over her shoulder to see Gabe Horton ambling down the boardwalk.

"Hello, Deputy. How are you this evening?" She hoped her voice was steady enough to conceal the turmoil roiling inside her.

"Can't complain." He halted by the buggy then tipped his head back to grin at Logan. "When are you going to relieve me?"

"Don't know," Logan mumbled as he shifted awkwardly on the seat. "I have to take dance lessons."

Gabe grinned broadly. "Good luck with those two left feet of yours."

Oh, dear, thought Tori. Teaching Logan to dance might be more difficult than anticipated.

Logan narrowed his eyes in warning. "Go make your rounds and stop tormenting me. Is Tanner still whining about not being released for the holidays?"

Gabe nodded his auburn head. "Yep. If he keeps it up much longer, I'll be tempted to hit him with a Yuletide log. He's definitely a pain in the—"

Logan cleared his throat loudly. "Language, Gabe."

"Not to worry," Tori spoke up. "I have, on more than one occasion, found it necessary to put curses to tongue. I'm not a prude."

"The hell you say," Logan teased devilishly as he snapped the reins over the horse.

Tori clutched his arm when the animal bolted forward and trotted away. She made up her mind, there and then, she was going to get their first kiss over with. She was not spending the evening battling nervous anticipation.

"Stop the buggy," she demanded when they zipped past the streetlights to become swallowed up in shadows.

"Why?" Logan stamped on the brake then turned toward her in concern. "What's wrong?"

Before he knew what happened, Tori flung her arms around his neck and kissed him right smack-dab on the mouth. Instinctive need bombarded him and he dropped the reins to clutch her voluptuous body against his. At first touch, his mind went blank. His body caught fire and need scorched him when her lips parted invitingly beneath his.

Logan told himself to be gentle because he could tell right off that Tori wasn't very experienced with men. But damn, he'd been without a woman for months and lust was running roughshod over him. Yet, Tori was an endearing novelty to him and he'd shoot himself before he frightened or alarmed her with impatient ardor.

The instant before he got carried away completely and devoured her like a famished fiend, he reared back to gauge her reaction to his kiss. She stared owlishly at him for a long moment. Then her fingertips skimmed over her mouth, as if analyzing their first kiss.

It nearly drove him crazy when she licked her lips in that naturally seductive way she had about her.

"Well..." she said unevenly, still gaping at him.

Logan didn't know if that was good or bad. "Well what?"

She suddenly came to her senses, scooted away then stared straight ahead. "Now that we have that settled and out of the way we can concentrate on dancing."

"Maybe you can," he mumbled under his breath. That quick taste of her made him want more, not less.

"Pardon?"

"Dancing. Right. Can't wait."

He drove off before he succumbed to the urge to toss aside the reins and reach for the green-eyed siren instead. Logan was pretty sure the holiday arrangement he'd made with Tori was going to be pure torment.

So much for the peace and serenity of the Christmas season, he thought sourly. Playing the role of Victoria Thurston's husband was guaranteed to test his willpower and resistance to its very limits.

Logan wasn't at all sure he could handle the pressure.

"Now then," Tori said as she scooted aside the chair and the rug in her living room. "The waltz is nothing more than one long step followed by two short ones. You can move any direction you please with the first step. Ready?"

She slipped into his arms and showed him where to place his hands. But the way he kept staring at her with those dark, smoldering eyes played hell with her pulse.

"Step, step, close. One, two, three. One, two, three—"

Her voice evaporated when he angled his head toward hers and narrowed the space until his powerfully built body brushed against hers. Tori went weak in the knees.

"We have a problem," Logan murmured huskily.

"We do?" she bleated.

He nodded and his lips hovered a hairbreadth from hers. She wanted him to kiss her so badly she could already taste him. She well remembered the feel of his sensuous lips moving expertly over hers and she savored the arousing feel of his masculine contours gliding provocatively against her.

"I'm going to have to kiss you again." He skimmed his lips over her mouth and her legs wobbled. "That first kiss came as too much of a surprise. I wasn't at my best. I can do better."

She almost smiled at that remark. She didn't want to have to tell him that if he was more devastating the second time than he was the first, he might reduce her to a pile of smoldering ashes. Logan Daniels left her hot and bothered, no doubt about that. He was beyond all previous experience and she reacted to him in shocking ways that obliterated her self-restraint as nothing else ever had.

Sure enough, the instant his lips settled on hers, burning sensations sizzled through her body. Her heart hammered against her ribs, making it difficult to breathe. She inhaled him, clung to him because she wasn't sure she could stand on her own feet if he suddenly released his grasp on her.

Sweet mercy! Is this what reckless desire felt like? Tori hadn't experienced it before. Mild attraction? Yes. Wild, breathless lust? No, definitely not.

When he deepened the kiss and lifted her off the floor to compensate for the difference in their height she gave herself up to the compelling hunger he aroused in her. She kissed him for all she was worth, until she had to come up for air.

"One, two, three," she murmured in rhythm, desperately trying to concentrate on waltzing. "Slow…quick, quick—"

Logan groaned as he clutched her closer. His lips skimmed her flushed cheek and his hand splayed over her derriere to caress her familiarly.

Tori had no idea what possessed her to hook her legs around his lean hips or why he settled her intimately against him. The maddening sensations prompted her to kiss him ardently. When she felt the hard bulge in his breeches pressing suggestively against her, need intensified immediately. She told herself that she should be alarmed because things between them were moving too fast and she was having one devil of a time controlling the wild sensations spilling through her.

Unfortunately Logan's thought-provoking comment about becoming more familiar with each other in an effort to convince her parents the marriage was legitimate kept buzzing in her brain.

Confound it, for over a year she'd wondered what it would be like to kiss him. And poof! She'd kissed him in the buggy and again in her living room. Now she was wondering what it would be like to be naked with him, to skim her hands over his brawny male body which was, at this very moment, gliding suggestively against her.

"Damn, I never dreamed I'd like dancing so much," Logan whispered against her lips.

"This isn't exactly how it's done in the ballrooms of high society." She arched shamelessly against him. A strange sense of satisfaction coursed through her when Logan moaned, clutched her tightly against him and ran both hands over her hips. "West Texas style waltzing, however, is beginning to hold tremendous appeal for me."

"You ought to be against the law," Logan murmured before he delivered a lip-blistering kiss that left her head spinning like a windmill. He set her away from him abruptly. "I better go before—" He clamped his mouth shut.

"Before what?" she asked as she rearranged her twisted yellow gown.

He sent her a squint-eyed stare. "Let me be blunt, pretend wife of mine. Unless you want to find yourself flat on your back and naked beneath me... Or above me... Or beside me... I don't care which. I had better leave. *Now.* This wasn't part of our arrangement."

She stared into his bronzed face and blushed a dozen shades of red while the vivid picture he painted with words exploded in her mind.

"Yes, you should definitely leave," she said shakily.

If he didn't leave, she might ask him to stay to teach her something that had nothing whatsoever to do with dancing.

"I don't think we should see each other tomorrow," he said in a clipped tone. "The day after, I'll pick you up in the wagon at seven o'clock and we'll ride off to catch a stagecoach in Shallow Springs that will deliver us to the train depot in Purple Sage Hollow."

Tori bobbed her head agreeably then noticed that her carefully arranged coiffure had somehow come unwound—much as she had—while they were kissing each other as if there was no tomorrow.

"Good night then." He whirled on his boot heels and strode toward the door.

"See you day after tomorrow," she called as he disappeared into the shadows. "And thank you for supper!"

Tori collapsed on the displaced chair to fan her heated face. "Convincing my family of the attraction for Logan isn't going to be a problem."

If she became more aware and aroused by him, she was fairly certain she would burst into flames and set the house on fire.

Logan stalked toward the jail cells, ready to bite off Tanner's head for whining and complaining about his cold meal and meager accommodations.

Tanner studied Logan's menacing snarl. "What's a-matter with you? You don't seem to be in the holiday spirit."

"Just clam up," Logan snapped before he slammed the door—good and hard.

"My, we're in a sour mood, aren't we?" Gabe taunted as he leaned a hip on the edge of the desk.

"Speak for yourself. I'm the picture of good tidings and holiday cheer," Logan grumbled sarcastically.

"Ha." Gabe smirked.

Logan rounded on his grinning friend. "You have to act in my stead." He spun about, unaware that he'd taken up Tori's nervous habit of pacing from wall to wall. "*You*'re going to be *me* for the holidays, Gabe. I'll stay here and keep a lid on this town."

The expression on Logan's face must have drawn Gabe's concern because he studied him closely. Too closely. "What happened tonight? Spread around too much Christmas cheer, did you?"

Logan had never been one to kiss and tell and he wasn't changing tack now. "All you need to know is that you're taking Tori to Fort Worth instead of me."

Gabe crossed his arms over his chest and grinned wryly. "Can't handle her, is that it? Or don't trust yourself?"

Logan and Gabe had been friends through thick

and thicker but this was the first time Logan itched to knock that teasing grin off his face. "Are you going to do me this favor or not?"

"Not," Gabe said. "You agreed to this. Plus, she picked you specifically. That means something. All you have to do is figure out what." He smiled playfully as he swaggered toward the door. "In case I forget to tell you before you leave town, Merry Christmas, Logan. Ho, ho, ho."

Scowling, Logan stormed across the office then down the street to the boardinghouse. The moment he closed the door and stood there in silence, every erotic sensation Tori had stirred in him returned in full force.

Gabe was right on the mark. Logan made the humiliating discovery this evening that he couldn't trust himself alone with Tori. Trying to restrain himself while she was underfoot was going to become the worst Christmas holiday on record.

"Some friend you are," Logan muttered to Gabe's taunting image. "You refused to help save me from myself. Merry Christmas, indeed!"

Chapter Three

Two days later, Tori was ready and waiting when Logan pulled up in the wagon. She had been dashing around like a madwoman, placing holiday decorations in the store windows and giving away Christmas cookies to her customers. She had seen nothing of the marshal since their dance lesson—if you could call it that. In addition, she'd lost a lot of sleep trying to figure out what there was about the dark-eyed, raven-haired Logan Daniels that prompted her to cast inhibition to the four winds when he came within three feet of her.

"Morning," Logan said in a neutral voice. He gaped at her when she clamored from the house with luggage dangling off her like ornaments on a Christmas tree. "Why so many satchels?"

"I have to bring morning dresses, evening gowns and such," she explained. "It's a different world in Fort Worth."

"Apparently." He hopped to the ground to load the luggage. "I didn't bring a single dress with me."

"Good. I'd hate to have to explain that to my family," she said, grinning. She handed over several satchels for him to place in the bed of the rented wagon. "Luckily you won't be on display to the same extreme that I am. I, after all, have to compete with the wardrobe of the Chosen One, who shops at the exclusive boutiques in Boston. She never fails to look freshly bathed, starched and pressed. Even when Cilla looks her worst, I can't match her when I'm at my best. My sister is an absolute marvel of fashion."

Logan tossed her a quick glance without meeting her eyes. "You look fine to me."

"Fine is not a satisfactory standard for the Thurstons," she said as she bounded onto the wagon seat without his assistance. She frowned warily when she noticed a rifle and shotgun at her feet. "Are we expecting trouble?"

"I always expect trouble." Logan plunked down on the seat. "This is still wide-open country where Mexican banditos, white outlaws and renegade Indians loot and plunder. Getting shot for Christmas is not on my wish list."

A brisk north wind prompted Tori to fasten her

jacket to ward off the chill. "I don't recall having much trouble with desperadoes when I first came to Lone Ridge."

"The area is more dangerous since the Rangers have moved their patrols northwest," Logan explained as he headed southeast.

Tori touched his arm to draw his attention. "Before we go any farther down the road I want to apologize for making you uncomfortable the night we went out for supper then practiced dancing—"

He flung up his hand to forestall her. "No need to apologize. What happened was my fault."

"Nonsense. I kissed you without warning and that started us off on the wrong foot," she insisted.

Logan blew out his breath and said, "Look, let's agree that we both got carried away. After what happened, I tried to persuade Gabe to replace me since we're similar in size, stature, age, profession and background. But he insisted on staying home."

Tori slumped dejectedly. Logan wanted to back out after she had practically thrown herself at him in a fit of lust. She had offended him and he probably thought his moonlighting job for Christmas was going to become more complicated than he originally anticipated. But Logan was much too honorable to go back on his word and abandon her.

"There is no need for you to pretend to find me intriguing or attractive until we arrive in Fort Worth."

He glanced up sharply then frowned. "I didn't say I—"

The report of a rifle shattered the crisp morning air. Logan grabbed the back of her head and shoved her to the floorboards.

"Stay down!" he commanded as he snapped the reins over the horse and launched off at breakneck speed.

Tori anchored herself to his legs as the wagon bounced over rough terrain. The jarring motion practically shook her teeth out of her head, but she huddled against Logan while several more shots rang out in the near distance. She craned her neck around the edge of the seat to see two Mexican desperadoes, dressed in serapes and sombreros, in hot pursuit. When she looked up at Logan, she noticed he'd clenched his teeth as he spared a quick glance over his shoulder to monitor the men's approach.

"I didn't know highwaymen got up this early in

the morning—" She ducked when another bullet whistled overhead.

"I'll try to take cover in the grove of cottonwood trees." He fired off two quick shots. "Just hang on for a few more minutes."

Logan didn't appear the least bit flustered by the attack, merely annoyed by the inconvenience. Tori greatly admired his ability to remain so calm under fire. She, on the other hand, was rattled. It was her first ambush. Nevertheless, she drew in a bolstering breath and vowed to follow his lead. She grabbed the shotgun and plunked down on the seat.

"I said stay down," he barked sharply.

"You aren't hunkering down so I won't either."

"Can you handle a shotgun?" he asked as he plunged downhill toward the protection of the trees.

"If it's loaded and ready to fire. I can't guarantee I can hit what I aim at."

"Just look vicious and convincing, is all I ask."

Another shot zinged past them and plugged into the wagon bed. That was close, thought Tori. Another six inches and she would have been hit!

She braced herself when Logan turned sharply, sending the wagon into a skid. The banditos didn't cease their attack but they veered west when Logan dropped the reins and began firing both peacemakers simultaneously.

"Blast away," he ordered.

Tori secured the butt of the shotgun against her shoulder, took aim then pulled the trigger. The loud explosion made her ears ring. The backlash of the weapon knocked her off balance. She squealed in surprise when she did a back somersault over the seat and landed on her satchels in the wagon bed.

"You okay?" Logan asked without taking his eyes off the banditos who had halted just beyond pistol range, to shout tauntingly at him.

"Hands up, hombre," one of the bandits called out. Then he commenced rattling in Spanish.

Tori couldn't translate what the outlaw said or what Logan replied when he shouted back in rapid-fire Spanish. Obviously the highwaymen understood because they stared wide-eyed at Logan. When he grabbed the rifle and fired a shot, the skinny bandito yelped. He curled over his horse's neck and grabbed his injured shooting arm. The next shot knocked the sombrero off the stout bandit's dark head. He growled what Tori assumed to be a foul curse at Logan who responded in kind.

Determined not to appear the helpless female—

a role she detested of her gender—she snatched up her shotgun, fired then braced herself for the painful kick against her shoulder.

"The next shot will be aimed at your gut!" she snarled threateningly.

"You don't have a next shot, unless you reload," Logan said aside. Then he handed over his rifle. "Go ahead. Give 'em hell, Tori."

She did. Her shot sent dirt and pebbles splattering around both horses' front hooves. The startled animals reared up then plunged forward, forcing the banditos to hang on or be catapulted through the air.

"I *always* want to be on your side when a fight breaks out," Tori declared. She readjusted her cockeyed bonnet then plopped onto the wagon seat. "This delay isn't going to cause us to miss our stagecoach connection, is it?"

"No." Logan took time to look her over carefully, as if to assure himself that she was still in one piece.

She smiled brightly and said, "I'm fine. Not to worry. Adventure feeds my soul. That's why I moved to Lone Ridge. Out here, women are not so confined to male expectations." She paused then glanced at him. "I don't know what you said to those banditos but they didn't seem so cocksure of themselves afterward."

Logan set aside the weapons then took up the reins to return to the road.

"What did those outlaws say to you?" she persisted.

"You don't want to know."

"Of course I do. Don't make me twist your arm. *Tell me.*"

He huffed out his breath. "They said they would spare my life if I gave them my whore."

"What!" Tori howled in outrage.

He grinned. "I told you that you didn't want to know."

"What did you say that struck a chord of alarm in them? And do not tell me that I don't want to know because I most certainly do."

"I told them you were a bona fide lady, not a whore. Then I told them where they could go and what they could do with themselves when they got there. Lastly, I promised to ride into Hades and strip the charred hide off their bodies." He cast her a quick glance. "Anything else you want to know, sweetheart?"

"No, dear." She settled her skirts around her. "I would have told them the same thing if they had threatened to take you away from me. And thank you for defending my honor. That was very gallant of you."

"That's me. Gallant as hell. And thank you."

When Tori settled in for the ride to Shallow Springs, Logan urged the horse into a faster clip to make up for lost time. She had impressed him during the perilous confrontation. She hadn't whimpered and wailed. She had tried to contribute to their defense.

Faint of heart she was not, he reminded himself.

Then he wondered how her parents could *not* be proud of her refreshing character, her accomplishments and her bravery.

Furthermore, if anyone referred to this strikingly attractive female as an ugly duckling at the soiree, Logan was going to pound them flat.

A few minutes later he realized that his feelings of inadequacy about rubbing shoulders with the upper crust of society during the holidays had dimmed in comparison to his crusade to make sure Tori was treated with the respect and admiration she richly deserved. She was her own woman and that counted for a great deal in the world according to Logan Daniels.

* * *

Tori was relieved that the stagecoach trip from Shallow Springs to the train depot in Purple Sage Hollow was uneventful. The instant the coach rolled to a halt, Logan clutched her hand, pulled her off the seat and into his waiting arms. Tori didn't have time to savor the brush of her body against his masculine contours before he set her to her feet and stepped away.

Odd, she mused. He had been keeping his distance most of the day. It was as if he was trying to avoid physical contact. Had she done something else besides pounce on him during the dance lesson that offended him?

While Logan towed her along at a swift pace to reach the train depot, she wondered if forward, assertive women put him off, wondered if he preferred timid females.

The possibility disappointed her. She was nothing if not independent-minded, straightforward and ambitious. Some men felt threatened by spirited women. She had hoped Logan was not among them.

Logan dropped the carpetbags and satchels at her feet. "We have an hour before the train arrives," he announced. "I have an errand to run before we board the train."

She cast him a muddled frown. He didn't say what the mysterious errand was. He simply lurched around and strode away. Surely he didn't think he had to buy her a Christmas gift to keep up pretense. Anyway, she had taken care of that yesterday by purchasing a small rhinestone pin for herself and a gold-plated pocket watch for him, so they could exchange gifts Christmas morning.

Her thoughts trailed off when she noticed how much female attention Logan received as he cut an impressive swath on the boardwalk. He drew attention because of his towering height in a crowd. Clean-shaven, and wearing a trim fitting shirt and breeches that accentuated his brawny physique, he had women stopping and staring appreciatively at him as he strode past.

Tori smiled as he disappeared around the corner. An unprecedented sense of pride and possessiveness overwhelmed her. A moment later, she gave herself a mental pinch and reminded herself that Logan was only her holiday husband. The charade would end the instant they stepped onto the westbound train to return to Lone Ridge.

"Need some help with all your luggage, ma'am?"

Tori pivoted to see a well-dressed man of average size and stature, sporting a blond mustache and goatee, smiling rakishly at her. Here, she thought, was the shining example of the upper-class gent that had previously tried to court her because of her parents' good standing in elite social circles. That type reeked of insincerity and hidden agendas. Watching the man ogle her, as if she was an appetizer for his upcoming Christmas feast, made her frown in irritation.

"Thank you, but no," she replied stiffly. "I am not in need of any help."

He sidled closer, all practiced charm and premeditated smiles. "Then perhaps we could share a seat on the train and get to know each other better, my dear."

"I am not your dear," she snapped then shooed him on his way. "Go pester someone else with your shallow charm."

He opened his mouth to reply then his gaze lifted over her head. A second later, he spun on his well-shod heels and zipped into the depot, lickety-split.

Tori glanced over her shoulder to see what—or who—had sent the Casanova of the High Plains scurrying off like the rat he was. Amusement pursed her lips when she saw Logan looming behind her like the rock-solid peak of Lone Ridge. She had to admit that Logan was very good at giving the evil eye. If she didn't know how gentle he could be when the mood suited him, she might have been intimidated.

When he eased around her to gather up their luggage, she watched him refocus on the gent who had taken a seat in the corner of the depot. The man fidgeted in his chair and looked everywhere except at Logan when he reacquainted him with The Look.

"Beautiful women are a lot of trouble because they attract too much attention," he said as he gestured for her to follow him away from the crowd gathered beside the railroad tracks.

Tori stood there, rooted to the spot. "Beautiful? *Me?*"

Her voice fizzled out when he clasped her hand to shepherd her along beside him. When they were out of earshot of the milling crowd, he pivoted toward her.

"Yes, you are," he insisted. "You're the only one who doesn't seem to know how attractive you are. I watched several men give you the once-over while I walked toward you."

"I saw dozens of women eyeing you when you walked away," she reported.

"That's just because I'm taller than average and tower above the crowd," he said dismissively.

She shook her head. "You are strikingly handsome and exceptionally masculine looking," she complimented. "It was the first thing I noticed about you when I arrived in Lone Ridge—" She clamped down on her runaway tongue when Logan arched a thick brow and grinned devilishly.

The sound of a distant whistle, signaling the approach of the train, wiped the smile from Logan's face. Bemused, Tori watched him dig into the breast pocket of his shirt. When he extended a shiny gold band, her jaw dropped open and she gaped at him in astonishment.

"It stands to reason that your family will expect to see a wedding band on your finger," he explained. "This is the best ring Purple Sage Hollow has to offer."

When he slipped the ring on her finger, it was a mite too big. She was still gaping at him when he tugged the ring off her finger.

"Wrong size. I'll be right back."

He took off like a shot then veered around the corner. Her heart squeezed in her chest, amazed that he'd purchased a wedding ring for her to wear. She had overlooked that aspect of her ruse, but Logan had spent his own money to make certain her holiday charade appeared authentic. She wanted to kiss him for his thoughtful attention to detail.

But you are not going to kiss him, she told herself. That's what scared him off. She was *paying* him to portray her husband. Just because she was becoming emotionally involved too quickly didn't mean he shared her growing affection. No, Tori reminded herself. Logan Daniels was a man trained to serve and protect. It was second nature to him. When he had a job to do, he did it. She was his job for the Christmas holidays and she better not let herself forget it.

She watched Logan cut another impressive swath through the crowd to rejoin her. She smiled when he slid the new gold band on her finger. It was a perfect fit.

"Thank you," she murmured, stunned by the odd sensation that trickled through her. The ring made their marriage seem all too real. A lump clogged her throat when she peered into his obsidian eyes. A jolt of sizzling awareness riveted her and she tried desperately to tamp it down. "I'll repay you for this."

"No, the ring is on me."

A vision of Logan naked, wearing the gold ring on his pinky finger, blazed across her mind, making her blush candy-apple-red.

He eyed her curiously for a moment then added, "You paid for the train ticket. Fair is fair."

Shortly thereafter, the train pulled into the station and they boarded as man and wife. During the trip, Tori spun the gold band on her finger and wondered what it would be like to be truly and legally married to Marshal Logan Daniels.

It would never happen, she told herself sensibly, as she peered out the window to admire the rolling hills. Logan and Gabe only planned to be in Lone Ridge until they were hired to tame another town. Logan would only belong to her while she was home for Christmas. Expecting anything more from him was inviting disappointment, she told herself realistically.

"Good Lord," Logan croaked in disbelief when he got his first look at the Thurstons' grand castle in Fort Worth. Home? He silently scoffed at the inaccurate description. Mansion was more like it.

Hell, he predicted that only the president of these United States lived in a palace equal to this estate on the edge of town.

Tori had grown up here, surrounded by luxury and every comfort imaginable. Logan had lived in a one-room shack and barely had enough food to stave off starvation. Their backgrounds had been drastically different.

"Logan? What's wrong?" She studied him worriedly.

Logan gave himself a mental shake then tried to shrug nonchalantly. "This is quite a place. A Christmas wreath on the door. Mistletoe hanging on the marble-tiled porch. Can't image what bells and whistles your father neglected to include here."

"None that I can think of," she said as Logan followed her up the front steps, laden down like a pack mule.

Which was what he was, he thought uneasily. He didn't belong in this setting any more than Tori belonged on a cattle drive or a shootout with desperadoes. Yet, on second thought, she had been pretty amazing during their morning confrontation with those Mexican banditos. She was no shrinking violet, that was for sure. Yet, he wasn't a proper gentleman who had been groomed for a life of brushing shoulders with Fort Worth's elite social circle.

What in the hell am I doing here?

Before he could bolt and run the massive, hand-carved front door—one that boasted a coat of arms—swung open.

"Miss Victoria, so good to see you again. We missed you last year."

The wiry, middle-aged butler with gentle gray eyes and strawberry-colored hair doubled at the waist. Tori stepped forward to give him a hug and peck on the cheek.

"It's *Mrs.* Logan Daniels," she corrected. "This is my husband, the marshal of Lone Ridge." She half-turned to continue the introductions. "Gerald Vickers and his wife, Marianne, run this household with impressive efficiency. I have Marianne to thank for my love and appreciation of cooking and baking."

"That answers that question," Logan replied as he shook Gerald's hand. "I can't wait to meet the woman who taught Tori to make those melt-in-your-mouth pies that are nothing short of heaven."

Gerald and Tori raised their eyebrows at him. Had he gone overboard in his effort to brag on his pretend wife?

"My sweet tooth is my downfall." He tried out his best smile on the butler who appeared to be judging him and trying to decide if he was worthy of the title of Tori's husband.

It was good practice for when he met the Thurstons, he decided.

"Is she here? About blasted time," came a booming male voice from the interior of the elaborately decorated foyer that was complete with an oversize chandelier that dripped with crystals sparkling in the light.

Logan appraised the man who strode toward them. He knew instantly where Tori had inherited her eye and hair color. Her father looked to be fifty-five, or thereabout, and he was dressed in expensive garments that put Logan's new wardrobe to shame.

"Papa, it's so good to see you." When Tori walked forward, the older man curled his arm around her and patted her shoulder.

It annoyed Logan that Thurston was more interested in surveying him astutely than greeting his youngest daughter.

"Logan Daniels, this is my father, Franklin Thurston," she introduced formally.

"A pleasure, Franklin." Logan gripped the man's hand firmly and looked him squarely in the eye.

They stared at each other for a long moment. Logan had stared down more than his share of outlaws and he was pleased to note that Franklin was the first to glance away.

"About time you arrived, darling. I wondered if you would make it before your sister arrived."

Logan glanced over Franklin's head to watch Mrs. Thurston make her grand entrance down the curved staircase. As Tori had said, her mother was fair-haired and fair-skinned. She was forty-five years old—give or take—and there was a regal air about her. She was petite, well dressed and her neck and earlobes dripped with diamonds.

He was most certainly mingling with a different class of people. When they regarded him critically, he doubted he measured up. And what was that ridiculous nonsense about arriving *before* Princess Priscilla and her merry band of elitists? No wonder Tori teasingly referred to her sister as the Chosen One.

"Hello, Mother." Dutifully Tori approached the reigning queen of Thurston Hall. "Logan, may I present Belinda Thurston. Mother, this is Logan Daniels."

Belinda inclined her head ever so slightly as she all but floated down the last three steps. Logan caught himself thinking that it was a wonder Tori had managed to break away from the hidebound traditions observed by the Thurston family.

Logan bowed gallantly then removed his hat. "Nice to meet you, Belinda. You have a magnificent home."

She preened, then gestured with a wrist that was encircled with enough diamonds to choke a horse. "The servants are a wonder. I couldn't manage without them."

I don't doubt it, thought Logan. Tori was an industrious worker. He doubted Belinda was.

"Come along and I'll show you to your suite so you can settle in before Priscilla arrives." Belinda pivoted on the bottom step to glance back at Franklin. "Did you send someone to fetch her from the train depot, dear?"

Logan frowned in annoyance. He and Tori had made their own arrangements for transportation. Apparently Priscilla received royal treatment. He muttered under his breath about Tori's parents behaving as if her arrival was less important than Priscilla's…

His thoughts scattered when he stared into the

expensively furnished suite that he'd occupy for the holidays.

"You and Logan will sleep here," Belinda decreed.

Oh, hell, thought Logan. He set aside the luggage then stared at the Victorian-style bed with its carved headboard that nearly scraped the high ceiling. The massive mahogany dresser, with its oversize gold-frame mirror, filled the opposite corner. A sitting area, with its tufted sofa that was nowhere near long enough to accommodate his six-foot-plus frame, graced the north corner. Priceless end tables and chairs completed the ensemble.

Logan might have remembered to purchase a ring, in an attempt to lend credence to their marriage, but he had been so damn busy trying to control his lusty urges toward Tori all the livelong day that he completely forgot about sleeping arrangements.

He could just hear Gabe Horton laughing his head off and saying, "Merry Christmas. Ho, ho, ho..."

Chapter Four

After her mother swept from the suite, Tori glanced apprehensively at Logan who stared at the massive headboard and the bed that was covered with a green satin spread and festive pillows. He looked as if he had been bushwhacked.

"Do you have a well-thought-out plan for this predicament?" he asked, still gaping at the frilly bedding.

She closed the door to ensure privacy. "No, I'm afraid not."

"Figured as much," he grumbled.

"I didn't think far enough ahead to consider sleeping arrangements. I'll sleep on the couch."

That was not where she preferred to sleep, she realized with a start. She wanted to cuddle up with her pretend husband. Somewhere between here and Lone Ridge, her feelings for Logan had exploded out of proportion. It was preposterous. Not to mention dangerously foolish. Nevertheless, she enjoyed being with him, appreciated his dry sense of humor, admired his courage, self-reliance and his ability to protect both of them.

Too bad her parents hadn't earmarked *Logan* for her. She would have snatched him up in two shakes.

"I'll sleep on the floor," Logan volunteered as his gaze circled the elaborate room for the third time. "I've camped out on the ground plenty of times during forays and cattle drives."

"We'll sleep together," she declared impulsively.

He looked horrified by the prospect, which hurt her feelings something fierce.

"I promise not to throw myself at you the way I did on our first date," she muttered, her face pulsating with color. "We'll barricade the space between us with Mother's embroidered Christmas pillows."

"I'd prefer the Great Wall of China," he mumbled.

The comment cut her to the core. He truly was worried that she would pounce on him. Well, curse it all. She should have taken his suggestion and hired someone who didn't appeal to her to portray the marshal of Lone Ridge. Then she wouldn't be fighting this impossible attraction for a man who was having serious second thoughts about masquerading as her husband.

"We'll take turns washing off the trail dust," she suggested, gesturing toward the tub behind the dressing screen.

"You go first," Logan insisted. "I'll take a grand tour of the house so you can enjoy your privacy."

He didn't even want to see her naked, she mused dejectedly. She knew this was no fairy-tale marriage, like Cilla's. It was as fake as the rhinestone pin she had bought herself for Christmas.

"Hurry downstairs!" someone called from the other side of the door. "Cilla and her family have arrived!"

Logan opened the door to see a young, sturdily built maid with frizzy brown hair poised in the hall. She curtsied and smiled politely at him.

"Sarah, this is Logan," Tori introduced quickly as she breezed from the room.

Logan was halfway down the steps when Gerald the butler opened the front door. The fairy princess from Boston had arrived to be fussed over by her adoring parents. Priscilla Thurston Spradlin appeared from the darkness like an angel on high, spotlighted by the golden light beaming down from the chandelier.

Tori was right. With Priscilla's fair skin, silky platinum blond hair and shapely physique, she was a sight of beauty to behold. However, Logan's tastes didn't center on fairy-tale princesses. He had acquired a taste for evergreen eyes, mahogany-colored hair that tumbled into lush curls and a voluptuous body that fit his contours as if she had been created precisely for him.

He watched Tori bound excitedly down the steps to hug her sister who seemed equally happy to see her. There it was, thought Logan. Family. Holiday traditions, festive decorations and an upcoming Christmas Eve ball to reunite the Thurstons' circle of prestigious friends and family.

This reunion was in sharp contrast to the kind of holiday Logan remembered. He'd grown up like an extra person in the world. There hadn't been colorful stockings hanging from the fireplace in a spacious drawing room. There had been no ceramic likeness of Santa Claus or a host of por-celain angels sitting on the mantel and end tables. Logan came from humble beginnings. He lived an unadorned life with unadorned holidays. He hadn't realized what he'd missed until now.

A five-year-old boy, wearing green corduroy knee breeches, jacket and a crisp white shirt, walked inside. He glanced peevishly from left to right then whined, "I'm hungry. Get me something to eat. Papa said I had all sorts of gifts waiting for me. Where are they?"

The little brat tolerated his grandparents' hugs with indifference, before tramping off to the drawing room to look for his Christmas stocking.

Logan bit back a smile when Randolph Spradlin made his grand entrance, followed by the butler who was burdened down with excessive amounts of leather luggage. Logan crossed his arms over his chest and leaned a hip against the banister to watch the six-foot-tall gent, who was dressed in the latest style and finest fashion, remove his kid gloves one finger at a time. He pulled off his Bowler hat then struck an arrogant pose as he nodded a stiff greeting to Belinda and Franklin Thurston.

Fierce possessiveness bombarded Logan when Randolph's hazel-eyed gaze landed squarely on Tori. He looked her over from head to toe. Then his gaze lingered on the full swells of her breasts before drifting to the flare of her shapely hips.

Logan reminded himself that nothing was exactly what it seemed—and here was the glaring example. Randolph wasn't the model husband. He had a wandering eye and it was presently focused on Tori in lusty speculation. The storybook life Tori presumed her sister led had a serious flaw. Randolph was a womanizer. Logan would bet his reputation on it.

When Randolph's attention finally drifted up the steps to survey his supposed brother-in-law, Logan was ready and waiting to meet his gaze. The stony stare he leveled on Randolph was one he'd perfected while staring down outlaws. Logan shifted his attention to Tori then back to Randolph, just in case the arrogant jackal was too stupid to understand that Logan would tolerate no one toying with his wife.

His wife. The thought echoed through his mind. He hadn't pretended to be a loving husband for even one full day and already he was thinking like a possessive married man. There was no telling how much this charade was going to affect his thinking by the time he exited this castle in fairyland and returned to the outpost of civilization near the panhandle of Texas.

"Allow me to introduce my husband," Tori announced.

Logan took his cue and ambled down the steps.

He halted to grasp Priscilla's dainty hand then pressed a kiss to her knuckles. "Tori has mentioned you fondly dozens of times. It's good to finally meet you."

Priscilla's smile displayed her dimples. Her clear blue eyes twinkled with amusement. "Did she mention the awful tricks I used to play on her when we were children?"

Logan glanced discreetly at Tori. "No, she had nothing but praise for you. But knowing my lovely wife as I do, I suspect she held her own with you. It's one of the many qualities I adore about her."

A genuine smile crossed Priscilla's delicate features as she glanced back and forth between Logan and Tori. "I'm pleased that you appreciate my sister for the exceptional person she is. Otherwise, I intended to have a heart-to-heart talk with you."

Unable to tolerate being out of the limelight, Randolph sauntered over to curl his arm around his wife. "Quite right, sweetheart."

Logan wondered how many other women Randy-the-rake referred to as sweetheart. More than one, Logan suspected.

"We want only the best for dear Victoria." Randy cast Tori an appreciative glance. "You have blossomed into a dazzling woman since I saw you two years ago. Logan is a lucky man."

When Belinda flapped her arms, her bejeweled necklace, bracelets and earrings glistened in the light. "Gerald, be so kind as to carry the luggage upstairs, please. The Spradlins will be using the two suites in the east wing."

She turned to Franklin. "Why don't you pour your sons-in-law a drink?" She motioned with her hand and added, "Tori, you can help Cilla settle in her rooms." She glanced around then frowned. "Now where did Timothy get off to, the sweet little darling?"

Just then, a female shriek erupted from the dining room. The family members moved as one toward the arched doorway. Sarah, the stout maid Logan had met earlier, was drenched with wine. She stood beside the sideboard where the "sweet little darling" held an empty bottle and snickered in devilish amusement.

"Timothy! Stop that!" Priscilla scolded as she stamped over to pull the boy off the furniture and set him on his feet. "Apologize to Sarah this instant!"

"Now, now, don't be so hard on him. Boys will be boys," Randolph insisted as he shouldered past his wife. "Timmy has been cooped up on a train for two endless days." He confiscated the wine bottle from the blond-haired holy terror and smiled charmingly at Sarah. "I'm sure you realize Timmy meant no harm."

Logan didn't think Sarah realized anything of the kind. She looked none too happy with father or son.

Randolph thrust Timmy's hand into Sarah's. "You're in charge of him." He glanced sideways at Franklin and said, "Now, how about that drink. I'm positively parched."

Logan strode up beside Tori and leaned close so he could whisper what looked to be sweet nothings in her ear. "If our pretend son, that we may have to produce in the future to keep up this charade, behaves as abominably as this sweet little darling, I'll make him behave. This brat is doomed to end up like the undisciplined outlaws I'm paid to hunt down."

Playing along, Tori glanced at him with a blinding smile and patted his cheek adoringly. "I agree, honey." Then she pushed up on tiptoe to kiss him on the chin and whispered, "Have two drinks for me. I'm going to need them to get through this evening."

Leaving him at the mercy of her father and brother-in-law, Tori grasped her sister's hand and darted toward the steps.

Logan snagged her arm on the way by. "One last thing. The price just went up," he murmured against the side of her swanlike neck—and became sidetracked by the tantalizing feel and alluring scent of her skin.

She chortled, her green eyes dancing with amusement and mischief. "We will discuss that in great detail later, love."

Then off she went. Logan looked at Randy-the-rake then at Franklin, the proper, transplanted Englishman. He was more than ready for a drink. Although he preferred to down a couple of jiggers of rotgut whiskey, he sipped his wine—plus two glasses for Tori.

"Oh, Tori, I'm so thrilled you could make it home for Christmas this year," Priscilla enthused as she lifted her blue silk gown from the luggage and hung it in the wardrobe closet. "Last year was nearly unbearable without you here. I told Mother I wasn't making the long trip unless you agreed to come home, too."

Tori rolled her eyes. "So that's why I was given

the royal ultimatum. There was an *or else* attached to my invitation." She scooped one of Cilla's expensive dresses and shook out the wrinkles. "Timmy has grown like a weed."

Cilla blew out an exasperated breath. "That's exactly what he's turned into. Randolph contradicts what I tell him, spoils him to the extreme and makes excuses for his bad behavior. He's at his worst when his father is underfoot. Which isn't often, thank goodness. Randolph spends most of his time at his clubs…and elsewhere."

Tori peered intently at her sister. "Does that mean what I think it means?"

Cilla bobbed her shiny blond head and looked so melancholy that Tori hugged her close.

"I'm so glad you weren't handed over on a silver platter to an upstart businessman," Cilla murmured miserably. "I'd go crazy if I weren't allowed to work with my charities. Seeing those orphans, who have nothing and no one to love them, breaks my heart. I invited them to our home last summer for a feast but Randolph canceled my plans. He insisted that he didn't want lice-infested, malnourished brats running around loose in his house. Neither did he want Timmy to associate with them. I rather thought Timmy might see that he had been blessed and that others in the world were suffering."

The perfect world and ideal life that Tori presumed her sister led shattered. Her nephew was spoiled rotten and self-indulgent. At age five, he had already learned that his father allowed him to get away with murder and would counter his mother's attempts to discipline him.

"How long have you known that Randolph has become unfaithful to you?" Tori questioned gently.

"*Become* unfaithful?" Priscilla sniffed caustically as she fluffed another of her elegant dresses with more vigor than necessary. "I swear he was born that way. Housemaids, casual acquaintances, you name them and he has approached them."

Tori was appalled and outraged for her sister's sake. "That weasel! I have a few words to say to him and none of them are kind—"

Cilla grabbed her arm before she breezed out the door. "You mustn't interfere. We have settled into our arrangement. I have established my own life and he has his. It's the best I can hope for without bringing down scandal on both families."

"I am so sorry. You know I only want the best for you," Tori assured her.

Priscilla nodded and smiled sadly. "I know, despite the ridiculous favoritism. I'm grateful our parents didn't lead you down the same path they designated for me."

"I've teasingly referred to you as the Chosen One because you were selected to become the extension of their lives and the keeper of tradition." She frowned pensively. "I think it's the ingrained English custom of grooming and favoring the first-born who will carry on the lineage. I was only the spare heir, but that was all right with me because I wanted no part of the regimentation foisted onto you."

"*You* trotted off to Houston to develop your independence and self-reliance and they permitted it," Priscilla continued. "*You* were allowed to strike off to open shop in a town of your choosing. You've made a successful career while I tolerate being window dressed for a man whose only interest is showing off his well-connected, well-heeled wife in public. You don't know how many times I've longed to exchange places with you."

Tori blinked, stunned. Her sister truly envied her? She longed for the life Tori had established for herself?

"Furthermore," Cilla went on to say. "You married a handsome, virile man who seems genuinely infatuated with you. I saw the way he glared at Randolph when he looked you over too thoroughly this evening."

"He did?" Tori scowled. "How dare Randolph think I would have the slightest interest in him when you are my sister and he knows I love you dearly!"

"I appreciate your loyalty, sis. Some of my pretentious acquaintances in Boston have succumbed to Randolph's shallow charm, just to spite me. Little did they know they could have him...with my blessing."

Tori chuckled in amusement when Priscilla carelessly tossed Randolph's luggage in the corner without airing out his clothing. Good for you, thought Tori. Let the bastard tend his own wardrobe.

Priscilla grabbed Tori's hand and led her toward the suite at the other end of the hall. "We'll stall a few more minutes by getting your belongings unpacked."

When Priscilla opened one of Tori's satchels to air out her dresses, she gasped in alarm. "What the blazes is this?"

Tori paused from her task of hanging up Logan's

new suit to note the horrified look on her sister's face. "That's a bullet hole."

Priscilla gulped, wide-eyed. "Sweet mercy!"

"Not to worry. I wasn't wearing it at the time."

"I should hope not." Priscilla poked her forefinger through the hole. "It would have gone straight through your heart!"

"We encountered two outlaws on the first leg of our journey by buckboard," she explained as she went back to unpacking Logan's garments. "Logan made short work of scaring them off. He even let me blast away at them with a shotgun."

Priscilla sighed whimsically. "I should have rebelled against the life our parents designed for me. I wish I would have left Randolph standing at the altar and struck off to enjoy the adventure and excitement that I only read about in dime novels."

"You should come for a visit. For thrills, I'll round up a few bandits and you can scare them away with a loaded shotgun," Tori teased playfully.

"Maybe Randolph should be my first target." Cilla smiled wickedly. "Then I could marry a man who cares enough to protect me from harm. Someone capable like Logan."

"Logan is definitely an expert at his job," she agreed, but she didn't confide that she had *paid* him to portray the devoted husband. Especially not while Cilla presumed Tori led the envied life of freedom and adventure.

After so many years of living in Cilla's shadow, Tori allowed herself to savor the moment. Coming home for Christmas was turning out to be better than expected. She only wished she could bundle up Cilla and Timothy and cart them off to a place where they were free to make their own choices and set their own expectations.

Meanwhile, downstairs in the study, Logan was sharing another drink with Franklin and listening to Randy boast—ad nauseam—about his accomplishments in factory management. Logan would have bet a year's salary the cocky rogue took credit for some of his underlings' innovative ideas then passed them off to Tori's grandfather.

"So, tell us about life in…where is it? Nowhere, Texas?" Randolph sniped insolently. "Does the little spot in the road merit a place on a map?"

Randolph's ridicule rolled off like water down a duck's back. "Lone Ridge," he corrected nonchalantly then finished the second glass of white wine. "You would like it, Randy." He noticed the arrogant gent pulled a face at the shortened version of his name. Even more reason for Logan to use it—repeatedly. "Lots of wide-open spaces and plenty of fresh air. Not the stench of huddled masses. There's plenty of game for hunting and spring-fed creeks for fishing. It's a man's paradise."

"Truly?" Franklin perked up, though Randy's pale face puckered with distaste.

"You should visit us sometime," Logan invited, then asked himself what the devil he thought he was doing besides asking for more complications with this charade. "The view atop Lone Ridge is nothing short of breathtaking. You can see for miles and it feels as if you're standing on top of the world. I'm sure it's like Fort Worth's beginning when your family ventured west to seek your fortune."

"Yes, I believe you're right," Franklin murmured pensively. "I had almost forgotten how much my father loved the challenge of investing and overseeing his financial interest in a nearby cattle ranch. He loved the idea of establishing a life for his family in a fledgling town."

"Much like Tori, who had the courage to make a life for herself," Logan said pointedly. "She has a thriving business, by the way. She has dozens of requests for pies, cakes and pastries for special occasions, besides furnishing desserts for local restaurants."

Franklin smiled. "I'll admit I was leery of her venture, but with you there to look after her I don't worry so much—"

His voice dried up when the sound of shattering glass exploded nearby. Logan sped off when he heard Belinda yelp in dismay. Out of the corner of his eye, he saw Tori and Cilla dashing down the steps. He made a beeline into the dining room and he scowled when he saw Timmy-the-terror standing by the china cabinet. Belinda was down on her knees, picking up the pieces of a hand-painted plate and gravy bowl.

"This was my great-grandmother's china," she said remorsefully. "It was my mother's cherished keepsake brought over from England."

"Timothy Spradlin! Apologize to your grandmother!" Priscilla demanded as she squatted down to help her mother, who couldn't see what she was doing because of the tears clouding her eyes.

"No," Timothy said stubbornly.

Logan had had enough. He was accustomed to taking charge of situations. The moment Randy opened his mouth to make excuses for the ornery brat, Logan grabbed the kid's hand and hauled him toward the front door. Despite Timothy's loud objections—which Logan ignored—he stepped onto the porch.

"This looks to be the perfect time for little Timmy to become better acquainted with his new uncle." Logan glanced back at Tori who bit back an impish grin that made her luminous green eyes sparkle. "If we miss supper, don't fret, sweetheart. We'll grab a bite when we return."

"I do not wish—" Randolph tried to object but Priscilla bounded to her feet and planted herself in her husband's path. "Timothy is in capable hands. Tori has been telling me what an exceptional, well-respected law enforcement officer Logan is." She glanced over her shoulder and nodded decisively. "You have my blessing, Logan. I would love for my son to spend time with you."

Logan left, tugging the brat along with him. He didn't know what Tori and Priscilla had discussed upstairs, but Priscilla was displaying newfound bravado. Obviously Tori's independent spirit had rubbed off on her. In Logan's opinion, the pretty blonde had received the perfect gift for Christmas.

Tori had bathed and dressed for bed by the time Logan returned. Garbed in her nightgown and a modest robe, she waited anxiously for Logan's report. "Well, did you have to lecture the precious little darling on the importance of good manners or threaten him by suggesting Santa Claus didn't stop by to see bad little boys?"

"Neither." Logan shed his jacket and stared eagerly toward the brass tub nestled behind the dressing screen in the corner. "I took Timmy to jail while I introduced myself to the local police commander. Then Timmy took a tour of the foul-smelling cells and I told him about the prisoners I chase down and lock up because of their bad behavior."

Tori chortled softly. "Did your tour and pointed remarks make an impression?"

Logan nodded his raven head and grinned. "I told the kid that I locked up people who stole, lied, cheated and broke precious possessions that belonged to others. I also told him that if he didn't behave himself he would grow up in a cell and his parents wouldn't be allowed to bring him gifts and provide the comforts he took for granted."

"And he actually listened?" she asked curiously.

"Yep." Logan unbuttoned his shirt then cast it aside. "We had the discussion over a loaf of stale bread and a cup of water in the park. After that we viewed the holiday decorations the city put on display."

Tori darted over to hug the stuffing out of Logan. "Thank you. For everything! The gold wedding band, your doting attention in front of my family and your willingness to help Cilla steer Timothy down the right path."

"You're welcome." He dropped a kiss to her lips then grinned. "But I told you the price went up. I wasn't kidding."

Tori stared into his obsidian eyes, his devilish grin and his bare muscular chest. Warm tingles danced down her spine as she impulsively traced her forefinger from one male nipple to the other. "Name your price, Mr. City Marshal. Whatever it is, you are definitely worth it."

His smile faded and sensual tension sparked through the air. "You wouldn't approve of my price, so don't be so generous with your offer."

When he stepped back, Tori yearned to reclaim her grasp on him, to caress his muscular flesh. "Try me."

"Don't tempt me. I don't think your idea of *getting into the Christmas spirit* is the same as mine."

Tori became hopelessly distracted when his bronzed skin rippled with muscles. She could stare at his masculine chest and washboard belly all night—and enjoy every tantalizing minute of it. Mesmerized, she speculated on how he'd look without a stitch of clothing. Then she gave herself a mental slap for allowing her thoughts to drift down such provocative avenues.

"I asked the maid to fill the tub for your bath, but the water might be cool by now," she chirped, unable to take her eyes off him.

He turned away, giving her a tantalizing view of his broad shoulders and lean hips. "The colder the better," he mumbled as he veered around the dressing screen.

She listened to the splash as Logan sank into the tub. Her imagination went wild, wishing she could join him. Good gracious! she thought. Suddenly she wanted much more for Christmas than Logan's willing participation in a charade. She wondered how much extra he'd charge for love lessons. If she was going to pretend to be married once in her life, she might as well enjoy the full benefits and discover what she had been missing.

Reining in her wild thoughts, Tori wheeled toward the door. "I'm going downstairs to fetch a drink," she called out.

"Better not go overboard. I already consumed two glasses of wine for you," he said wryly.

"It wasn't enough. Can I bring you something?"

"Yes, but not that colorless wine. It's for sissies," he insisted. "Make it something strong."

As strong as the wild, reckless sensations bombarding her? she wondered as she fled the room. She was absolutely certain that sharing the bedroom with Logan would tempt and torment her to no end.

"Torment. That isn't what Christmas is supposed to be about," she muttered on her way down the steps.

She surveyed the liquor cabinet in her father's study then grabbed one bottle for her and one for Logan.

Her thoughts circled back to the man sloshing around naked in the bathtub. Suddenly he was all she wanted for Christmas. She didn't think the substituted brandy she sipped on her way upstairs was going to be enough to satisfy her, either.

Chapter Five

Tired, frustrated and unsure how to keep his hands to himself while sharing a bedroom with Tori, Logan stepped from the bathtub. He grabbed the towel when he heard the door open and close. Tori might as well have been wrapped up in ribbons and bows, like the special gift she was, he thought, exasperated. Unfortunately she was the one Christmas package that did not have his name on it.

"This is going to be one long damn night," he mumbled.

"Come again?" she called from the other side of the dressing screen.

"Nothing. Just talking to myself." *And I better listen to the voices of noble intentions and propriety,* he warned himself harshly.

He cocked a curious brow when he heard the clank of a glass against a bottle. He walked around the screen to see Tori propped up on the bed—in a sheer golden nightgown. Desire hit him like an unseen fist. Despite his discomfort and torment, he frowned warily while he watched her pour another drink and down it in three swallows.

"How many of those brandies have you had?"

"Not sure."

Her gaze locked on his half-naked torso then dropped to the private parts of his anatomy that were covered by the towel. Having Tori's gaze roam over him and watching her blush profusely made him grin. He walked over to retrieve the bottle from her hand but she thrust her glass at him.

"More."

Logan downed his own drink in one swallow first. Then he reluctantly refilled her glass.

She offered him a toast. "To Christmas."

"I'll drink to that." He filled his glass to the brim.

"You and me both."

She thrust her empty glass at him again but he didn't refill it because he noted a slight slur in her voice.

He held the bottle away from her when she

reached for it. "You need to slow down so I can catch up."

"I don't want to slow down…Logan?"

"What?" he asked between gulps.

"I've thought it over and I've decided I want you to make love to me for Christmas."

Her forthright comment made him choke and sputter.

While he wheezed to catch his breath, she levered herself upright to whack him on the back. "How much will the love lessons cost me?"

He couldn't speak. His tongue was stuck to the roof of his mouth and his brain froze up like an icicle.

"It has occurred to me that the only way to *act* intimate, as you suggested, while we're under my family's scrutiny is to actually *be* intimate. I must admit the prospect has become most appealing to me."

Logan's willpower took a direct hit when he peered into that exquisite face, surrounded by frothy mahogany curls that tumbled enticingly over the peaks of her breasts—that were barely concealed by the near-transparent fabric. Damn! How was he supposed to deny her request when it was at the very top of *his* wish list? And how could he even think of accepting her offer when he knew she had drowned her inhibitions and usual good sense in brandy?

All these years he'd thought he'd suffered through one sad excuse after another for what *should have been* happy holidays. But this had to be the Christmas from hell. What he wanted most was the one thing he knew he shouldn't have.

"Logan, I want you. It's as simple as that."

Tell her no! the noble side of his brain shouted.

His thoughts scattered like buckshot when she reached over to grasp the towel tied loosely around his waist. Hungry need exploded inside him when her hand brushed his abdomen. Her gaze flowed unhindered over his body when she tossed aside the towel and left him exposed—mind and body.

"Victoria Thurston, if we do this, you are going to hate yourself…and me…in the morning," he rasped as she stared at his arousal.

"My goodness…"

Her gaze finally lifted to his amused smile. He wondered if it was possible for her face to turn a deeper shade of red than it was now. He couldn't imagine how.

"Should I douse the light?" he asked.

"The first time, yes," she mumbled as she set aside her glass.

"*First* time?" he croaked as he snuffed the lantern. "How many times are you planning to do this?"

"As many as it takes. I never do anything half-way."

Logan could feel the sexual tension buzzing around him like a hornet. Moonlight sprayed across the room, guiding him to her. Not that he needed light to lead his way, he realized as he stretched out beside her. His body was a compass and she was magnetic north.

He pulled the nightgown over her head so he could do what he'd wanted to do since the first time he'd kissed her a few nights earlier. He wanted to savor every tantalizing inch of her satiny flesh by taste and by touch.

He began his journey of discovery by feasting on her dewy-soft lips, her perfectly arched brows then the elegant column of her neck. When he dared to caress her nipples with thumb and middle finger, she moaned huskily and arched toward him.

"More," she demanded, not that she had to ask because he was all in favor.

"My pleasure." He flicked at her nipple with his tongue then suckled gently.

"Ah, Logan…"

Her voice fizzled out when his wandering hand glided down her rib cage to swirl over her concave belly. When his fingertips drifted over the silky flesh of her inner thighs, he groaned in torment. The hot desire he'd called from her was so close yet so tormentingly far away. The things he wanted to do with her might shock her, he knew. But he'd had enough to drink—and all too quickly—that it was difficult to restrain himself. He shifted sideways to spread a row of moist kisses from the crests of her breasts to her navel then to her abdomen.

When he parted her heated flesh with his thumb then skimmed his lips over her, he felt her body tremble and he heard her breath whoosh out on a shattered sigh. When he kissed her intimately, repeatedly, she clamped her hand over his forearm. Her nails bit into his flesh while she whispered his name like a chant.

Logan had never spent much time seducing a woman. None of his previous encounters had been as magical as discovering what Tori liked, discovering what made her come undone in his arms. Logan never realized that sharing this kind of intimate passion even existed. Or that it would satisfy and fascinate him quite so much.

"Come here...please..." she gasped when he glided his fingertip inside her to caress her slowly and deliberately.

"Don't rush me," he teased then skimmed his lips over her hot flesh.

She moaned when he caressed her with his tongue then inserted two fingers to stroke her. She was so tight, so warm and inviting that need roared through him, demanding that he take what she offered and appease the ravenous hunger gnawing at him.

"Logan, I need you like crazy," she panted as her sensitized body all but melted around him.

He twisted above her then eased between her legs. He looked down at her while he brushed familiarly against her. He could feel the warm rain of her desire bathing him. Mesmerized, he stared into evergreen eyes that glowed with passion in the moonlight. He saw the mahogany cloud of curly hair that fanned her beguiling face and he was hopelessly, completely lost.

He wanted to be one with Tori more than he wanted his next breath. Of all the holidays he had endured and survived in his hardscrabble life, this was the one he would cherish in all the years to come. The gift of this unique, amazing woman's desire was every fantasy come true—

Logan stopped breathing when Tori wrapped her hand around his engorged flesh and caressed him.

"I want you now," she rasped. "I don't think I'll survive another minute if you don't make this maddening ache go away."

Tori measured him with gliding fingertips, stroked him repeatedly. She guided him closer, aching to satisfy the need burning deep inside her. When his powerful body surged toward hers, she hooked her legs around his bare hips, desperate for him to fill the empty ache he had aroused in her.

She hissed out her breath when he plunged inside her, stretching her, consuming her. The fire in her blood blazed higher as she instinctively moved toward him, meeting thrust with urgent thrust.

She had never understood what total abandonment or overwhelming desire was like. But now she knew. She would never forget the incredible feeling of her body locked intimately to Logan's muscular flesh.

The faint twinge of discomfort was no match for

the hot sensations building like a fiery crescendo inside her. Pleasure intensified and she struggled to breathe over the wild pounding of her pulse. She clung desperately to Logan as he drove into her, creating even wilder needs with each penetrating thrust.

She heard him groan, felt his panting breath against the side of her neck. He tensed, as if holding back. Which was the last thing she wanted. She clutched him closer and arched into him, gyrating impatiently in an attempt to capture some elusive need that teased and tormented her.

"Oh, damn..." he mumbled.

Oh, damn is right, thought Tori. She felt him shudder uncontrollably—triggering the most indescribable sensation imaginable. She swore she had been lightning-struck. No part of her was left untouched by the electrifying passion that sizzled through her and melded them together.

Tori tumbled through time and space—stunned, amazed, completely sated. Pleasure radiated from her as she nuzzled her head against Logan's muscled shoulder. She held on to him until the last of her strength and energy drained away.

A moment later, she sagged against him like a rag doll. Her last thought before she collapsed in the afterglow of all-consuming pleasure was that sharing Logan's passion was the best holiday gift she'd ever had.

Logan awoke with a vague headache to find himself half-draped over Tori's lush, naked body. Reality hit him like a doubled fist to the jaw. He had taken Tori's innocence. He hadn't been able to stop himself, even when he realized that he was her first experiment with passion.

"Damnation," he muttered when he remembered how he and his pretend wife had guzzled liquor then broke every rule of propriety by creating a bonfire of flaming passion that burned him alive.

This was to have been his finest hour, he told himself disdainfully. It had been more than fine, but not in the noble way he'd intended. His desire for Tori had outmuscled his willpower. He wasn't sure what he had been doing the past decade when he'd scratched an itch, but it was nothing compared to the pleasure he'd shared with Tori.

The disturbing thought of creating a little Timmy of his own, who ran around pouring wine on a maid's head and breaking heirloom dishes, made him wince.

Damn it, for a man who dealt in dispensing

consequences for bad behavior he had fouled up royally. He might have caused complications that extended long past the Christmas holidays and changed the course of Tori's life.

One thing was for sure and certain: he never wanted Tori to marry him because she *had* to. He wanted her to marry him because—

When that runaway thought galloped through his head, Logan recoiled, careful not to wake Tori. Scowling silently, he raked his fingers through his tousled hair and asked himself at what point last night had he discarded the good sense he'd nurtured for three decades. It only took a moment to pinpoint the instant that he'd thumbed his nose at consequences like a thief on his way to rob a bank.

He had looked down at Tori, lying on the bed, her lush body bathed in moonlight, and he'd known there wasn't enough noble restraint in the world to prevent him from living out his wildest fantasy.

Although she was the best mistake he'd ever made, it was still a mistake. He predicted she would hate him, and herself, when she woke up. She had become entrapped in her own scheme and the price had been excessively steep.

Mentally kicking himself repeatedly, Logan eased from bed then freshened up with the cool water left in the tub. Then he dressed hurriedly. He wasn't sure he wanted to be on hand when Tori roused and realized he had failed to protect her from her worst enemy—her pretend husband.

Worse, he had no idea how to make this up to her.

Easing the door shut behind him, Logan went downstairs. He hoped a cup of coffee would clear his head. Something damn well better. He needed to *think*. Unfortunately the exceptionally good time he'd had last night was the one thought that kept parading through his mind while Franklin chattered on—and on—about the ins and outs of the newspaper business.

Tori had been bustled around the estate most of the day, involved in last-minute arrangements for the Christmas Eve ball. She hadn't had the chance to be alone with Logan. She hadn't seen much of him, either. Her father had taken the menfolk—Timmy included—on a tour of the estate, the newly expanded newspaper office and to view the Christmas decorations the city council had set up in the parks.

"I'm truly sorry about your broken heirloom dishes," Priscilla told her mother while the threesome set up additional tables in the foyer and dining room.

Her mother smiled ruefully. "They were sentimental favorites but I have another piece that I will display behind glass on the top shelf of the china cabinet."

"At least Timothy seems better behaved after his evening jaunt with Uncle Logan," Priscilla remarked, casting Tori a meaningful glance. "In fact, Timothy seems to have taken a liking to Logan. I'm glad of that."

Tori rather thought that Timmy, even at his young age, had learned to respect discipline and a firm hand. She predicted Logan would make an exceptional father because he didn't sit back; he resolved problems before they got out of hand.

The thought of a child of her own gave her pause. She had been focused on making a success of her bakery and avoiding the long arm of her family's unacceptable expectations. She had intended to be a spinster. However, the consequences of last night's intimate tryst could change her future plans.

Tori swallowed uneasily, wondering if she would be forced to tell another white lie to her family. She would have to dispose of Logan—figuratively speaking, of course—so he wouldn't have to be involved in future charades.

Well, she told herself. She would deal with whatever consequences she encountered. *She* had insisted Logan teach her the meaning of passion, after all. The thought of her lack of restraint, the unbelievable intimacy, and the incredible pleasure she'd discovered put a crimson blush on her face.

"Are you feeling okay, sis?" Cilla asked attentively.

Tori pasted on a bright smile. "I'm fine. It's just a bit stuffy in here. I'm not accustomed to the heat given off by these oversize fireplaces. I rarely use one at home. Even Decembers are mild because the protective bluff of Lone Ridge blocks the wind and moderates the temperatures."

"I am definitely coming for a visit," Cilla declared. "Boston is positively frigid. Besides, I would like Timothy to develop an appreciation for wide-open spaces."

"Name the time," Tori offered generously. "You're always welcome. Plus, I could use helping hands since my business is expanding rapidly."

Good gracious, she thought a moment later. As much as she delighted in Cilla's company, she would have to break down and confide to her sister that she wasn't married. Not that Cilla would betray her, but Randolph was another matter entirely. The unfaithful cad.

"I doubt Randolph can make the trip with us, though," Cilla went on to say. "According to him, he has too many responsibilities to visit Texas more than once a year."

Good for you, thought Tori, smiling wryly at Cilla. *Leave the bastard at home and develop a strong, independent streak that he can't stifle.*

"That is so sweet of you, Cilla," said their mother. "Despite your busy schedule you are willing to make the journey to help your little sister."

Tori rolled her eyes. Some things changed, but others remained the same. Cilla was Belinda's little darling who inherited her coloring and delicate good looks. Tori knew she would always be compared to her sister. It didn't bother her as much as it used to. It just didn't matter anymore that her parents could not see her for who she was.

She realized that because she lived a rewarding, productive life, she had learned to accept and appreciate her family for who they were. She was her own person. The thought made her smile. Coming home for Christmas was turning out to be an epiphany.

* * *

"Are you feeling all right?" Tori asked while Logan tried to tie the fashionable cravat in place. "You've been exceptionally quiet this evening."

Logan tossed out what he hoped was a non-chalant smile. Truth was that he'd beaten himself black and blue the whole livelong day while Franklin hauled him around town. "I'm fine. Perfect. Having the time of my life."

"Pfftt!" she sniffed in contradiction. "You spent most of the day with Papa, Randy-the-unfaithful-bastard and Timmy-the-terror."

Logan frowned curiously when Tori walked over to rescue him by tying his cravat properly. "Did Cilla tell you Randy was prone to sleeping in other beds besides his own?" he blurted out of the blue.

Her long lashes swept up to meet his gaze and it was all he could do not to take her in his arms and kiss her until he appeased the lingering desire that hounded him.

"When did you figure that out?" she asked curiously.

"Last night when Randy ogled you like his next meal. If he touches you improperly tonight, don't be surprised if I shoot off his wandering hand."

Tori grinned. "How very chivalrous of you, dear.

And yes, Cilla confided that she had an unhappy marriage. I invited her to Lone Ridge. She can come as often as she wants and stay as long as she pleases. Timothy, too. That child will be better off without Randy's negative influence."

"Amen to that."

"In addition, I'm sorry about last night," she remarked then quickly looked the other way.

He'd wondered when regret would get the best of her and she'd bring up their reckless tryst. "It was my fault."

"No, it wasn't." She stepped away then turned her back to him. "*I* insisted and you darn well know it... Fasten these tedious buttons, will you? I don't want to call in a maid. The servants are busy with last-minute preparations."

Logan enjoyed the feel of his knuckles brushing over the bare skin of Tori's back. As enchanting as she looked in the eye-catching, form-fitting silver gown that displayed her breasts to their best advantage, he'd prefer to have her *out* of it and *in* bed with him.

Christmas Eve ball go hang, he thought. He'd made a gigantic mistake with Tori last night. So why not do the holidays up right with another colossal one tonight?

Are you out of your mind? the voice of reason railed at him. He felt guilty about taking her innocence. Now he was contemplating the prospect of skipping the party and spending the evening in bed with Tori. That would impress the hell out of his pretend in-laws, wouldn't it?

"Brace yourself," she forewarned as she pirouetted to face him again. "Father informed me that he intends to use the party to introduce you to his friends and announce our recent marriage. We'll dance the first waltz."

"Oh, hell!"

"Do you want to practice before we go downstairs?"

He snorted. "You know where that first dance lesson ended up. And no more toasts to Christmas, either. Last night, I—"

She pressed her index finger to his lips to shush him. Despite her telltale blush she said, "Don't you dare apologize for the best night of my life."

He blinked, enormously pleased with her remark. Then he reminded himself that he was the *only* night of her life. She had nothing for comparison—and he didn't want her experimenting, either. The very thought roused his deepest feelings of possessiveness.

Mercy, what was happening to him? He had agreed to be Tori's holiday husband and poof! All sorts of troubling sensations and emotions overcame him. This charade felt too real and he was enjoying his role entirely too much.

When she pushed up on tiptoe to kiss him, every thought flew out of his head. Impulsively he wrapped her in his arms and drank the sweet nectar of her lips. This kiss had to be enough to get him through this evening and through this charade, he told himself determinedly.

"Ready?" she asked as she backed from his arms.

"As I'll ever be. Let's get this over with."

Tori smiled so often she feared her face would crack. Her parents kept hauling her from one guest to the next, forcing her to be as charming as she knew how. If she heard another person say it was a relief to see that she'd emerged from her ugly duckling stage to blossom into a lovely woman she was going to resort to Timmy's tactic of dumping wine on people's heads.

And poor Logan, she thought in dismay. He had been bombarded by teasing remarks about how he was lucky he hadn't met Tori during her awkward adolescence. A time when she had skinny arms and legs, her eyes seemed too large to fit her face and her mouth practically stretched from one ear to the other.

She was excessively pleased when Logan had his fill of the comments and told one of her spiteful childhood chums that dredging up memories bored him and that as breathtakingly lovely as he thought Tori was, it was her inner beauty, character and lively personality that intrigued him most. Then he gave several of her former school classmates The Look he was famous for. They backed off, turned tail and poured themselves a glass of courage before daring to face him again.

"Ladies and gentlemen! I want to introduce my new son-in-law, the highly respected marshal who has made an impressive name for himself in West Texas!"

"I see why Franklin is in the newspaper business." Logan remarked as he came to stand beside Tori. "He can turn a phrase and dress up facts like nobody's business.

"May I formally present Logan Daniels." Her father swept his arm in an expansive gesture to single out Logan, who nodded graciously during the applause.

"Victoria and Logan, we wish you many happy

holidays together. The floor is yours," her father declared then signaled for the band to strike up a waltz.

Tori forgot this was a charade when Logan took her hand and drew her familiarly against his broad chest. He lowered his head to drop a quick kiss to her lips, drawing smiles from the attentive crowd.

He nuzzled her neck in a display of affection and whispered, "Start counting the cadence of the waltz, sweetheart, and don't stop until this damn dance is over. I'll give you anything you want if you can prevent me from looking like a clumsy fool."

"You are too light on your feet for that to happen," she assured him then counted the steps while he whirled her around the room.

For the next few minutes, while she stared into Logan's fathomless eyes and felt his body moving provocatively against hers, she realized that it was no longer enough to fool her family and friends into thinking she was married to a capable law officer and that she owned a popular bakery in Lone Ridge. What she really wanted for Christmas was Logan's genuine love and devotion—forever.

How was it even possible that she'd fallen so hard so fast? She supposed that she had been infatuated and had admired him from a distance for a year because he appealed to her physically. In addition, he had earned her respect because of his invaluable service to the community. Plus, he had a wry sense of humor and he was an amazingly skilled and considerate lover. Tori was certain she could spend the next hundred years with him—

"May I cut in?" Priscilla asked during the second waltz, after her father invited everyone to dance.

Logan studied Tori questioningly. It was her call, she knew. He was here for *her*. The realization made her love him even more.

"Of course." Tori backed from Logan's powerful arms. "Handle my sister with care. She means a lot to me."

Logan winked and said, "I just hope she can count."

Tori made it halfway to the refreshment table before Randolph swaggered over, as if he were God's gift to women.

"This is the perfect time for us to become better acquainted," he purred as he snaked his arm around her waist to give her a suggestive squeeze.

Tori bent his wrist backward until he grimaced in pain. "I didn't like you when I first met you and I think even less of you now that I know you. The only reason I'm tolerating your presence is that it's Christmas. If you make my sister unhappy, I will sic my husband on you. He will have my orders to crush you like the roach you are."

"You always did have a sassy mouth," Randolph scowled. "Too bad it overshadows the fact that you've become amazingly attractive the past two years."

She flashed him a mocking smile and said, "You've become less attractive with each passing year. I think it's due in part to your noticeable lack of character. For the life of me, I cannot fathom what you think you have to be arrogant about, either. Now go away, Randy. You're bothering me."

Take that, she thought as she left him standing by the refreshment table, gaping at her in astonishment.

Chapter Six

"Whew, I'm glad that's over," Logan gushed in relief, and then closed the bedroom door so he could remove the cravat that felt like a hangman's noose around his neck.

He glanced at Tori who stepped behind the dressing screen to change into her nightgown. When she emerged, his thoughts stalled out. The overwhelming feelings of desire that destroyed his self-control the previous night flooded over him again. He made a noble attempt to stay where he was but Tori walked over to unbutton his shirt then cast it carelessly aside.

"Have you forgotten what happened last night?" he asked as she unbuttoned his breeches.

"No, it's all I've been able to think about while playing nice to my parents' guests." She grinned impishly at him then added, "I fully intend to get my money's worth for hiring a pretend husband."

He sucked in his breath when she glided her hand inside the open placket of his breeches. Logan swore the top of his head was about to blow off when she caressed him, arousing him to the extreme.

A string of discarded clothing—his and hers—led the way across the room. They tumbled across the bed in their haste to get their hands on each other. Tori spread a row of moist kisses over his shoulder then shook her head when he tried to snuff the lantern. When he turned back to stare questioningly at her, she kissed him with the kind of hungry impatience he knew and understood because it was hammering away at him. He nearly blacked out when she kissed her way down his chest and belly to brush her open mouth over his pulsating arousal.

He gasped for breath then groaned in defeat while she seduced him one exotic kiss and caress at a time. He couldn't resist her touch and he no longer cared if his conscience railed at him until his ears burned. Tori's gentle lovemaking compensated for every gift he'd done without at Christmases past. He would gladly relive those lonely holidays if they paved a path to her arms. She bombarded him with sensations that spun his world off its axis and left his body quivering with ineffable pleasure.

"You are killing me, woman," he gasped as another frayed strand of self-restraint escaped his grasp.

"Am I? I swore I died at least twice last night," she murmured against his throbbing flesh. "You should know that I have every intention of compensating for all I've been missing these past few years."

"I swear I've unleashed an irresistible, seductive siren." Logan wrapped his hand in her long hair, using it like a rope to draw her face to his.

He kissed her ardently, and he could taste his own desire for her on her lips. The intimacy of the moment sent him toppling over the edge into wild abandon. He hooked his arm around her waist and set her above him. His breath came out on a ragged sigh as she sank down upon him and he became the pulsing flame inside her.

"This is where I want to be for Christmas," he said as he moved erotically against her. "All I want is you."

Logan wasn't even aware that he had voiced the confession until the words echoed around him. When she smiled down at him then wiggled suggestively above him, he didn't care that he'd given himself away. And why not? He'd given all he was—the best of what he was—to Tori already.

After all, a man could fall no farther when he was already at the bottom of his heart.

When Tori awoke Christmas morning, she could feel Logan's warm strength beside her. She smiled contentedly at the thought. Opening one eye, she noted Logan had propped his head on his hand. He'd been staring down at her, waiting for her to wake up.

"Merry Christmas. I've never said that to anyone, first thing in the morning." He frowned pensively. "Maybe, Gabe, but this is a lot different."

Tori didn't know why she felt sentimental suddenly, but his comment touched her. Impulsively she levered herself up to give him a loud, smacking kiss on the lips. "Merry Christmas to you, too. I've never said that, first thing in the morning, to anyone but you, either. But then, I've never been in—"

She clamped her mouth shut before she blurted out her affection for Logan. She didn't want him to feel awkward or pressured before they descended the steps to unveil the traditional Christmas tree and gifts that her parents insisted on saving until Christmas morning.

He arched a curious brow. "What were you saying?"

Flushing, she grabbed the edge of the sheet, wrapped herself in it then bounded to her feet. Logan didn't move, just lay there—naked. She stared appreciatively at his masculine physique. Every sensible thought flew out of her head, replaced by the erotic memories they had made last night.

"I forgot what I intended to say. Seeing you naked does that to me," she hedged as she turned her back to him.

"Tori...?"

She flapped her arm at him. "Don't distract me again. I need to dress and so do you. Timothy will be anxious to open his gifts. I don't want to keep him waiting."

"What's the traditional procedure?" Logan asked as he rolled off the bed to freshen up.

"We wait in anticipation while Father opens the door to the sunroom. He keeps it locked up tight until Christmas morning. Then we *ooh* and *ahh* over the magnificent tree and the decorations. Next, we open gifts then we have a light breakfast in the sunroom. Then we retire to our rooms to dress for an early lunch feast."

Logan nodded as he buttoned himself into one of his new shirts. "This is nothing like my usual tradition of crawling from bed to meet Gabe at jail for coffee. If it's an uneventful day without crime, we entertain ourselves by playing checkers or poker."

Tori moved swiftly across the suite. She wrapped her arms around him from behind then nuzzled her cheek against his muscled back. She suddenly felt petty for complaining about her family and dragging him along to redeem herself in her parents' eyes. For better or worse, she had a family and Logan had none at all. Because of her charade, she had left Gabe Horton with no one to greet on Christmas Day.

"What's that for?" he asked as he turned in her arms.

"Must be the season that's getting to me." She displayed an overly bright smile and blinked back the mist of tears that welled up in her eyes. "I know I've asked a lot of you, but I'm glad you're here with me. Next year, we are going to include Gabe. Somehow or other. I don't want to leave him out. We'll form our own family in Lone Ridge."

Logan chuckled as he dropped a kiss to her lips. "If you're baking for the holidays then count me in."

The impatient pounding at the door prompted them to glance sideways.

"Uncle Logan? Aunt Tori! Come quickly! Santa Claus has been here!"

"Yes, I know," Tori called out to her overanxious nephew then smiled mischievously. "I saw him last night."

Logan grinned conspiratorially at her then said, "We'll be there in one minute, Timmy. Count on it."

Logan swore his eyes nearly popped out of his head—same as Timmy's—when Franklin swung open the door with a dramatic flair to reveal the monstrous pine tree encircled by yards of shiny tinsel and decorated with hand-carved and hand-painted ornaments. In addition, teacup-size cakes of various flavors dangled from the tree limbs. Candles flickered, casting fascinating shadows on the tree. The morning sun glowed molten gold through the windows, giving the tree an incandescent, supernatural quality, the likes of which Logan had never seen. The peaceful silence that filled the room made it seem as if the world stood still to announce the existence of a presence beyond their understanding.

He surveyed the delighted expression on Timmy's face then he appraised the adults who smiled appreciatively at the splendid tree. Something unfamiliar tugged at his heart and he reached over to clasp Tori's hand. Her glistening evergreen eyes reminded him of the lighted Christmas tree. He swore, until the day he died, he'd never get through another Christmas without thinking of the enthralling expression that encompassed her lovely face.

His heart contracted and a lump clogged his throat when she turned that dazzling smile on him then gave his hand an affectionate squeeze. Unconcerned about what was considered inappropriate behavior in the Thurston house, he leaned down to kiss Tori, right smack-dab in front of her family. To his relief, his supposed in-laws merely smiled indulgently.

"There is nowhere I'd rather be except here with you this morning," Logan whispered for her ears only. "You're the best Christmas I've ever had."

Timmy, at the end of his patience, yelped excitedly then bounded toward the gaily-adorned packages that awaited him. Logan wondered if the boy would ever appreciate how good he had it. For sure, Logan would never forget this special Christmas. He had become part of a family.

While Timmy played with the toys his parents and grandparents had given him, Logan pulled the small box from his pocket then handed it to Tori. She frowned, bemused.

At his urging, she opened the box. Her mouth dropped open wide enough for a partridge to roost. She gaped at the delicate emerald ring that matched the gold band Logan had purchased for her in Purple Sage Hollow.

"When? Where?" she bleated in amazement as he slipped the ring on her finger.

"Yesterday, while your father gave me the grand tour of Fort Worth," he reported. "The ring reminded me of the color of your eyes."

Tori blinked rapidly, trying not to cry and reduce herself to sentimental mush. The moment she glanced at her sister, who was trapped in a loveless, arranged marriage, Tori fully appreciated her own marriage, pretend though it was. Her time with Logan overflowed with enjoyment, amusement, passion and happiness.

When she handed Logan his gift, he unwrapped

it quickly then gave her another kiss. She was certain her family believed her marriage was real because Logan played his part as the devoted, adoring husband to the hilt.

"You always know what I want," he said as he brushed his thumb over the gold pocket watch. "I'll never lose track of time so I can come home to you."

While Timothy and Cilla untied the small cakes and Tori brought in the tray of coffee, she surveyed the sunroom with a newfound appreciation. No matter what childhood disappointments she'd endured. No matter what differences of opinions, conflicts of personalities or unreasonable expectations, this was her family. And family was family. She knew she could count on these people for assistance if necessary, just as she would lend support if they needed her.

The holiday season was a reminder of the importance of belonging to a family. Having Logan here with her made the moment incredibly gratifying. Together they could celebrate the special magic and true gift of Christmas—the bright promise of unconditional love and hope for the future. Tori vowed never to let herself forget that.

Her gaze lingered on Logan and she watched

Timmy crawl onto his lap to show him the toy locomotive and freight cars Santa had left for him.

"That man is a keeper," Cilla murmured on her way by.

"I know." Tori wished she could keep her pretend husband because he was the only gift worth having for Christmas—and all yearlong.

Two hours later, when everyone hiked upstairs to bathe and dress for a formal Christmas dinner, Tori surged into the suite to fish into her purse.

"Here's the money I owe you for being my holiday husband," she said. "I added more banknotes to cover the cost of this lovely ring. Your thoughtfulness overwhelms me."

When he grasped her hand, palm up, to return the money, she frowned, puzzled.

"There's no charge," he insisted. "I told you, this is the best holiday in living memory."

Emotion swamped her like a flash flood and she swore she'd drown in it. She flung her arms around Logan's neck and blurted out, "I love you!"

She slammed her mouth shut so quickly that she nearly clipped off the end of her tongue. Before he could break her heart by smiling sympathetically and trying to let her down gently, she presented her back and struggled for hard-won composure.

"I'm sorry, Logan. That isn't supposed to be a part of our arrangement. I just can't help myself."

"Tori—"

Before he could voice a comment that was sure to leave her bawling like a baby, she shook her head. "You don't have to worry. I won't complicate your life more than I have already. I'll work up the courage to tell my family the truth before next Christmas rolls around."

"Listen, Tori, I—"

She spun around and marshaled her bravado. "Don't think you have to explain anything. You played your role so convincingly that I became carried away. I will survive. I got myself into this—"

When he clamped his hand over her mouth, she had no choice but to shut up. He grinned at her, his onyx eyes dancing with amusement.

"If you'll stop interrupting me, chatterbox, I'd like to say that I'm in love with you, too. I want you to be more than my Yuletide bride. I want you for always, if you'll have me as your forever husband."

He loved her? His words rang in her ears and all

she could do was stare at him in stupefied astonishment.

"Marry me, Tori. I don't want to return to a life
where I don't get to see you first thing every morning and last thing every night."

Logan wasn't sure where he'd found the nerve
to lay his heart on the line. He felt self-conscious
and awkward because he'd never voiced the words
to another woman. But emotion just kept pouring
out of him like eggnog spilling from an upturned
pitcher.

He chuckled when Tori squealed in delight then
leaped up to fling her arms around his neck and
her legs around his hips. It instantly reminded him
of their first dance lesson so he waltzed her around
the room. He was hopelessly lost in the moment
and in his all-consuming love for her. He didn't
care if he banged into the furniture and kerplopped
on the floor.

Before that happened, however, he tumbled with
her onto the bed so he covered her lush body with
his.

"Is that a yes?" he asked as he combed his fingers through her silky mane of mahogany hair that
tumbled across the pillow.

"*Yes!*" she whispered emphatically. She traced

the delicate skin around the corners of his eyes. "You will always have my heart, Logan. It's my gift to you this Christmas and all the Christmases to come."

"I give my soul to you forever and ever," he promised faithfully.

He sealed his solemn vow with a kiss brimming with so much love and affection that one erotic, breathless moment led to another.

They were noticeably late for Christmas dinner.

It became a Daniels' family tradition.

* * * * *

THE HOMECOMING
Elizabeth Lane

Dear Reader

Christmas is more than a time for presents, parties, decorations and carols. For some of us it's a time when painful memories are most deeply felt—loss, loneliness and alienation. But if we open our hearts Christmas can also be a time of healing, a time to reach out, to bridge chasms of separation and bitterness and come together in the spirit of love.

THE HOMECOMING is a story about three good people who need to forgive each other in order to forgive themselves. It isn't a pretty tale—but then, it wasn't meant to be. Clay, Elise and Buck are trapped in a cycle of blame and remorse that can only be broken by one act—the act of total forgiveness and love. Only then will they be able to heal and move on with their lives.

It's my hope that this story will move you to think, to feel, and perhaps even to act. If I hear that it's inspired even one of you to reach out and begin the healing of old wounds, I will know it was well worth the writing.

With my heartfelt wishes for a joyous, loving holiday season.

Elizabeth Lane

To those of us who need to be forgiven...
And to those of us who need to forgive.

Prologue

Kansas State Penitentiary
Leavenworth County, Kansas
December 4, 1878

"You've served your time, McAllister. You're free to go."

Clay McAllister shivered as the iron gates clanged shut behind him. The December cold cut to his bones. His cheap prison-issue coat was too thin for the weather, but it would have to do until he got back to Texas.

Back home—if he still had a home.

A lot could change in three years, Clay knew. His wife hadn't written to him once. The only thing he'd received from her were his own unopened letters, with a terse Return To Sender penned on each envelope. The returned letters had told him, at least, that she was still living on the ranch. But they answered none of his other questions.

Why was Elise so angry? Didn't she know what had happened to him?

What in hell's name had gone wrong?

The memory of that awful night still darkened Clay's dreams. He and his eighteen-year-old brother, Buck, had driven a thousand head of longhorn cattle up the trail to Abilene. After selling them for top dollar, they'd paid off the hired vaqueros and set out for an evening of celebration. A bath, a good meal and a couple of drinks had been enough for Clay. With the cash in the hotel safe, he'd retired early to rest up for the trip home.

He'd drifted off to sleep with a smile on his face. The money from the cattle sale—almost twenty thousand dollars—would pay off the debts on the ranch and give them a good start for next year. It would also buy the new furniture Elise had been wanting, as well as clothes and toys for their two-year-old boy, Toby. They'd been living on the ragged edge of poverty for so long. What a pleasure it would be to buy nice things for his wife and child.

Sometime after midnight he'd awakened to

discover that Buck's bed was empty. His brother hadn't returned to the hotel.

Worried, Clay had dressed and gone out looking for him. Buck was a strapping lad, able to do a man's work on the trail. But at eighteen he had a lot to learn. Abilene was as rough as any cow town on the map, a place where a young man could get into no end of trouble. As he searched the saloons and gambling dens and checked the drunks passed out on the boardwalk, Clay had lashed himself for leaving Buck on his own. If anything had happened to the boy, he would never forgive himself.

He'd lost track of the time it took to work his way toward the far end of the street. Here, even at this late hour, the discreetly shuttered houses swarmed with activity. Half-opened doorways offered glimpses of seductively clad women. Raucous female laughter and the notes of a tinny piano drifted through the darkness.

Damn him! Clay didn't relish the thought of dragging Buck out of a whorehouse. But he was getting worried—and angry. He'd raised his kid brother after their parents died, and he'd tried to teach him decent values. But it appeared that the lessons hadn't taken. When he found the young whelp, by heaven, Buck was going to get the tongue-lashing of his life!

He was mounting the steps of the first house when he heard the commotion. Upstairs, in the place across the street, a fight had broken out. Glass shattered as a chair smashed through a window. Shouts and screams erupted in the night, accompanied by the sound of crashing furniture and bodies.

Thinking only of his brother, Clay plunged across the street, shoved his way inside and charged up the stairs. By then the whole place had become a melee of shrieking women and their scrambling customers. In a lamplit room at the end of the hall he found Buck, half dressed and fighting off three men. A tired-looking redhead, her makeup smeared, cringed in a corner, clutching a sheet against her body.

One of the men, a stocky, redheaded fellow in a checkered suit, had drawn a hidden knife. The blade flashed as he made a lunge for Buck. Reacting instinctively, Clay seized a cast iron boot jack and swung it against the man's head. The man sagged to the floor, collapsing without a sound.

Seconds passed before someone realized he wasn't breathing.

A sudden hush fell over the room. Rough hands seized Clay from behind, holding him fast. Before they dragged him away, Clay managed to mouth a few words to his brother.

"Get out of here, Buck. Take the cash from the hotel and ride for all you're worth. Give the money to Elise and tell her what happened. I'll come as soon as I can."

His trial was speedy. Under different circumstances Clay might have gone free on the grounds of defending his brother. But the man he'd struck down was a city councilman, and the town was screaming for justice. With a verdict of manslaughter, he was sentenced to serve five years in the state penitentiary. Good behavior had gotten him out in a little more than three.

Clay had never learned what the fight was about. And he'd never heard from Buck again.

Now, mounted on an aging buckskin horse that was all he could afford, Clay headed through swirling snow—south by southwest, along the empty cattle trails to the high Texas plains he called home.

With luck, he would be there by Christmas.

Chapter One

North Texas
December 21, 1878

"Mama! There's a man riding up to the gate!" Five-year-old Toby burst in through the front door, his cheeks ruddy with cold.

"Anybody we know?" Elise glanced up from the iron skillet she was scrubbing.

"Don't think so. He's riding tired, like he's come a long way. Maybe he's a tramp."

Elise's eyes flashed to the shotgun she kept above the door. "You know the rule. Go into your room and stay there until I find out who it is."

"Yes'm." Toby closed the front door, shutting off a blast of wind that fluttered the homemade ornaments on the tiny Christmas tree. As he scampered to his bedroom, Elise walked to the front window and stared down the road.

The approaching stranger was still some distance away. She couldn't make out his features beneath the slouch-brimmed hat, but she could see that he was a big man, tall in the saddle, his broad shoulders hunched against the cold. His buckskin mount plodded wearily along beneath him. Toby had been right. Both horse and rider looked as if they'd come a long way.

Elise kept her eyes on him as he approached the gate. She'd learned to be wary of strangers. But something about this man was familiar—the rangy body, the shadowed face...

Her hand crept to her throat. "No," she whispered. "No, it can't be..."

Beneath the high arch of the gate, Clay paused to gather his courage. With each day of the long ride from Kansas, the hunger to be home had grown deeper. He'd yearned for the feel of his own land beneath his feet, his own roof over his head, his woman and child in his arms. That burning desire had kept him moving through cold and wind, through gnawing hunger and fatigue.

Now that he was here, all he could think of was turning away and riding on.

Only the thin curl of smoke from the chimney told him the place was lived-in. Aside from that…Lord, what had happened here? The fences and outbuildings were in disrepair, the pastures untended, the cattle gone. A single milk cow stood in the corral with its head to the wind. A few scrawny chickens pecked in the yard.

What had become of the men he'd hired to stay and take care of the ranch? What had become of the stock?

What had happened to his family?

Dread constricted his chest as he nudged the horse to a walk. It wasn't like Elise to let the place go like this. She was the one who'd planted flowers, bordered the pathways with whitewashed rocks and hung bright calico curtains in the windows of their little house. Clay could see those curtains now, limp and faded as if no one cared about them anymore.

Maybe Elise had taken the money, sold the ranch and moved away, leaving the place to some squatter family. One of the newcomers, a woman most likely, could have returned his letters. That would explain a lot. But Clay could've sworn the handwriting on those envelopes was his wife's.

Braced for anything, he dismounted at the porch, climbed the front steps and knocked on the door.

On the other side, footsteps creaked across the floor planks, their cadence achingly familiar. Clay forgot to breathe as the latch turned and the door opened inward.

"Hello, Clay." Elise's voice was cold. "I suppose you'll want to come inside."

Clay's eyes drank her in. She was still beautiful, but thinner than he remembered, her blue eyes sunk into tired shadows. Tendrils of wheaten hair had escaped her hastily twisted bun. They framed her face, softening the angry set of her jaw.

The old hunger knifed through him, the pain almost bringing him to his knees. He wanted to seize her in his arms, to crush her against him and devour that stubborn mouth with kisses. But even a fool could see that it wasn't what she'd want.

"I'll put my horse away first if that's all right," Clay said. "He's carried me a lot of miles. He deserves a rest."

"Fine. There's hay in the barn. I'll warm up some soup." She sounded as if she were speaking to a stranger, not her husband. "Why didn't you let me know you were coming?"

"I did. I'm guessing you didn't bother to open the letter." Clay turned away and walked down the front steps. He should've known Elise wouldn't be happy to see him. From the looks of the place, she'd fallen on hard times. He could understand her blaming him for that. But she should've had more than enough money to live on. He'd seen to that when he'd sent Buck home with the cash from the cattle sale.

Hadn't he?

By the time he'd stabled, fed and watered the tired buckskin, Clay was churning with questions. What had happened to the money? Where was Buck? And what about Toby? Surely if anything had happened to their son, Elise would have let him know.

Something had gone terribly wrong here. Until he knew what it was, he'd be wise to step softly.

Willing himself to stay calm, he turned back toward the house. By now the sun was low in the sky. The landscape was a cheerless sweep of yellow grass and gray hills beneath a brooding winter sky. The chilling wind seemed to whistle between his ribs as he bent to wash up at the pump.

Hesitating, he mounted the porch and rapped lightly on the front door. It rankled him that he needed permission to enter his own house. But until he knew where things stood between himself and Elise, Clay knew better than to take liberties.

The door creaked open. He found himself staring down into the clear, blue eyes of a young boy.

Clay's breath caught in a silent gasp. Toby had changed a lot in three years. But Clay would have known his son anywhere.

"Come on in, mister," he said. "Mama doesn't like leaving the door open. It lets out the heat."

He stepped aside to let Clay enter—a handsome child, tall for his age with a sprinkling of freckles across his nose and a thick mop of fair hair like his mother's. Clay's heart contracted at the sight of him. Only one thing kept him from gathering the boy into his arms.

Toby had called him "mister."

Ignoring the sting, Clay closed the door behind him. The small parlor was much as he remembered—the cheap Mexican chairs he'd promised to replace, the hand-braided rug, the tattered books crowding their shelves. The portrait of Elise's parents hung on the far wall. The wedding photograph, taken the day he and Elise were married, was missing.

The Christmas tree stood in one corner. It was little more than a twig anchored in a flowerpot, hung with strings of popcorn and snowflakes cut from old wrapping paper. There were no presents underneath.

Elise had always loved Christmas. Clay remembered how she'd used to spend weeks planning the day, decorating the house, wrapping little gifts and baking treats for any visitors who might come to call. He remembered her childlike anticipation, the songs and laughter, the sheer joy of the season.

What had happened to that joy? Where had it gone?

From where he stood, he could see Elise working in the kitchen, setting the table, unwrapping the bread and stirring the soup kettle on the stove. The aroma of fresh-baked bread lingered in the air, awakening memories of the old days when love had spilled like sunlight through their little house. The longing for those days was like a knife in Clay's gut.

Everything he wanted on this earth was right here in plain sight. And he didn't know how to get it back.

Elise's hands shook as she sliced the coarse wheat bread. How dared Clay show up here after what he'd put her through? His betrayal had broken her heart. And the tragedy that followed had crushed what was left of her spirit. If she lived to be a hundred, she would never, ever forgive him.

Looking up from her work, she stole a furtive glance into the parlor. Clay was standing a few steps inside the door, his stone-gray eyes intent on Toby. Dread clutched at Elise's stomach. Toby had been a two-year-old when Clay rode off on the cattle drive. Would he remember his father? Had she been wrong not to tell the boy right off who their visitor was?

Sooner or later Toby would have to know. After all, Clay wasn't just passing through. The ranch was his property and it was clear enough that he had no place else to go. But that fact raised a whirlwind of questions. What would Clay expect of *her?* If he thought she was just going to fall into bed with him—

"Oh—!"

Pain shot up Elise's arm as the bread knife sliced her left thumb. She uttered a little cry as blood spurted onto the cutting board.

"Here, hold still." Clay was at her side in two strides. Grabbing the flour sack she'd used to wrap the bread, he pressed it to the cut. His sudden nearness undid her. He was so big, so powerfully male with his chilled fingers clasping her wrist, his stubbled jaw almost brushing her forehead. A long-forgotten heat stirred in the depths of her body. Elise struggled to ignore it. Heaven help her she didn't want these feelings. She didn't want *him.*

"Hold the cloth there till the bleeding stops." His voice was a low rasp. "I'll get something to wrap your thumb."

"Are you all right, Mama?" Toby stood in the doorway, a worried look on his face.

Elise forced herself to smile. "It's nothing. Just a little cut."

"Find us a clean handkerchief, son," Clay ordered. Toby scurried off to the bedroom, giving them a few seconds alone. "He doesn't know?" Clay asked.

Elise shook her head. "There wasn't time to tell him."

"Doesn't he ask about his father?"

"I've always told him his father was away on a long trip."

Clay's weathered face creased into a scowl. "Well, I'm back, and the sooner he knows it the better."

"Please." She met the coldness in his eyes. "He's such a sensitive little boy. Give him some time to get used to you."

"How much time?"

"Until I think he's ready."

Clay's shoulder's sagged in acquiescence. "We need to talk, Elise," he said.

"I know. We will." Her heart shrank at the thought of it but some things had to be faced.

Toby returned, waving a cotton handkerchief that Elise recognized as one of Clay's. She'd kept all Clay's clothes, planning to make some of them over for the boy when he grew bigger. The idea of Clay's return had been pushed to the back of her mind. According to the marshal's report he'd been sentenced to five years. How could she have known he'd be back in three?

And why, as she stood there confused and hurting, did she find herself wanting Clay to take her in his arms? After reading the report of his arrest, she'd had no desire to ever be touched by him again.

"Hold still." Bracing her hand against his palm he peeled away the cloth he'd pressed against the wound. The bleeding had stopped, but the cut was long and deep, running from the tip of her thumb to the first joint. Elise quivered as he bound it tightly with the handkerchief and knotted the ends. "Should be good as new in a couple of days," he said, "but only if you keep it dry and don't do anything to open it up. Hear?" He glanced down at Toby. "Your mother's going to need some extra help. What can you do?"

"I can feed the chickens and get the eggs," Toby

said. "I can carry in the wood, too. But I can't chop it. Mama always does that."

A muscle twitched in Clay's jaw. "Don't worry, son. Your mother will never have to chop wood again."

Elise felt the trembling beneath her skirts. So there it was. Clay was back and he was taking over. He would take care of things, as he always had. But what about her? How could she be a wife to Clay when his betrayal haunted her every waking moment?

The soup had begun to steam. Pulling away from Clay's nearness, she slid the kettle off the burner. Her voice shook as she spoke. "Supper's ready. Sit down and I'll dish up the soup."

Her bandaged hand moved awkwardly as she struggled to lift the heavy soup kettle off the stove. Clay stopped her with a touch on her wrist. "You sit down. I'll do the rest. You can bring me the soup bowls, Toby."

Toby's eyebrows met in a small V above the bridge of his freckled nose. "How did you know my name? Did Mama tell you?"

"Yes." Clay spoke the lie as if he'd just been forced to swallow vinegar. Denying his own son would chafe him hard. But the truth would open Toby to hurt. Elise couldn't allow that to happen.

While Clay ladled the soup into the bowls, she and Toby took their accustomed places on either side of the table. Elise had set Clay's place at the end. He handed out the bowls, sliced more bread and sat down.

"Say grace, please, Toby," Elise said, and the boy murmured a short prayer. Stealing a glance from under her lowered eyelashes, Elise studied Clay where he sat with bowed head. His face was lined, and his water-slicked hair showed strands of gray that hadn't been there before the fateful cattle drive. Prison would be hard on any man. But then, hadn't Clay brought that punishment on his own head? Surely he'd gotten no worse than he deserved.

"Do you go to school, Toby?" Clay broke off a chunk of bread and dipped a corner of it in the soup.

"I can't go till next year." The boy imitated his father, dipping his bread the same way. "But I can read a little, and I know my numbers. Mama taught me."

"Your mother must be a good teacher." Clay's eyes rested on Elise. Her face warmed at his praise, but she willed away the pleasure of it. If Clay thought he could win her through flattery, he was mistaken.

"I'm hoping the teacher will let me help out at school," Elise said. "That way I could take Toby into town and be there to bring him home. If I do a good job, the city council might even pay me a little."

"We'll see about that next year." Clay reached for another slice of bread. There was no butter. What little cream Elise was able to get from the poor cow, she churned and sold to the hotel in town.

They finished the meal in awkward silence, interspersed with even more awkward snatches of conversation. Afterward Clay insisted on washing the dishes while she got Toby ready for bed.

"He's a nice man," Toby mumbled as she tucked him in. "Is he going to stay?"

"We'll see. Just go to sleep." Elise kissed his forehead, breathing in the sweet little boy smell she loved so much. A tear scalded her cheek. So many things had gone wrong in her life. But at least she had her wonderful son.

She sang until Toby's eyes closed in slumber. When she returned to the parlor, Clay was warming himself by the blaze he'd kindled in the fireplace. He was seated in the big wooden rocker he'd always favored, looking so much at home that for an instant it seemed as if he'd never left. Then Elise saw the tense expression on his face, and she knew the time of reckoning had come.

Settling into the chair he'd drawn up to face him, she stared down at her hands. A spot of crimson had oozed through the makeshift bandage on her thumb.

"Look at me, Elise." His voice was rough and hard. Elise forced herself to meet his granite eyes.

"Why did you return my letters?" he demanded. "Do you hate me that much?"

Her breath sucked in, hurting. She shook her head. "I could never hate you, Clay. I just don't understand how you could have done what you did."

A muscle twitched in his left cheek. "So what is it you think I did? Where's Buck? Didn't he tell you what happened?"

"I haven't seen your brother since he left with you on the cattle drive."

He stared at her. "And the money? The twenty thousand dollars from the cattle sale?"

"Look around you, Clay. Would Toby and I be living like this if we'd had money?"

He sagged in the chair, looking as if he'd just been shot through the heart. Seconds passed before he found his voice. "Tell me," he said. "Tell me everything."

Everything? Elise drew a ragged breath. She didn't trust herself to tell him the worst. But she would tell him as much as he needed to know.

"I waited for you to come home," she said. "When the time came, I watched the road every day, praying I'd see you. Weeks went by, and more weeks, with no word. Finally I drove the buggy into town to see the marshal. He offered to contact the authorities in Abilene."

Her throat tightened, threatening to betray her emotion. She stared down at her tightly clasped hands.

"Elise, it wasn't—"

"No. Let me finish." She forced herself to meet his tormented gaze. "Two weeks later the marshal rode out to the ranch. He gave me a copy of the official report."

Clay's grip tightened on the arm of the chair. "What did it say? I want to see it."

"I burned it. I couldn't stand the thought of Toby ever reading the words on that paper." Elise shook her head. "I only wish I could burn them out of my mind as well. Then I might be able to welcome you home."

"What did it say?" Clay's whispered words were etched in steel.

"You should know. You were there, in that awful place, with that woman when the fight broke out. Every time I close my eyes I can imagine you lying with her."

Clay's face had turned the color of alkali dust. His voice emerged as a hoarse whisper. "Damn it, Elise, if you'd read my letters—"

"How could I, after what I'd learned? How could I open those envelopes and read more of your lies?"

Clay rose to his feet, looking angrier than Elise had ever seen him. Only the awareness of his sleeping son, in the next room, kept his voice low.

"Listen to me," he growled. "I wasn't with any woman. I went into that house looking for Buck. When I followed the sounds of a fight, I found three men trying to beat him up. One of them drew a knife. If I hadn't come to his rescue, Buck might've been killed."

He loomed above her, terrible in his silence. Elise rose to face him, her knees quivering beneath her skirts. "You've had three years to concoct that story, Clay. How can you expect me to believe you?"

He exhaled, his shoulders sagging. "Buck was supposed to tell you everything," he said. "I made sure he got out of there before the law showed up—told him to get the money out of the hotel safe and hightail it back to you."

"Well, Buck isn't here. And neither is the money. All I have is your word, and after three years that isn't worth much."

He sank back into the chair. The firelight cast his face into harsh relief, deepening the lines of weariness and despair.

His hands were nicked and scarred in ways Elise didn't remember from before. Prison must have been hell for a man like Clay. What had he done to survive? How had he found the courage to make it home?

She fought the urge to go to him, to brush the lank, untrimmed hair back from his face, to creep into his arms and feel his strength holding her close. It had been so long, and she had suffered so much hurt. But she had her pride. Even if he was telling the truth, how could she take him back again?

Lifting her chin, she forced herself to speak. "This is your ranch, Clay. And Toby is your son. I can't force you to go. But I'm not ready to be your wife again. You can sleep in the bunkhouse. There are blankets on the beds and wood by the stove. Tomorrow I'll gather up your clothes, so you'll have something clean to wear."

"Fine." He rose from the chair, unfolding his long limbs with effort. "Don't worry, Elise, I'm too tired to give you any trouble. Thank you for supper."

Turning away, he opened the front door. His back was erect, his head –high and proud, but his feet betrayed him. He was stumbling with exhaustion.

"Wait, you'll need a light." She thrust a straw into the fireplace and transferred its flame to the spare lantern that hung by the door. Clay accepted it with a silent nod and stepped out into the night. The door creaked shut behind him and closed with a subtle click.

Legs giving way, Elise sank into the rocking chair. The cushion still held the warmth of Clay's body. His masculine touch lingered on her skin.

An avalanche of questions caved in on her. She hunched into a ball, her hands clutching her knees. Could she believe Clay's story after all this time? Could she put the past behind her and forgive him? Even now, with her world shifting like river ice, Elise knew it was what she wanted. She'd wanted Clay from the minute he'd stepped into the house.

But what if he was lying? How could she let him make love to her while her mind was picturing where he'd been and what he'd done?

And what about their son? How much of the truth

could she tell Toby, and how soon? He was such a tender little boy, and she would be giving Clay the power to break his heart.

As she sat up, Elise's gaze fell on the sad little tree that stood in the corner, its needles already drying. She didn't have the means for much of a holiday, but she'd done what she could. She and Toby had cut the pine in the far pasture where a stray seed had sprouted. In the past weeks she'd unraveled wool from an old afghan and knitted Toby a warm sweater. She'd also planned to stay up Christmas Eve making him some gingerbread men. Maybe she'd even cook one of their precious hens and make a pie for dinner. She could only hope that would be Christmas enough.

Clay's arrival had turned everything upside-down. But that didn't mean she should change her Christmas plans. The day was too important to a boy who had too little brightness in his life.

In the few days that remained, Elise resolved, she would try to remain calm and cheerful. When Christmas was done, she and Clay would confront their differences.

Maybe then she'd be able to tell him everything.

Chapter Two

Clay lay on his back, staring up into the darkened rafters of the bunkhouse. He hadn't bothered to light the stove. After three years in an unheated cell, he was used to the cold. And compared to his prison bunk, the sagging mattress that cradled his bones felt downright luxurious. Stripped down to his long johns and covered in blankets, he was more than ready for a long night's sleep. But his churning emotions had kept him awake for hours.

He'd hoped to spend the night in a different bed, but he should have known Elise wouldn't welcome him there. She'd been through a devil of a time. He couldn't blame her for feeling betrayed. But, damn it, the woman had to know he was telling the truth. He loved her with his whole heart. He would never look twice at another woman, let alone sleep with one. Why couldn't she trust him?

And Toby? Lord, the boy didn't even know his

own father. Three years ago he'd been a toddler. Now he didn't remember that time. Clay ached with love for his son. But how could he show that love if the boy only saw him as a stranger?

How was he going to fix this godforsaken mess?

The rafters creaked as wind buffeted the roof of the bunkhouse. Sleet spattered the panes of the high window. Clay closed his eyes, listening as the fast-moving storm swept in. After three long years he was safely home where he belonged. But he felt as if he'd stepped into someone else's life.

Everything had hinged on Buck's making it home with the money. But something had clearly gone wrong because Buck had never arrived. Had he been robbed? Arrested? Even murdered? Clay's fists clenched in the darkness. There could be no resolution until he learned what had become of his wild young brother.

He was beginning to drift. Tomorrow he would take stock of all that needed to be done on the ranch. Then, in the spirit of putting things right, he would begin. This was his land. This was his family. Somehow he had to make it all work.

Clay could feel himself sinking. He sighed as the darkness closed over his mind. He had come such a long way, and he was tired. So tired...

She leaned over him in the darkness, her moonlit hair hanging loose, brushing his face. When his hand reached up to touch her cheek he felt the wetness of tears.

"Elise—"

She hushed him with a finger; then, shifting closer, she lowered her sweet mouth to his. Her lips were warm. She tasted of peaches, cinnamon, summer rain and all the things he'd missed in that hellhole of a prison. With a low moan he drank her into his senses, breathing her aroused woman scent, tasting, touching. A shudder passed through her body as his tongue invaded her mouth, its tip stroking the silken surfaces in a thrusting pantomime of what he'd yearned to do for three long years. He caressed her body through the gossamer thin cotton nightgown, his palms molding the softness of her breasts and tracing the jutting curve of her firm little buttocks. She was his wife, so warm, so beautiful...

Easing away from him, she moved her hands to the fastening of his long johns. Her nimble fingers freed his arousal from the confines of fabric and buttons. His swollen shaft sprang upward, quivering in readiness as she raised her nightgown and straddled his thighs. Clay's breath stopped as she

poised herself above him and, with a little whim-
per, lowered her hips. As her satiny wetness slid
over him, he groaned...

And woke up alone in the narrow bunk.

Fully awake once more, he lay staring into the darkness. His crotch was damp from the dream, his gut knotted with the pain of wanting what he couldn't have. Whatever it took, he had to work things out between himself and Elise. This craziness couldn't go on much longer.

The storm had passed, brushing the landscape with glittering ice. The waning moon shone through Elise's bedroom window, casting ghostly patterns on the whitewashed wall. Too restless to sleep, Elise lay curled on her side. Except for a few familiar creaks and rustlings, the night was still. Toby would be fast asleep. But what about Clay? Was he warm enough? Would he be able to rest after his long ride?

Had she done the right thing, insisting that he sleep in the bunkhouse? Some men would consider it a woman's duty to lie with her husband, whether she felt like it or not. But Clay wasn't like that. He wouldn't force her. Not if he knew she didn't want him.

Clasping her knees, she huddled beneath the quilts. A tear pooled on the muslin pillowcase as the memories swept over her—Clay's arms around her, his mouth on hers, his lean hard body filling her, loving her, the smell and feel and taste of him…

For a moment it was all she could do to keep from pulling on her boots, flinging a quilt over her nightgown and rushing across the yard to the bunkhouse. But no—the fears were already returning. Her heart might want him. Her body might ache for him. But the memories and the hurt would be there, driving them apart like a wedge.

How could she believe him?

And even if she did, how could she forgive him, when nothing could bring back what she'd lost?

It was too much to ask of any woman.

Morning was clear and bitter. Clay was up before dawn, breaking the ice off the watering trough and feeding the meager stock. All he found was the one milk cow and a horse that had been too old to take on the cattle drive. The other animals he'd left behind—the longhorn cows and their calves, the herd bulls, the pigs and the draft horses—were gone. He could only guess that Elise had sold them to pay the bills on the ranch. Lord knows what she and Toby were living on now. He would have to find a way to get money, even if it meant working in town or selling the strip of pastureland that bordered his neighbor's property. Land was precious but he couldn't let his family go wanting.

The house was quiet, with no smoke coming from the chimney. Clay gathered up some firewood and piled it on the back porch. Then he cleared the pump of ice, filled a bucket and carried it into the kitchen. Before leaving he made a fire in the stove. At least his wife and son would awaken to a warm house.

Elise's bedroom door stood ajar. He fought the urge to open it a crack and look at her. Seeing her asleep, so soft and vulnerable, would only deepen his hunger. Likewise, he refrained from looking in on Toby. It could frighten the boy to wake up and see a strange man in his room.

A strange man...

Clay's mouth tightened as he turned away from his son's door and went back outside.

There was plenty of work to keep him busy. The woodpile was down to a few logs. Clay pried the ax from the chopping block and started on a gnarled cedar trunk that looked as if it had been horse-dragged out of the foothills. How had Elise managed the heavy work with no hired help? The thought of his dainty, petite wife chopping wood, hauling water and plowing the hard ground made him seethe. If he ever found out what had become of that money from the cattle sale...

He channeled his fury into every ax blow. By the time he was finished he was sweating beneath his long johns and the ground was littered with chunks of stove wood. Clay took a moment to gather the wood into a pile. Then he strode toward the corral to herd the cow into the milking shed.

He found a clean bucket next to the milking stool. Leading the cow into the stall, he tossed a forkful of hay into the feed box, gave her a moment to settle down, then crouched onto the stool and began pulling at the teats.

He hadn't milked a cow in more than three years, but it wasn't the sort of thing one forgot. His hands settled into the easy rhythm, squirting the milk into the tin pail. The aroma of fresh milk was strangely soothing. He closed his eyes, resting his head against the cow's warm side.

The prickle of some sixth sense told Clay he was being watched. Slowly he turned around. A small figure, silhouetted against the sunrise, stood in the doorway.

Clay spoke in a whisper, half fearful that the boy might bolt at the sound of his voice. "Toby, what are you doing up so early?"

Toby inched into the milking shed. His hair was cowlicked from sleep, and it appeared he'd gotten dressed by himself. His coat was crookedly buttoned, his shoes on the wrong feet.

"Do you want to watch me milk the cow?" Clay's question sounded awkward in the stillness.

The boy nodded. Clay returned to milking, conscious of the round blue eyes following his every move. After a long moment he felt a light touch on his shoulder. Toby was standing at his side.

"You're my papa aren't you?" the boy asked.

Clay's throat jerked tight. "What—gave you that idea?"

"I sort of remembered you. So I thought about it and figured it out."

Clay suppressed the impulse to gather his son into his arms. It was too soon. They were both too raw, too tender.

"Your mother didn't tell you?" he asked.

Toby shook his head. "Why is she mad at you?"

"Did she say she was mad?"

"No, but I can tell. Is she mad because you were gone so long?"

"I'd say that's a good guess." Fearful of betraying his emotions, Clay turned back to the milking. Warm milk splashed into the pail.

"Where have you been?" Toby asked.

Clay hesitated. Lying would only make things worse later on. "I was in a place where I couldn't leave," he said. "I'll tell you more when you're older."

The boy was silent. Clay fumbled for a diversion. "When I was your age I used to watch my father milk cows," he said. "Let me show you something he used to do. Step back a little and open your mouth."

Toby looked uncertain, but he did as he was asked.

"Ready?" Clay raised one teat and directed a squirt of milk into his son's mouth.

Startled, Toby jumped back. He licked his lips. Then, like the sun coming out, his face lit up. He giggled. "Do it again, Papa!" he said.

Elise stood at the kitchen window, watching her husband and son walk out of the shed together.

Toby was bouncing like a puppy, laughing as he tried to keep even with his father's stride.

There could only be one explanation for what she was seeing. Clay must have told Toby the truth. Even though she'd asked him to wait, the man had ignored her wishes. He'd betrayed her trust again!

The coffeepot was boiling over. Steam hissed as coffee spattered onto the hot stove top. Grabbing a dish towel, she slid the pot away from the heat and checked the bacon in the skillet. Her neighbor had given her a smoked side after he'd bought and butchered the last of her pigs. Elise had hung it in the springhouse and rationed each sliver, knowing that when it was gone there would be no more. That she'd lavished three precious slices on Clay's breakfast was beyond the limits of common sense.

When she returned to the window, Clay and Toby were washing up at the pump. The boy was watching his father, imitating the way he soaped his hands and splashed his face. Elise had never seen her son look so happy.

With a sigh she turned away from the window and began setting the table. Reality was bitter medicine, but some things just had to be accepted. It might be her prerogative to deny Clay his wife. But she had no right to deny Toby his father.

Minutes later they came in through the back door, their faces damp and glowing with cold. Elise shot her husband a glare across the kitchen. *You told him,* her look said.

Clay answered her as if she'd spoken out loud. "I didn't tell him, Elise. He figured it out. You can ask him if you want. How's your hand?"

"Better. Sit down and I'll dish up your breakfast."

Toby sniffed the air. His face lit up. "Yum! Bacon! I love bacon!"

"One piece for you." Elise scooped the cooked strips onto a saucer. "And two for your...father." She cracked fresh eggs into the simmering bacon grease. "Sunny side up, right?"

"You've got a good memory." Clay took his seat at the head of the table with Toby on one side. Elise slid the cooked eggs onto a pie tin and transferred them to the table, along with sliced bread and a pot of warm beans. As if by prearranged signal, the three of them bowed their heads while she took her turn at saying grace. It was almost like being a family again, Elise thought—except for the bitterness that had made their marriage a hopeless sham.

"It's been a long time since I sat down to a breakfast like this one." Clay broke off a chunk of bread and dipped it in his egg yolk. Toby, Elise noticed, did the same.

"We usually just have mush," Toby said. "Mama must've wanted to make this special."

"I see." Clay's eyes rested on Elise, triggering a surge of heat to her face.

Picking up one of his two bacon strips, he laid it on her plate. "No more self-denial, Elise," he said. "We'll share and share alike in this family, even if it's just bacon."

"I'm afraid you won't find much to share around here," Elise said.

Clay's mouth tightened. "I can see that it's been a rough three years. But now I'm here, and I'm ready to take care of you both. It may take a while to get things back to where they were, but it can and will be done. I promise you."

Elise glanced down at her plate, avoiding his earnest gray eyes. Some things could never be as they were. Sooner or later she would have to tell Clay what had happened after he left. But she wasn't ready yet. She was still reeling from his sudden return.

Toby reached across the corner of the table and

tugged at Clay's sleeve. His blue eyes were dancing. "Tell her," he said. "Tell her what we want to do."

Clay cleared his throat. "Toby and I were thinking, we'd like to ride up into the hills and get ourselves a real Christmas tree, a nice, fresh bushy one. And we'd like you to come with us."

"How can I?" The protest was out of Elise's mouth before she had time to think. "I've washing to do and bread to mix, and the house hasn't been swept in—"

"You can't do wash and mix bread with your bandaged thumb. Leave it and come."

"Oh, but I—"

"Leave it, Elise. We've got two horses, and I know you can ride. Once the sun's higher it shouldn't be too cold. Come on. When was the last time the three of us had any fun together?"

Elise glanced at Toby. The anticipation in his eyes melted her resistance. "Oh…all right," she sighed. "But I'm going to need some extra help from you two."

Clay's grin deepened the creases in his face. "Fine. As soon as we're finished with breakfast, Toby and I will get started on the dishes. Right, son?"

Toby grinned back at him. "Right, Papa!"

* * *

By early afternoon the sun had melted the glaze of ice off the ground. Quail called from the sleeping orchard behind the house. Where wildflowers had grown, sparrows fed on dried seed heads, twittering from stem to stem.

Bundled into Buck's old sheepskin jacket, Elise guided the horse up the winding trail. Clay rode ahead, holding Toby on the saddle in front of him. She could hear the pleasure in the boy's voice as he chattered away, pointing, asking questions and listening to Clay's answers. How blessedly easy it had been for Toby to accept his father. It was as if the one piece missing from his young life had fallen into place. In Clay, he had found a needed friend and hero.

What would it be like for him when he learned that his hero wasn't perfect?

Elise forced the thought from her mind. Christmas was a time for children to feel loved, secure and happy. The last thing she wanted was to spoil it for her little boy. For this holiday week she would put aside her differences with Clay. She would be patient and civil toward him, and she would take pleasure in their son's happiness. Sooner or later the reckoning would come.

But as long as Clay kept his distance, it could wait until after Christmas.

And if he didn't keep his distance?

Elise's mouth went dry at the thought of his touching her, holding her. She steeled herself against the tugs and tightenings in the core of her body. She wasn't ready to let Clay make love to her again. With so many secrets between them, it would be a mockery of the trust they'd once shared.

On the higher, shaded slope, there was a dusting of snow. It clung to the aspen branches and dry undergrowth, creating a lacy fairyland. A doe raised its head and bounded up the hill, leaving a shower of white in its wake. Toby had fallen silent. Now he spoke, breaking the winter stillness. "It looks like Christmas up here," he said.

Clay chuckled, a rich, warm sound that Elise felt all the way to her bones. "Come on," he said, nudging the horse forward. "Let's get that Christmas tree."

They found the perfect tree just below the ridgeline. Clay cut it with the hatchet he'd brought. Then he used two felled aspen trunks and some rope to fashion a makeshift travois. Lashing the tree in place, he tied it behind his horse.

"Here you go, son," he said, boosting the boy into Elise's arms. "My old horse might decide he doesn't like pulling a tree. If he bucks, I don't want you on him."

Elise unbuttoned her coat and snuggled her son into the warm lining. Clay stood looking up at her, a naked hunger in his eyes. He was doing his best to please her, to win her back; but she wasn't ready for that to happen. Tearing her gaze away, she stared into the pattern on Toby's knitted cap. "Thank you," she murmured. "It's a lovely tree."

He gave a slight nod, then turned aside, mounted his horse and started down the trail. The travois trailed behind, leaving twin ruts on the frosted ground. Nudging her own horse into motion, Elise followed at a safe distance. One arm held the reins. The other clasped Toby securely against her.

"We don't have enough decorations for the new tree," Toby said. "Can we make more?"

"We'll see." Elise was already racking her brain for things they could use. Colored yarn? Scraps of bright calico? The brass buttons she'd salvaged from an old army coat?

As the boy chattered on about Christmas, her spirits began to sag. A homemade sweater wasn't much of a gift for a small boy, but it was the best she could do. She would give anything to see Toby's eyes sparkle on Christmas morning, but she had no money to spare. Neither did Clay, she was sure. They'd be lucky to afford food on the table this winter, let alone Christmas presents.

What had happened to the money Clay swore he'd sent home with Buck? Having that money would have made all the difference.

All the difference in the world.

Clay sat by the fireplace, resting his boots on the hearth. A crackling blaze filled the parlor with warmth and cheer. From the corner where the new tree stood, the aroma of fresh-cut pine drifted on the air. He closed his eyes, letting the sounds and smells of Christmas seep into his senses. His homecoming had been far from perfect. But anything would be better than the lonely hell of the past three years.

In the kitchen, Elise was giving Toby his Saturday night bath. Through the open doorway, the sound of splashing water blended with the voices of the two people Clay loved most in the world.

He'd forgotten about the Saturday night ritual until Elise had stumbled into the kitchen carrying the big tin washtub she kept propped against the back of the house. Clay had taken the tub from her and insisted on bringing in the pump water and putting it on the stove to heat. But the thought of her lugging that tub and all that water every week for the past three years had eaten at him the whole time. A delicate little flower of a woman, Elise wasn't made for heavy work. But somehow she'd managed that and more. Lord, how hard it must have been for her.

He would make it up to her, Clay vowed, if it took him the rest of his life.

He heard the swish as she helped Toby out of the tub. After the boy was in bed, Elise would bathe. Then it would be Clay's own turn. By then the water would be cool, but never mind that. In prison he'd had nothing more than a bucket and a rag, and there'd been no chance to bathe on the road. Washing in a real tub would be a treat.

Clay's clean long johns, stockings and trousers lay folded on the hearth. Earlier Elise had bundled his stored clothes and carried them out to the bunkhouse. Her message was clear. For the foreseeable future he would not be sleeping in her bed. Much as her stubbornness chafed him, Clay had resolved to respect her wishes. The desire to have her was slowly driving him crazy. But he would not take her against her will.

Only when the door between the kitchen and parlor clicked shut did Clay realize he'd been dozing. The faint sounds beyond the door told him that Elise was climbing into the tub. He stared into the flames, trying not to imagine the water flowing over her naked skin, pooling in the hollow between her breasts, settling over her petal-soft belly.

The torment was more than he could stand. Swinging his feet to the floor, he rose and stalked out of the front door, onto the porch. His breath misted in the cold night air as he stood with his hands thrust into his pockets. Damn it, he'd done nothing wrong! Not unless saving his fool brother was a sin. The woman had been through a bad time, but he'd never meant to hurt her. Why couldn't she put the past behind her and welcome him home?

He stayed on the porch long enough for his frustration to cool. When he returned to the parlor, he saw that the kitchen door was open and the door to Elise's bedroom was closed. A kettle of water steamed on the stove, ready to be added to the tepid bath. A clean, dry towel hung over the back of a chair.

Be thankful for small favors, Clay told himself as he stripped off his clothes. At least she'd cared enough to think of his comfort. The gesture was small, but it was better than nothing.

Elise tugged her nightgown over her head and covered it with her flannel wrapper. She'd kept her bedroom door closed all day to provide more heat for the rest of the house. By now thc room was so frigid that her teeth were chattering. Her hands quivered as she knotted the sash around her waist. She'd planned to sit up in bed and read awhile; but her skin and hair were still damp. The thought of crawling between icy sheets made her shiver.

The parlor would be deliciously warm. But to get there, she would have to walk through the kitchen. And the splashing sounds beyond the door told her that Clay was still bathing.

Don't be a goose, she lectured herself. *The man's your husband. There's nothing wrong with your seeing him naked.*

She knew she was being silly, but three years was a long time. Her stomach fluttered as she opened the door and stepped into the lamplit kitchen.

Clay sat with his back toward her, his knees buckled against his chest. The size of him took up so much space in the round tub that water sloshed over the rim. At first he didn't seem aware of her. He was struggling to wash his hair, scooping the water into his hands and losing most of it before it reached his head. His cramped position in the tub made it impossible to bend over. His helplessness tugged at her heart.

"Wait." She stripped off her long-sleeved wrapper and tossed it over a chair. Dressed only in her thin muslin nightgown, she stepped behind him, took a tin cup from the counter and scooped it full of water. He groaned with relief as she poured the water over his head. "I always used to do this for you, remember?"

His chuckle sounded strained. "I remember. I just wasn't sure you did."

Taking a sliver of lye soap, Elise lathered her hands and began to soap his head. His thick brown hair was stiff with dust and sweat. She massaged the suds all the way to his scalp, scrubbing with the cushions of her fingers.

"Lord, that feels good," he muttered.

"Somebody's got to keep you looking presentable."

He laughed, a comfortable sound. Too comfortable, she thought. She could feel the deep stirrings, the awakening desires she had no wish to feel. Scooping a cup of water, she poured it slowly onto his hair. The water trickled down his neck and over his broad shoulders. His skin was the warm gold of polished maple. She had always loved his skin, seeing it, touching it.

She remembered the times she'd washed him all over while he stood in the tub, soaping his powerful frame from head to toe, touching every part of him. Those baths had always ended with both of them in bed, their bodies locked in a glorious tangle. But she couldn't think of those times now. She couldn't let herself want them.

Clay was still her husband. But her innocent passion for him was dead. It had faltered when she'd read the report of his arrest. And it had died forever that spring night in a windblown orchard—the night she had buried her heart.

Chapter Three

"Elise, are you all right?"

Clay's question snapped her back to the present. The empty cup clattered to the kitchen floor.

Hot-faced, she bent to pick it up. She was losing her hard-won self-control. She needed a diversion to get it back. "I'm fine," she said. "I just remembered something I wanted to ask you, that's all."

"What's that?" He sluiced his fingers through his streaming hair.

"I usually take Toby to church on Sunday. This time there'll be Christmas songs and a special program. He's been looking forward to it." Elise took a deep breath. "I was hoping you'd want to come with us."

Clay hesitated, as she'd expected he would. Her husband had never been much of a churchgoer. And she could just imagine how uncomfortable he'd feel walking into church after a three-year absence, with the whole congregation knowing where he'd been. But she could hardly go and take Toby without inviting Clay to come along.

After an awkward pause, he shook his head. "Afraid I'm not up to church yet. But I'd be happy to drive you into town."

"There's no need," Elise said. "The weather's clear and the road's safe. I can drive the buggy myself. I've been doing it long cnough."

His jaw tightened, and Elise realized how her words had struck him. "Fine," he said. "I can find plenty to do around here. I'll have the buggy hitched by the time you're ready to go. Now, if you'll excuse me—"

Shifting in the tub, he rose with his back toward her. Water cascaded down his body in glistening drops. On his arms and shoulders there were new scars, mute testament to what he must have suffered in prison. Clay was no longer the gentle, laughing husband who'd ridden away from her. The years had changed him into a lean, hard-edged stranger, someone she no longer knew. Even so, the sight of him took her breath away.

Turning, he reached for the towel she'd hung where the stove would warm it. Elise willed her hands to remain clasped at her waist. To reach out and touch him, as she yearned to do, would mean total surrender. It would mean giving up everything—her pride, her trust, her hard-won defenses against pain.

A pain so deep she could hardly bear it.

As he wrapped the towel around his hips, Clay turned back toward her. Elise glimpsed his arousal before he pulled the towel tight and tucked the end to hold it in place. She felt the dampness of her muslin nightgown where it clung to her torso, revealing every curve. Heat flashed upward from the core of her body.

His eyes probed hers, questioning, seeking. She saw the hunger in their stormy depths. A word from her, a touch of her hand and all resistance would end.

"Elise—" His hand reached out for her.

No—it was too soon. If she let him into her bed before she was ready, what had once been an act of love would become an act of submission, or worse. She could find herself lying beneath him, thinking of what he'd done and hating him for it.

Seized by unreasoning panic, she snatched up her robe, darted into her bedroom and closed the door behind her.

Heart pounding, she lay in the darkness. She

heard the splash of water as Clay emptied the tub out the back door. Then his footsteps died away and the house was quiet.

Clay had the buggy hitched by the time his wife and son came outside. Toby's hair was slicked into place. He wore a dark woolen coat that strained at the buttons and showed his bony little wrists below the cuffs. Elise was wearing a plain gray dress with the navy blue cloak she'd owned since her teens. Her hair was twisted into a coiled braid on the back of her head. Her eyes avoided Clay's as he helped her into the buggy for the two-hour drive to town.

"There's oatmeal on the stove," she said. "You'll want to eat it before it cooks dry and sticks to the pan."

"Fine. I'll do that." Clay handed her the flour sack that held bread and apples for their lunch. "Sorry I didn't make it inside for breakfast."

She ignored his apology. Things were strained between them after last night. A few hours apart might do them both good.

"We usually get back around three o'clock," she said. "I'll start supper then."

"Take your time." Clay boosted Toby onto the

seat and tucked a quilt around him. A glance at the early morning sky confirmed that the weather was clear.

"Aren't you coming with us, Papa?" Toby asked.

"Not today, son," Clay said. "Stay warm and mind your mother. I'll see you when you get home."

The boy waved as Elise guided the one-horse buggy down the drive toward the gate. Clay returned the wave, feeling an unexpected pang of separation. How had he survived the past three years without his family?

Toby would enjoy the Christmas service, he reminded himself. And there'd likely be other children at the church. Maybe he'd get a chance to play with them. The boy needed friends.

Clay finished the routine chores and sat down to a breakfast of oatmeal and fresh milk. Even cold, it was better than the slop he'd been forced to eat in prison. Afterward he scrubbed the pan to save Elise the trouble and went back outside.

By now the sun was up, a glittering diamond bright on the frosted pasture. Clay stood on the porch, warming his hands in his pockets as he surveyed the yard. There was plenty of work to do be done on the fences and outbuildings. But maybe he'd start by bagging a mess of quail for

Tuesday's Christmas dinner. The birds were small and a bother to dress. But their dark, succulent breast meat was like a taste of heaven.

Taking the shotgun down from the rack above the door he checked the chambers, pocketed some extra shells and headed around the house to the orchard, where the quail liked to winter.

The orchard was older than the house. Planted years ago and abandoned, Clay had found it untended and dying when he homesteaded the ranch. Seasons of pruning and care had made the trees as productive as they were beautiful. But now the branches were thick and tangled. The orchard would need pruning again in early spring if it was to bear a decent crop.

This morning the orchard was silent. The chattering flocks of quail were gone. Clay discovered the reason when a rooster-size goshawk flapped off a high limb to circle into the sky. With a predator in the neighborhood, the birds would be scattered and hiding. His quail hunt would have to wait for another time.

Clay shouldered the gun and began walking from tree to tree, checking each one for disease and pondering which limbs to cut away come spring. Morning light shone through the branches, casting sun-dappled shadows on the ground. Long yellow grass, stiff with frost, crackled under his feet.

The largest tree stood in the middle of the orchard. It must have been planted long before the others because its thick trunk was gnarled with age. Elise had always favored that tree, he recalled. Many was the time he'd found her there on warm summer days, curled in its shade with a book or with Toby on her lap. Now, as he looked up into the branches his eyes lingered on an abandoned robin's nest. He remembered how, in the spring, Elise had hung out strands of bright yarn for the birds to use in their weaving. This nest was drab, with no traces of color.

Where had she gone, his beautiful, joyful wife? What could he do to bring her back?

Winning his way into her bed was something he wanted badly. But Clay knew that wouldn't be enough. He wanted to hear her laugh, to see her smile and know that Elise was truly happy.

But how could he get past that wall of bitterness she'd thrown up between them?

Only when he stubbed his boot on a rock did Clay happen to look down. At his feet was a small mound of weathered earth, cleared of leaves and bordered by carefully placed stones. Anchored to its center with a forked twig was a shriveled bouquet of cornflowers, bound with a faded pink ribbon.

He stared at it, uncomprehending for an instant. Then the truth sank home.

Clay's knees gave way beneath him. The gun slipped from his shoulder as he dropped to the ground, fists balled against belly. His face twisted with grief as he grasped the meaning of what he'd found. He wanted to scream curses at the sky, to howl like a wounded animal.

It all made sense now—Elise's anger, her refusal to forgive him, everything.

But why, in God's name, hadn't she let him know?

Elise stood by the buggy, her cloak wrapped tightly against the chill. Her gaze followed Toby as he raced around the churchyard, playing tag with a half dozen other children. Some older members of the congregation disapproved of such behavior on the Sabbath. But most parents welcomed the chance for their youngsters to burn off energy between the long church service and the ride home.

The Christmas program had been rich in tradition, with candles, carols, a choral reading from St.

Luke by the older children, and a sermon on the spirit of Christmas. In the past, Elise had loved the holiday. Now the message was bittersweet. How could she celebrate in the true spirit of love and forgiveness when her heart felt as cold as a stone?

"Merry Christmas, Mrs. McAllister." Marshal Sam Dodson had been at the service. Tall and raw-boned, with iron-gray whiskers and one bad eye, he had served at his post for as long as Elise could remember. "I hear Clay's come home."

Elise didn't ask him how he knew. Maybe the authorities in Kansas had sent him word of Clay's release. Or maybe someone had seen Clay on the road.

"Yes, he's home." Elise kept her eyes on Toby's blond head as he dodged among his playmates. "When I told him about the arrest report, Clay said he'd gone into that place looking for Buck, and that the man he struck down was going for Buck with a knife."

The marshal fingered his moustache. "Now that makes sense," he drawled. "Clay's a good man. I had a feeling he wouldn't have done what he did without a good reason."

"So you believe him?"

"I've never known Clay McAllister to lie." The marshal's gaze narrowed. "Have you?"

Elise shook her head. "It's just that, all this time, I've been imagining him in that awful place with one of those women. And then after what happened with the baby—"

"Have you told him about the baby?"

"Not yet. I'm waiting for the right time."

"Lord's mercy, woman!" the marshal growled. "Your husband's home! Get the poison out of your system, forgive him and move on! If you can't do it for Clay's sake or your own, do it for that boy of yours!"

Elise blinked away a tear. "Don't you think I want to? I love Clay. I want to believe him, but…" She shook her head, pressing her lips into a thin line. "Clay says he sent Buck home with the money from the cattle sale. But Buck never arrived, so I never got to hear his side of the story. Maybe if we could find out what happened—"

"Well, that's easy enough. Buck can tell you himself—that is, if he's sober enough to remember."

Elise stared at the marshal. "You're saying you know where he is?"

"I've known all along. Buck's over in Ridgeview City. He sweeps the livery stable for a few scraps of food and a place to sleep. From what I hear, he spends most of his time bumming drinks at the saloons."

Elise felt her knees go slack. She sagged against the side of the buggy. Seconds passed before she could trust herself to speak. "Why didn't you tell me?" she demanded.

"You had your own troubles, girl. I figured you didn't need any more."

With a farewell nod, the marshal drifted off to join his wife. The tag game drew to an end as parents called their children to the buggies. A biting wind raked the trampled grass where they'd played.

Toby came bounding toward the buggy, his plump cheeks red with cold. Elise caught him in her arms and swung him onto the seat. He yawned as she snuggled him into the quilt. With luck he would doze off and sleep all the way home.

As she climbed into the driver's seat, the weight of what she'd learned pressed on her like a load of granite. Buck was living in disgraceful circumstances, just a few hours away from the ranch. In all this time he'd made no effort to contact her.

What had happened to him—and to the money? If Buck had come back to the ranch, even without the cash, both of them would have been better off. He could have told her the truth about Clay's arrest. And he could have stayed to help her with the heavy work. Maybe if she hadn't been chopping wood that day—"

The guilt that welled inside her was as sharp as acid. She should have been resting. But she'd taken one chance too many and had no one to blame but herself.

All that remained now was telling Clay what had happened, and telling him about his brother.

Clay was a good man, but he did have a temper. Lord help her, what would he do when he learned the truth?

Clay stood on the front porch, watching as the buggy came down the road and turned at the gate. Relief swept over him at the sight. With clouds moving in, he'd begun to worry about a storm. But now his loved ones were safely home.

How was he going to begin with Elise? There were so many questions to be asked and answered. What had gone wrong? Had the baby lived? Did it have a name? Would Toby remember what had happened?

His throat tightened as he imagined his wife standing beside that lonely little mound, bending to lay flowers on the earth. Had she dug the grave herself? Had anyone else been there?

Had she meant to keep it a secret?

Emotions churning, he strode out to meet the buggy as it pulled up to the corral. Toby was sitting up, bouncing and waving as his father approached.

"So how was church?" Clay lifted the boy and swung him off the seat.

"Good. I got to play tag. Nobody caught me."

"Fast, are you?" Clay lowered his son to the ground. "Well, let's see how fast you can run into the house and change your Sunday clothes."

As Toby dashed for the porch Clay walked around the buggy to help his wife to the ground. He was still weighing the wisdom of telling her what he'd found when he looked up and saw her face.

Strain was visible in every line and shadow of Elise's expression. Something had happened in town. Until he knew what it was, he'd be wise not to stir up more trouble. Maybe later, after Toby was asleep, he could get her to sit down and talk. Only when the slate was washed clean could they hope to make a new start.

Clay reached up and took her hand. Her fingers were icicles through her thin wool mittens.

Her eyes avoided his gaze as he helped her to the ground. In the old days he'd joked that he could read her thoughts. She'd been so transparent then, so trusting. Now, when Elise looked at him, it was as if she'd covered her face with a mask.

What was behind that mask?

If he wanted his family back, he needed to find out—soon.

Elise washed the last of the supper dishes and dried her hands on a towel. The cut on her thumb had healed to a thin pink line. Since she no longer needed the bandage, she'd insisted on cleaning up while Clay told Toby a bedtime story.

From the parlor, she could hear the rumble of his deep voice, interspersed with Toby's giggles over the misadventures of a baby bear named Benjamin. She'd forgotten what a gifted storyteller her husband was—just one of the many things she'd loved about him.

She and Clay had known each other since they were children, growing up in the same Kansas town. Elise had loved him for as long as she could remember. She'd loved the powerful size of him, the dimple in his left cheek and the way his sandy-brown hair curled low on his neck. She'd loved his gentleness, his humor, and the way he'd taken responsibility for his young brother after their parents died. Four years older than Elise, Clay hadn't paid her much attention. Then one day, when she was eighteen, he'd noticed her, and all her dreams had come true.

She had loved Clay with every beat of her heart. And she'd truly believed he loved her, too. Maybe that was why the arrest report, and all it implied, had left her shattered.

The day after tomorrow would be Christmas. If she could have one wish it would be to feel that love and trust again—to forget the past and know the peace of forgiveness. But how could that be, when so much damage had been done—not only from his side but from hers?

The story had ended. Dressed for bed, Toby scampered into the kitchen ahead of his father. "Can Papa tuck me in?" he asked.

Elise nodded. "Yes, but only if you promise to go right to sleep."

"I will." Catching Clay's hand, the boy tugged him toward the bedroom. A moment later Elise heard the murmur of their voices as Toby said his prayers.

With a sigh, she untied her apron and laid it over

the back of a chair. Her nervous hands smoothed her hair into place. Most nights, Toby fell asleep soon after his head touched the pillow. She wouldn't have long to wait before Clay returned to the parlor. Then the moment of reckoning would come.

The logs in the fireplace were still burning. Elise pulled her chair close to the hearth and picked up the basket of straw she'd gathered. She'd come up with a way of tying the stems together in the middle, so the ends radiated outward like the points of a star. Hung on the tree, the makeshift decorations looked dainty and festive. But she was going to need a lot of them. Tomorrow Toby could help make paper chains and some figures out of salt dough. But the straw ornaments were too fragile for his young fingers.

Picking up a few straws she fixed them in place, gauged their center and picked up a length of thread. But her hands were shaking. Straws and thread tumbled into her lap. She pressed her palms to her eyes, wiping away furious tears. Christmas was supposed to be a happy time. Why couldn't she just put the past aside and celebrate her husband's return?

"Elise?" Clay's hand brushed her shoulder. She

hadn't even heard him come into the room. How long had he been standing behind her?

"Are you all right?" he asked softly.

Elise's only answer was a little choking sound. She struggled for composure as he turned his chair to face her and sat down. The burning logs crackled in the silence.

"I found the grave today," he said. "Do you want to tell me about it?"

She pressed her lips tight, waiting for the words to come.

"When were you going to let me know?"

"Soon." She forced herself to meet his gaze. His expression was unreadable. "The baby was yours, if that's what you're wondering," she said.

His breath rasped in his throat. "Lord, girl, that question never crossed my mind. Just tell me what happened."

She stared down at her hands, gathering courage before she spoke. "I didn't know about the baby until a few weeks after you left. I was so excited, Clay. I knew you'd be happy, too. Then I found out you weren't coming back, and I found out why."

"Elise, it wasn't—"

"Let me finish while I can. The money was running low. I had to sell most of the stock and let the hired hands go. By the first snowfall, it was just Toby and me here alone."

She stared into the burning coals. "As I got bigger the chores got harder," she said. "The ones I could, I let go. But we needed water in the kitchen. We needed to bathe and wash clothes. And we needed firewood."

Clay's big hands had tightened on the arm of the chair. "Couldn't you have gotten someone to help you? Someone from the church, maybe?"

Elise raked back a strand of damp hair. "I could have, if I'd asked. But I was proud. Too proud to ask for charity with a husband in…prison." Her voice faltered. Clay was staring at her as if he already knew what she was going to say.

"By my reckoning, the baby was due in May. It was early April. There was a spring storm moving in, and I wanted to lay in a good store of wood. I spent most of the day chopping. By suppertime I could barely drag myself into the house." She sucked in her breath. "After I got Toby to bed, the pains started. The rest happened fast—too fast to get help. By midnight it was all over."

"Elise—" He was half out of his chair, uncertain whether to go to her. She motioned for him to sit.

"It was a little girl, Clay. A beautiful, perfect little

girl with the tiniest fingers and toes…" The tears had welled over. They spilled down her cheeks as she spoke. "As soon as I could get up I wrapped her in a baby blanket, took her outside and dug the grave. Toby never saw her. I don't believe he remembers any of it."

Clay was on his feet, looming over her now. "For the love of heaven, Elise, why didn't you write? Why didn't you let me know?"

She rose to face him, meeting the anguish in his eyes. "Don't you see? If I'd had the sense to rest, I wouldn't have lost the baby. It's my fault our little girl isn't here. That's what I live with, Clay. It's what I'll live with for the rest of my life!"

Chapter Four

Clay's awful silence hung between them. The anguish in his eyes was as damning as a curse. Under his gaze, Elise felt herself begin to crumble. Her knees dissolved beneath her. Her hand clasped the back of the chair. Her body shook as sobs welled in her throat.

Blinded by tears, she sensed that he was moving. Maybe he was turning to walk away. She wouldn't blame him if he did. What she'd allowed to happen was unforgivable.

She waited for the sound of footsteps and the click of the door latch. But what she felt was his hands drawing her close. His arms went around her, supporting her, rocking her like a child. His lips traced her hairline, nibbling kisses between muttered words. "It wasn't your fault, girl. If I'd been there you wouldn't have been working like that—like a man. I'd have taken care of things. I'd have made sure you rested."

She raised her damp face. "But don't you see? I should have known better than to—"

His seeking mouth muffled her words. For the barest instant she resisted. Then her need for him, a need denied for three lonely years, surged like a flood and swept her away. Her body softened. Her arms went around him. Her fingers furrowed the thickness of his hair, pulling him down to her.

With a groan, he jerked her tight. His kisses crushed her, devoured her. "Lord, girl," he muttered. "You don't know how much I've wanted to hold you, to touch you…to have you."

Her tears were salty on his face. Elise tasted them, felt them. The tears would always be there, as would the sorrow, the guilt, even the anger. But their need for each other was too compelling to be denied any longer.

Where his hips pressed hers, she could feel the jutting ridge of his arousal. The contact ignited a bonfire between her thighs. She ground against him, whimpering as currents of flame shimmered through her body.

It was too soon, the voice of caution shrilled. There were too many unresolved questions between them. Elise ignored the warning. She wanted her husband—his skin against hers, his hands and mouth possessing her, rousing her to a frenzy, his heat filling that cold and empty place inside her— the place that belonged only to him.

With arms that were even stronger than she remembered, he scooped her up and strode toward her bedroom. It was *their* bedroom once more, Elise reminded herself. After tonight, there was no way Clay would go back to the bunkhouse.

They undressed frantically, their clothes falling in rumpled heaps on the floor. Clay reached back to fasten the door latch. Then he turned and lowered his wife to the bed.

She clasped him in her arms, drowning her senses in the sweet male aura of his body. Her hands caressed the well-remembered curve of his back, the firmly muscled shoulders and buttocks. Her mouth savored the saltiness of his skin, the clean, musky aroma of his sweat. "I love you, Clay," she murmured. "I've missed you so much…"

His kiss was hard and deep, his erection a swollen ridge against her belly. She could feel her own wetness slicking her thighs. Her legs opened beneath him, knees spreading to cradle his hips. "Don't wait," she whispered.

"I won't." Clay shifted lower, pushed inside and came home. She gasped as he filled her. Fresh tears flooded her eyes. Loving him was like a familiar dance she'd never forgotten. She lifted her hips to meet him, pulling him deeper, again and again as sensations swirled and mounted toward a dizzying climax. She muffled her cries against his shoulder as he drove into her again and again. There was no way to prolong the act—they were both too raw, too needy. As she toppled over the edge she felt him shudder inside her. He relaxed with a groan. They lay in warm darkness, wrapped in each other's arms.

It was only later, as Clay slept beside her, that Elise remembered.

She'd neglected to tell him about Buck.

Clay opened his eyes. The dawn was leaden gray through the high window. Flecks of hail spattered the glass. It was early yet, and cold outside. Staying in bed a little longer would be a welcome luxury.

Elise slumbered next to him, her body as soft and warm as a child's beneath the covers. As she stirred in her sleep, he felt his loins tighten. For a moment he was tempted to wake her and begin again where they'd left off last night. But it would soon be time to start the day. Toby would be stirring, and there'd be chores to do. With the Christmas baking she'd planned, Elise would have a long day ahead. Best let her sleep while she could.

Shifting onto his side he studied her sleeping face. She was so beautiful, so tender and vulnerable. He thought of her here alone, having to do a man's work as well as a woman's, hauling heavy loads and chopping wood until her tired body gave out and lost its precious burden. She could have died along with the baby, leaving Toby alone to starve.

A slow, burning anger began to grow in him.

None of this tragedy was Elise's fault.

He should have been here.

Buck, at least, should have been here. Even if something had happened to the money, he could have returned to take care of Elise and Toby.

For that matter, if Buck hadn't gone off whoring in the middle of the night, both of them would likely have been here. His brother's folly had cost him three years of freedom and the life of a child he would never know—to say nothing of breaking Elise's innocent heart.

Whatever it took, Clay vowed, he would find out what had happened to his brother. If Buck was alive, so help him, he would track him down and make him pay. There was no way to bring back what was lost. But he would get some degree of justice if he had to whip the young fool within an inch of his life.

Thin rays of morning sunlight filtered through the window. Crows called from the orchard as Elise blinked herself awake. She'd slept later than usual. But after last night who could blame her? She stretched her legs, savoring the unaccustomed twinge between her thighs.

Had she done the right thing, letting Clay back into her bed so soon? The dreaded imaginings of her husband with another woman hadn't come between them, thank heaven. But there remained hurts to resolve. If she and Clay allowed lovemaking to serve as a substitute for talking, those hurts could fester like buried splinters. Somehow she needed to make him understand that.

With a drowsy yawn, she reached toward Clay's side of the bed. The empty sheet was cool beneath her hand. From the kitchen she heard the clank of an iron stove lid dropping into place.

"Clay?" She sat up, clutching the sheet to her

breasts. Footsteps approached the door. An instant later it swung open.

"Sorry to wake you. I was just trying to warm the house." He was fully dressed, his thick hair uncombed, his expression troubled. Was he already regretting last night?

"What's wrong?" she asked. "Is Toby all right?"

"Toby's asleep. I just looked in on him."

"Then come and sit down." She motioned to the foot of the bed. "I can see that something's bothering you. I won't stop worrying until I know what it is."

His gaze took in her bare shoulders and tousled hair. Hunger flickered in the depths of his granite eyes. "If I take one step closer, I won't be held responsible for what I do to you."

Elise gave him a smile. At least it wasn't her he was unhappy with. "Then perhaps you'd better speak from where you are," she said.

Clay's jaw tightened. His face reflected his inner struggle as he spoke. "It's Buck. I can't stop thinking about what he did—to me, to you and Toby and to the baby. If he hadn't gone into that blasted cathouse—" His fist balled against his thigh. "Damn it, he was only eighteen. I should've made him come back to the hotel with me. I should never have turned him loose in that town!"

"Buck was of age. He was responsible for his own decisions." Elise felt the weight of her un-shared knowledge. Dared she tell Clay where he could find his brother?

"Then why didn't he take care of things the way I told him to?" Clay spat out the words. "I'm not proud to say it, but there's a part of me that hopes the young fool's dead. At least that might explain why he stayed away. Otherwise, he's got no excuse!"

Clay was working himself into a fury. This was the worst possible time to tell him, Elise knew. But she'd already kept the secret too long. She owed her husband the truth.

She forced her gaze to lock with his. "What if I told you I knew where to find Buck?" she asked.

Clay reeled as if she'd struck him. His lips mouthed something she couldn't hear. "How long have you known?" he demanded.

"Only since yesterday, when the marshal told me. Buck's over in Ridgeview City. It seems he's been there all along."

"What about the money? Did the marshal know anything about that?"

"No. But Buck doesn't have any of it. I'm sure of that much."

Clay's expression wavered between outrage and disbelief as Elise described his brother's beggarly condition. "Something terrible must have happened," she said. "Otherwise, why wouldn't Buck have come back to the ranch? At least he would've had a home here."

"The damn fool boy probably drank up every last cent of that money!" Clay growled. "Don't worry about making breakfast for me. I'll be leaving for Ridgeview City as soon as the chores are done."

"But tomorrow's Christmas day! Can't it wait?" Elise was on her feet, struggling into her clothes.

"I've already waited too long. So have you."

"What are you going to do, Clay?" Half dressed, she flew to him. Her hands clutched his shirt, as if she could hold him back.

The eyes that glared down at her were the stony eyes of a stranger. "My brother could've been killed that night in Abilene," he said. "Saving his worthless life cost me three years in hell. The only thing that kept me from losing my mind was my trust that he'd take care of you and Toby. Turns out, I couldn't even count on him for that."

"But what are you going to *do?*" She gripped his shirt, determined not to let him walk away without an answer.

"I don't know. I'll figure that out on the way. But it won't be something you'll want to see."

"You could get hurt, Clay." She was pleading now. "You could even end up back in jail. Whatever Buck did or didn't do, I don't want to lose you again!"

"Let me go, Elise." His voice was as cold as his eyes.

Startled, she dropped her hands. Without another word he strode across the parlor, lifted his hat and coat off the rack and walked out the front door. As the latch clicked behind him, Toby tottered out of his room, rubbing sleepy eyes.

"Is Papa mad at us?" he asked.

"Not at us," Elise reassured her son. "He just needs to go somewhere today."

"So why did he act mad?" Toby persisted.

"Grown-up business." Elise scooped him up in her arms. "How would you like to help me get ready for Christmas? We can bake pies and cookies and finish decorating our tree."

Toby's round little face spread into a grin. "Can we make gingerbread men?"

"We'll see. First you need to get dressed and have some breakfast. Then we'll get to work."

Whooping with delight, Toby raced back to his room. The floor chilled Elise's bare feet as she moved to the window. Her breath frosted on the glass as she leaned close. Clay was in the corral, using a shovel to clear the watering trough. His jaw was set, his mouth grim. The blade slammed again and again into the stubborn ice.

She remembered the coldness in his eyes when she'd tried to keep him from leaving. It was as if the prospect of confronting Buck had driven all tenderness from his mind, leaving nothing but rage.

She would never have described her husband as violent. But Clay had spent the past three years locked up with criminals. How could any man help but be changed by such an ordeal? Watching him now, Elise had little doubt that, in his present state of mind, he was capable of killing his own brother.

And she had no power to stop him.

Clay had planned to ride his horse the ten miles to Ridgeview City. But when he checked the supply of feed for the stock he found the bins perilously low. He would need to pick up some hay and grain.

Otherwise the horses, the cow and the chickens could be left with nothing to eat.

As he hitched up the wagon, he mentally counted the cash in his pocket. He'd earned a little money doing odd jobs on the way home from Kansas. With what was left, he'd hoped to buy small Christmas gifts for Toby and Elise. But the animals had to come first. Paying for a few weeks' worth of feed would take all he had.

Damn this poverty that ate like lye at his soul! By now he should have been doing well, with cattle on the land and money in the bank. But Buck's crazy, irresponsible behavior had cost him everything.

Tossing some old quilts into the bed of the wagon, he climbed onto the driver's seat. For a moment he paused, gazing back at the house. He'd half expected Elise to come running out and beg him to stay. But he'd spoken harshly to his wife, and she had her pride. He could only hope that once he'd settled the score with Buck, they could put the past behind them and make a new start. Elise was a queen among women, and she deserved better than the hard life she'd been dealt. She deserved a comfortable life with pretty clothes and nice things for the house—things he was too poor to give her. That thought rankled Clay most of all.

Clucking to the horses, he swung the wagon down the drive. The sky was overcast, with muddy clouds drifting in above the western hills. Clay gave the clouds a thoughtful scowl. The trip to Ridgeview City and back would take most of the day. He could end up driving home in a storm.

It flickered through his mind that maybe he shouldn't go. Elise was upset with him for leaving; and tomorrow would be Christmas—their first Christmas together in three years. If anything delayed him he might miss the day with his family, not to mention the worry his late return would cause.

But no, the feed shortage was critical. And the need to confront his brother was burning through him like rattlesnake venom. The sooner he got it out of his system the better.

At the gate, he paused and looked back toward the house, hoping for a glimpse of his wife and son. But the porch was empty, as he should have known it would be.

Raising his collar against the wind, he turned the wagon onto the road. The wheels creaked as they settled into the frozen ruts. Overhead, a pair of ravens spiraled against a sunless sky. The day promised to be as bleak and cold as Clay's mood.

He wasn't looking forward to the showdown with his brother. There was no way to predict how it would go. But Clay was certain of one thing. Once their score was settled, he would turn his back and walk away.

He never wanted to set eyes on Buck again.

Elise had spent the morning mixing bread, baking two apple pies and helping Toby fashion a small army of gingerbread men. Now it was past noon, and the little house was a wonderland of delicious aromas. Cinnamon, ginger, apples, pastry and pine perfumed the air.

It smelled like Christmas.

But it didn't feel like Christmas.

Dead on her feet, Elise sank into the rocking chair and closed her eyes. She'd kept busy all morning, chatting with Toby and trying not to think about her husband. But now the worry she'd held at bay for hours came crashing in.

Anytime now, Clay could be arriving in Ridgeview City. Once he found his brother, anything could happen. Clay was not armed—the shotgun was all they had, and he'd left it here with her. But Buck could easily have a weapon. If he felt threatened he might use it. Clay, on the other hand, had always been the stronger of the two. If his temper got the best of him, he could literally beat his brother to death.

Why had Clay insisted on rushing off like a madman, without taking time to think things over? Hadn't there already been enough grief in their family?

"Mama, can we finish the chain now?" Toby was standing at her side, holding the length of paper chain they'd used on their first small tree. Elise had promised him they would make it longer to go on the new tree. She'd already cut a stack of paper strips from her store of old magazines and wrapping papers. Now, she supposed, was as good a time as any.

"Let's make some paste," she said. "Then we can get to work."

In the kitchen, she mixed flour and water in a cup. When it had been stirred to a gluey consistency, she sat down at the table with Toby and they went to work. The boy already knew how to loop a paper strip into the chain and glue the ends. By the time Elise took her seat he was finishing his first link.

"Since you're working on that end, I'll start on the other," Elise said. "How far do you think our chain will reach when we're done?"

Toby gazed beyond the kitchen, into the parlor. "All the way to the door, I bet," he said.

Elise picked up a strip of paper and dabbed the end in the paste. "Let's find out," she said.

Little by little, the chain grew longer. The task kept her hands busy but did little to occupy her mind. One link, then another, joined like the links that had formed their family tragedy.

Clay's arrest. Buck's disappearance. The loss of the baby. She and Clay and Buck had fashioned the dark chain of events together.

Now Clay was about to add another link.

Outside, the wind had risen. Gusts of hail, as fine as river sand, blasted the kitchen windowpane. The very sound of it made Elise shiver. Being on the road in this weather would be misery.

Why couldn't Clay have stayed home today? Whatever Buck's sins, he was already suffering for them. Why not leave him to his own punishment and get on with their lives?

Elise's hands had torn the paper link she was pasting. Too restless to sit, she pushed away from the table, rose and walked to the window.

"Are you all right, Mama?" Toby's blue eyes were wide with concern.

"Fine. Just stretching my legs."

"When will Papa be home?"

"Not for a while. Maybe before dark." Anxious to distract the boy, Elise turned toward the stove. "How about some pearl tea to warm us up?" She moved the kettle over the heat and set two cups on the counter. Elise had loved pearl tea as a child. Made with hot water, milk and a pinch of sugar, it was one of Toby's favorite treats as well. "Let's see how many links we can make before the kettle boils," she said.

The diversion helped, but only for a few minutes. As they sipped their tea, her thoughts returned again and again to Clay. The sense of foreboding was so deep it almost made her ill.

It was Christmas Eve—and the future of their family hung in the balance.

Ridgeview City, an untidy sprawl of tin and clapboard, had never lived up to the promise of its name. Set amid colorless hills, it served as little more than a wayside stopping place for travelers. Scattered along its dusty main street were three saloons, a run-down hotel, a bathhouse, a jail, a dry goods and feed store and a livery stable. Ramshackle cabins and dugouts littered the treeless countryside. There was no sign of either a church or a school.

By the time Clay arrived in town it was midday and the wind had turned biting cold. He stopped first at the feed store and laid down the little cash he had for a bundle of hay and a few sacks of grain and oats. He was a stranger here. The weasel-faced man behind the counter waited on him without asking his business.

"I'm looking for Buck McAllister," Clay said. "Do you know where I can find him?"

The clerk shot a stream of tobacco into a brass spittoon at the foot of the counter. "Passed out drunk somewhere, most likely. If not, he'll be in one of the saloons tryin' to get that way. You kin of his?"

"Do I look like it?" Leaving the question to hang, Clay went out to the loading dock. He laid the feed bags in the bed of the wagon and covered them with quilts against the weather. Then, leaving the rig behind the store, he set out on foot to look for his brother.

Wind whipped his coat as he walked along the frozen street. A fine hail, stinging cold, spattered his cheeks as the memory of that awful night in Abilene rushed over him. It seemed he'd come full circle, searching the run-down bars and gambling houses for his brother. When he caught up with the young fool, Clay swore, he would collect his due for all the misery Buck's careless ways had caused.

With each step, anger rose in Clay's throat. By the time he walked into the first saloon, he was seething.

Lit by the glow of a potbellied stove, the place looked crude and dingy. Men with unshaven beards and bloodshot eyes slumped on a side bench or played cards at the single plank table. The bar itself was a rough cut board laid on sawhorses. Jugs and dirty glasses lined the shelf behind it.

The bartender glanced up as Clay approached. "Buck comes in here regular like," he said in response to Clay's question. "Sometimes I give him a glass for sweepin' up. But he ain't been in today, or yesterday neither, come to think of it. Is the lad in some kind of trouble?"

Clay muttered a noncommittal reply, thanked the man and walked out into the cold. In the other two saloons the answers were the same. Everyone seemed to know Buck. But no one had seen him within the past two days. On a hunch, Clay checked the jail. He found the door unlocked, the marshal's desk vacant and the cells empty.

Hands thrust into pockets, Clay narrowed his eyes against the wind. Maybe Buck was hiding somewhere. Or maybe he'd heard his brother was home and left town. But that explanation didn't make sense. There was no way Buck could have known Clay was looking for him.

Something here wasn't right.

An empty wagon creaked past, the driver hunched over the reins. Two skinny dogs nosed for morsels in a pile of rubbish. What was he doing in this godforsaken town? Clay asked himself. It was Christmas Eve. He belonged at home with his wife and son.

He would pick up his rig, check the livery stable and maybe ask at a few of the cabins. If there was no sign of Buck, he would head back to the ranch. With luck he might be there in time to tuck Toby into bed.

And then what? Even after last night things were still rocky with Elise. Likely as not, he'd return home to find himself banished to the bunkhouse again.

For all he knew, she could still have doubts about

his reason for being in that Abilene brothel. Then, too, there was the loss of their baby. Did she blame his absence, or did she blame herself for what had happened? Either way, the tragedy would lie between them for the rest of their lives.

Clay sighed as he turned back toward the feed store, where he'd left the wagon. If he could have one Christmas wish, it would be to wipe the slate clean, to erase the mistakes of the past and be at peace with himself and his loved ones. But that would be asking for a miracle. And not even God could undo what had already happened.

Climbing into the wagon, he headed for the far end of town. Like the rest of Ridgeview City, the livery stable was a tumble-down structure. Wind whistled through the plank walls. The sagging roof looked as if it might collapse under the weight of the next snowfall. The proprietor, big-bellied, and smoking a blackened pipe, came outside as Clay pulled into the yard. "Nasty day to be on the road, ain't it?" he muttered.

Clay answered with a nod. "I was told I might find Buck McAllister here," he said.

The man glanced back toward the rear of the stable. "Try the stall on the far end. Last time I checked, he was sleepin' off a bender. Snorin' like a hog, he was. If you can get the lazy bum to open his eyes, tell him he's got a day's work to do." He stalked back into the warmth of his office, leaving Clay alone.

Clay's mouth had gone dry. He'd spent most of the long drive planning what he would say to Buck; but now that the moment had come, his mind could not piece together two coherent words.

The first two stalls contained horses. The next two were empty, their floors swept and scattered with clean straw. From the last stall came the rasp of labored breathing.

"Buck?" Clay rounded the corner to see a tangle of dirty, ragged quilts on the straw. They covered a long body, far too thin to belong to the vigorous young man Clay remembered.

"Buck?" Clay pulled back the quilt to see a hollow-cheeked face, crowned by a tangle of dark hair. The body stirred. Bloodshot eyes flickered open. Chapped lips worked to form words.

"Clay…? 'That you? 'Must be dreaming…"

"No, you're not dreaming, boy. It's me." Clay reached down and touched the dry, flushed forehead. The heat startled him.

His brother was burning up with fever.

Chapter Five

"Wait!" Clay sprinted to the wagon and found the canteen he'd brought along. Resting Buck's head against his knee, he twisted out the stopper and drizzled the water between his brother's cracked lips.

"Whiskey..." Buck coughed, a harsh, racking sound.

"No, damn it, no whiskey! Drink this!" Clay tipped the canteen. Buck choked down a little of the water, but not enough to help much. Clay had spent time assisting in the prison infirmary, and he knew pneumonia when he saw it. Buck's body would be dehydrated from the fever, but his lungs were filling up with fluid. In his weakened condition, he could easily die.

Propping Buck against the wall to ease his breathing, Clay raced for the livery stable office. Heat from the glowing stove surrounded him like a blanket as he opened the door. "My brother's sick! He needs a doctor!" he gasped.

The proprietor glanced up from tamping his pipe. "No doctor in these parts. No undertaker, neither. We ain't got no choice but to tend to our own. And if that fool's your brother, he's your problem, not mine."

A pot of coffee bubbled on the stove. It wasn't medicine but at least it might revive Buck a little. Clay swore under his breath as he filled an earthenware mug with hot, black coffee. The man let him take it but showed no inclination to move from his chair.

Clay returned to find Buck shivering in the straw, his body racked by chills. Cooling the coffee with a little water, he roused his brother, cradled his head and forced sip after sip between chattering teeth. What Buck really needed was willow bark tea for the fever and steaming to ease his lungs. Back at the ranch he could be treated. But what chance did he have in this hellhole of a town?

The coffee seemed to revive Buck a little. He was struggling to speak. "Clay…about that money…"

"Don't worry about it. Not now," Clay growled.

"No…got to tell you now. Might not last much longer." He cleared the phlegm from his throat.

"Lost it in a poker game. Bastard cheated, took it all…beat me up when I tried to get it back…damn near kicked me to death. Never been right after that…"

"Don't try to talk. Save your strength." Clay fought back a surge of tears. He didn't want to think about what had happened. He didn't want to feel what he was feeling. Right now nothing mattered except saving his brother.

"And Elise…" Buck gasped out the words. "Lord, I couldn't face her. Wasn't man enough to tell her what I'd done. Hated myself for it. Been drunk ever since."

He didn't know the half of it, Clay thought. Being young and foolish might excuse some things. But given the consequences, Buck's mistakes were damned near beyond forgiving.

All the same, Clay knew what he had to do.

Rising, he strode out to the wagon and rearranged the feed sacks to make a protected hollow. He cushioned the space with hay and lined it with one of the quilts. Buck might not survive the long ride back to the ranch. But leaving him here was out of the question.

Only as Clay bent over his brother again did he realize they weren't alone. A small brown puppy squirmed out from under the straw, stretched, shook and wagged its tail. The pup couldn't have been more than seven or eight weeks old.

"Found him in an alley," Buck said. "Good dog. Doesn't eat much. Take him with you. He might be nice for your boy."

"Hang onto him for now." Clay settled the little dog in Buck's lap. Then, reaching underneath his brother's legs and shoulders, he lifted him in his arms. Buck's thin, dehydrated body felt almost weightless.

The fevered eyes widened. "Wh—what in blazes are you doing?" he gasped.

"The only thing I can do, little brother," Clay replied. "I'm taking you home."

Elise stood on the porch, gazing toward the road. In the west, the sun lay like a burning coal above the barren hills. Thinning clouds glowed like embers, turning ashen with the slow end of day.

The storm had passed, leaving a frosty sheen on the trees. The windless air was bitter cold. Elise shivered beneath her woolen shawl. It was time to go inside, get Toby into his nightclothes and tell him a Christmas bedtime story.

Once more she peered down the drive, straining to see through the winter dusk. She held her breath, listening for the nicker of a horse or the faint jingle of harness brass. Maybe if she waited a little longer, Clay would be here to share his son's Christmas Eve.

But no, she'd given him enough time. If he'd met with some delay, he might not be coming back until tomorrow. If the worst had happened, he might not be coming back at all.

Furious tears blurred her eyes. She wiped them away with her shawl. Why had she let Clay go off angry this morning? She should have pleaded, threatened, hung onto the wagon, whatever it took to stop him. Better yet, she should have waited to tell him about his brother. If anything had gone wrong, she would never forgive herself.

"Mama?" Toby had opened the door behind her. "Is Papa coming? Can you see him?"

"Not yet." Elise followed him inside and closed the door. "Come on, let's get you ready for bed. Then you can hear a story and hang up your stocking."

"I want Papa to tell me a story." Toby was tired enough to be whiny. "Can't I wait for him?"

"No, it's getting late." Elise was tired, too, her nerves frayed with worry. She struggled to remain patient and cheerful. "I'll wake you when your father gets home, so he can kiss you good-night."

"Promise?"

"I promise." How would it affect the boy if he woke up to a Christmas morning without his father? What would she say to him? "Hurry now," she said, forcing a smile. "While you brush your teeth I'll get your nightshirt. Then you can choose the stocking you want to hang."

Toby obeyed, dragging his feet. It wasn't fair, Elise thought as she unfolded a fresh nightshirt. Tonight was Christmas Eve, a magical time for children. But her boy knew nothing of magic. His innocent eyes mirrored only her own fears.

"I hear something!" Toby dashed past her to fling open the front door. "It's Papa!" he shouted. "He's here!"

The nightshirt dropped from Elise's hands. Heart in her throat, she hurried into the parlor. Icy winter air rushed in through the door that Toby had left open. Ignoring it, she flung herself outside, onto the porch.

Instead of stopping at the corral to unhitch the horses, Clay had pulled the loaded wagon up to the house. Swinging down from the driver's seat, he reached into the back and handed a wriggling bundle down to Toby. "Here's a Christmas present for you, son," he said. "Take him inside and get him warm."

For a moment Toby was speechless with surprise. Then he scampered back to the porch clasping the pup, who was plastering wet kisses on his face. For the first time, the magic of Christmas shone in his eyes. "Look, Mama! He already likes me! This is the best present I ever had!"

Clay was still standing next to the wagon. Elise was about to thank him for Toby's gift when she saw the look on his face. Something had happened.

"Your dog must be hungry, Toby," she said. "Why don't you get him some bread and milk in the kitchen? And please close the door when you go inside."

Toby carried the pup into the house, pushing the door shut behind him. Elise was left to face her husband alone.

"What is it?" She started down the steps, then paused. "Did you find your brother?"

He exhaled, his shoulders sagging. "Come on down here," he said.

She followed him around to the back of the wagon, her apprehension growing. When he pulled the quilts aside, she saw a face—the face of a man she had every reason to hate. Bone-thin, filthy and unshaven, Buck was so still that for a moment Elise thought he might be dead. Then his eyelids fluttered open.

I'm sorry, Elise. His lips formed the words but no sound emerged from his throat.

"Pneumonia. It's pretty bad." Clay turned away from his brother to hide his words. "I know how you must feel. But I couldn't leave him to die. I'm not asking you to nurse him. I can build a fire in the bunkhouse and tend him by myself, if that's what you want."

If that's what you want.

He hadn't asked her in so many words. But Elise knew that Clay needed her help. The bunkhouse was cold and drafty. The quilts were thin. The stove was too small to heat enough water, and Clay looked ready to drop.

In the bunkhouse, with no one but Clay to tend him, Buck would be lucky to last the night.

Elise gazed down at the man whose youthful mistakes had shattered her life. She looked into her husband's eyes and saw the weariness, the desperate need. It was as if they stood at a crossroads, and the choice of which way to go had fallen on her.

She lowered her gaze, probing the depths of her pain-scarred soul. She had suffered a terrible injustice. For three long years she had fed on that suffering. It had become part of her. It had hardened her heart.

Now she was being asked to let it go.

"Elise?"

Clay's voice roused her. She raised her head. "He'll be better off in the house," she said. "Let's get him inside. I'll heat some water while you get him out of those dirty clothes and put him in our bed."

There was no time for gratitude. They worked together now. Elise kept willow bark in the cupboard for fevers. While she brewed the tea and tucked Toby into bed with his new pup, Clay stripped off his brother's filthy rags, helped him into a clean flannel nightshirt and eased him into the warmth of the bed. Then Elise brought a damp cloth to sponge his face and sat beside Buck while Clay went out to take care of the horses.

Buck's skin was burning, but his body shook with chills. His breath came in shallow gasps through chattering teeth. Now and then his eyes would blink open. They were gray like Clay's eyes, but lighter and gentler. He was twenty-one years old, barely into manhood, and this Christmas Eve could be the last night of his life.

She thought of the lonely little grave in the orchard, the lost money and the wasted years she and Clay had spent apart. Links in a chain of sorrow that the three of them had forged together. *It's over,* a voice whispered in her mind. *It's in the past, and nothing can change it. Let it go.*

A stray tear welled in Elise's eye and spilled down her cheek. She was so tired of being angry, so weary of reliving old hurts.

"Are you all right?" Clay's cool hand rested lightly on her shoulder.

She tilted her head to rub against his arm. Her eyes looked up to meet his. "We need to forgive him, Clay," she whispered.

"I know. I'm trying, love." He bent down and kissed her hair. "For now, what we need is to save his life."

They set to work, using dampened sheets to rig a makeshift tent. Stripped to the waist, Clay hunched underneath, supporting his brother and holding pans of steaming water close enough for Buck to breathe the vapor. Elise trailed back and forth, carrying the cooled water to the stove, reheating it and passing it back to Clay in a cycle that seemed endless. Her eyes were shadowed with exhaustion. Her hair hung in steamy, wet tendrils around her face. Her tired feet dragged across the floor.

Clay had never loved her more. She was his angel, his reason for living. He would do anything for the miracle that would bring the sunshine back to those beautiful blue eyes.

We need to forgive him, Clay.

Forgive him? Clay shook his head. Forgiving what Buck had done to *him* might be possible. But for what Buck had done to Elise? No, that was too much to ask.

We need to forgive him.

Elise's voice echoed in Clay's memory, repeating like a whispered chant. Something in his heart shattered like spring ice. And suddenly he understood what his wife, in her womanly wisdom, was trying to tell him.

Only by forgiving Buck could they hope to forgive themselves.

There was no other way.

Clay gazed down at his brother's ravaged face, the sunken eyes, the cracked lips, the stubbled cheeks. Buck was so young, little more than a boy. He deserved the chance to grow and learn and make something of his life. For that, he would need the support of a loving family.

"Listen to me, brother." Clay touched the fevered cheek. "I love you, and you're going to make it. You've got a life to live, and we've got a ranch to rebuild. I'm going to need your help, hear?" He hesitated, gazing down at the unresponsive face. Fear tightened his throat. "Buck, can you hear me?"

There was a beat of dreadful silence. Then the pale eyelids fluttered. Buck stirred and coughed, loosening the congestion in his lungs. "'Lo, Clay," he muttered hoarsely. "Can I have that in writing?"

Over the next hour his breathing steadily improved. The makeshift tent was taken away, the steaming mercifully halted. Sometime after midnight the fever broke. Soaked with perspiration, Buck eased into a healing slumber.

As Clay stood beside the bed, he felt Elise's arms slide around him from behind. "Merry Christmas," she said softly.

Turning, he pulled her close. His lips found hers in a kiss that went soul deep. Her mouth was warm and damp and welcoming. Her arms twined around his neck, holding on as if she never wanted to let him go.

Unspeakably weary, they clung to each other, the curves and hollows of their bodies melding in warmth and need. The barriers of blame and doubt had crumbled away. Nothing remained between them but love, trust and perfect peace. For the first time, Clay felt as if he had truly come home.

"We're going to be all right, aren't we?" Elise whispered.

Clay nodded, his stubbled chin brushing her temple. "If we weren't so damned tired, and if we had a bed, I could make love to you here and now."

She laughed, and the sound was music in his ears. "There'll be time for that later. For now, we'd better get some rest. Something tells me Toby and that pup will be waking up early."

Tossing a quilt over the rug, they stretched out in front of the fireplace. As the dawn of Christmas stole over the land they slept in each other's arms, dreaming of good times to come.

Epilogue

Christmas Morning, 1882

What a difference four years could make.

Elise surveyed the spacious parlor of her new home, with its sunny windows and big stone fireplace. This morning the room was a mess of happy clutter. Toys, empty stockings and bits of wrapping paper littered the rug. Nine-year-old Toby sat by the hearth reading his new storybook. His dog, Brownie, shaggy, lop-eared and devoted, dozed with his muzzle on Toby's shoe. Three-year-old Maggie squealed with laughter as her kitten pounced on a string. One-year-old Luke, who'd just begun to walk, was having a grand time pulling ribbons and candy canes off the Christmas tree.

"What a beautiful sight!" Clay's arms slipped around her from behind. Elise leaned back against him, resting her head in the hollow of his shoulder.

His lips nuzzled her ear. "Mmm, you smell good," he murmured.

"I think what you smell is the turkey. It's almost done." She raised her face for his kiss. Their lips met and lingered, rekindling the memory of last night's love.

The past four years had been far from easy. There'd been times when she and Clay had feared that the ranch might not make it. Clay and Buck had worked from dawn till dark repairing the fences and outbuildings. Clay had sold off his best pasture to buy more cattle. Over the winters, Buck had taken jobs in town to help out with money. Elise had done her part, as well. It had taken all three of them, working together, to make the ranch a success.

They'd started on the new house last summer and finished it after the fall cattle drive. Clay and Elise had moved just in time to turn their old house over to Buck and his bride, Celia, a pretty girl he'd met in town. Today the newlyweds would be arriving to join them for Christmas dinner.

Early that morning, before the children were awake, Elise and Clay had walked hand in hand to the old tree in the orchard. There, on the little grave, they'd laid a sprig of pine and a tiny jingle bell, bound with a thin red ribbon. This had become their yearly custom. Their lives were happy now, but they would never forget their lost angel.

Elise's musings were cut short by a rap at the front door. Celia and Buck stood on the threshold, their faces flushed with cold and laughter. They made a striking couple—dark-eyed Celia, as delicate and shy as a spring violet, and Buck, tall, handsome, radiating energy and confidence.

Together they would sit down at the dinner table and count their blessings as a family. And perhaps, in a silent moment, they would remember the bittersweet Christmas when they'd received the most precious gift of all.

The gift of forgiveness.

* * * * *

THE CATTLEMAN'S CHRISTMAS BRIDE

Pam Crooks

Dear Reader

It has been such fun to head for Montana Territory and delve into these characters' lives. That it's during Christmas makes it even more fun!

THE CATTLEMAN'S CHRISTMAS BRIDE is Allethaire Gibson and Mikolas Vasco's story. As you will soon see, Allie and Mick's lives are not perfect—yet!—but when they discover their unexpected love for one another they find the completion only two lost souls can experience together.

By the story's end Allie has decided upon the most perfect gift for Christmas. I based that gift upon a monument that still stands today in Great Falls, Montana. Originally built as a vision for education and culture, Paris Gibson Square represented great vision and hope for the time. Today, it lives on as a community cultural centre and museum, and—well, keep reading to learn more about this historical gem.

The mystery of the missing library money will be solved in Jack Hollister's story, coming soon. Until then, I wish you and yours the joy and peace of the Christmas season, now and always!

Pam Crooks

Chapter One

Montana Territory
December 23, 1886

Ever since Allethaire Gibson had been kidnapped and held for ransom three years ago, nothing in her life had gone right.

But *this* was the worst.

She stared miserably through the train's frosty window into the darkness outside and wondered how she'd fallen so low. What had she done to deserve such humiliation? And just when she'd begun to pull herself together, hold her head high and prove to everyone she was the same person she'd always been.

She'd tried. So hard.

After her horrific ordeal as a hostage in the wilds of Montana, she'd wasted no time in returning home to blessed civility in Minnesota. She'd gone to the usual parties with her friends, young and wealthy like herself. She'd frequented her favorite shops and restaurants. Had even indulged in a lavish European vacation—all to prove she was the same honest and upright woman as before.

Allethaire Gibson, daughter of Paris Gibson, the respected and forward-thinking industrialist.

Except it wasn't long before she discovered everything had changed.

She had changed.

Minnesota didn't feel like home anymore. At least, not like it used to. And Allethaire knew why. What everyone thought. What they said when her back was turned.

That her reputation was ruined. That she'd become a fallen woman while living with a band of outlaws.

It wasn't true.

It wasn't fair.

Allethaire thought she'd found her salvation in the Ladies Literary Aid Society. She'd worked tirelessly to promote her idea for a new library to be built in Minneapolis. The design had been breathtaking, exciting, modern. With the city's growing population, the need for such a fine exhibit of civilization and culture had been clear, and eventually, after more of her hard work raising funds, the money had rolled in by the fistfuls.

She should have succeeded in restoring respectability to herself. But something had gone wrong, and she was too blind, too naive, to see it coming.

Her fingers closed over the slender, brown bottle tucked in her handbag. Now, here she was, fleeing in the middle of the night like a common criminal—back to Montana, of all places.

Her despair begged for solace in the brandy she kept hidden, but she didn't dare allow herself the privilege of taking a swallow. Not even a little bracing one. No one on this crowded train could see her need to cope. Her abominable weakness.

She had to stay alert, even though she hovered on the edge of exhaustion. She had to appear strong and not the coward she really was.

Her eyes welled on a wave of renewed misery, and she leaned her head back against the thin cushion, letting her body absorb the rocking motion of the wheels hurtling along the tracks. In her haste to leave Minneapolis, she'd been forced to take one of the few remaining coach fares left on the St. Paul, Minneapolis & Manitoba Railway train headed west, a far cry from the comfort of the Pullman private car in which she was accustomed to traveling. No reclining chairs, no warm berth, no plush and pampered privacy.

But what did it matter?

As far as everyone was concerned, Allethaire was just another ordinary passenger, a woman journeying alone and packed into her seat with other wayfarers, like a sardine in a can.

For the first time in her life, she was glad no one knew who she was. It was easier that way.

Feeling little of the heat from the stove behind the long row of seats, she crossed her arms and huddled deeper inside her wool coat. Snores from the slack-jawed travelers stretched out around her warred with her tired brain. How could anyone get comfortable under such tight quarters? How could anyone sleep?

Amazingly enough, however, her lashes drifted closed, and she did.

She awoke, disoriented and cold, and flooded with a sense that something wasn't right.

Sunlight stretched in through the dull windows. Allethaire sat bolt-upright and grappled to find her purse, then discovered it was exactly where she'd kept it. Tucked against her chest. A quick check revealed nothing missing—her money, her hand-kerchief, her hand mirror, a few folded papers. Her brandy. They were all there, and oh, thank God, she hadn't been robbed while she slept.

"Someone is riding along the tracks." Sitting next to her, a matronly woman with cheeks pinkened from the chill leaned forward and rubbed at the glass with her coat sleeve. The accent threading her words revealed her German heritage. "Ach! That is strange."

Allethaire blinked in confusion. She scrambled to focus. "What?"

"See him?" The woman tapped a gloved finger against the pane. She peered closer. "What is he doing out there?"

Allethaire stared like an owl at the man indeed riding close to the train, but in the next moment, he was gone, left behind by the propelling locomotive.

Distracted, she swiveled her glance toward the opposite set of windows. Toward mountains and unforgiving range sprawled beneath somber gray clouds as far as she could see.

Montana Territory, as wild and desolate as ever.

She'd hated this part of the country once. Three years ago. She hated having to come back now.

"Where are we?" she asked to no one in particular.

"Helena, coming up." A scholarly-looking man in spectacles and a wrinkled tweed suit stared out the window, too.

Allethaire's heart tripped. They were closer to Great Falls than she thought. One more stop, and her journey would end. A wary desperation from seeing her father again—and telling him all the things he didn't yet know—fluttered through her, leaving her feeling sick to her stomach.

The woman beside her settled back into her seat. "My name is Margaret Butterfield," she said, venturing a smile.

Allethaire endured a stab of guilt. She'd made no attempt to be friendly since boarding the Manitoba; in fact, she made a pointed effort to keep to herself, but to refuse to respond to Margaret's friendliness now would be blatantly rude.

Still, she chose a careful response. "Mine is Allie."

She hadn't been called that since she was a child, but the less anyone knew about her, the better. Especially her name, which had always been much too distinctive.

"Are you coming to Montana to celebrate Christmas with your family?" Margaret asked.

"No." Allethaire had given little thought to the holiday, though it was only a couple of days away. "I won't be staying out here long."

Not any longer than she had to. Besides, her father's social calendar was likely filled with a wide array of Christmas gatherings. Just as hers would be had she stayed in Minneapolis, and if her life hadn't taken such a horrifying turn for the worse. Her father wouldn't have time to be with her anyway. Even if he wanted to.

Which he wouldn't, once he learned the truth.

A sudden craving for the brandy hidden in her purse gripped her.

"Oh?" The woman nodded, encouraging Allethaire to continue. "Then where will you go?"

"South." The word dropped from Allethaire's tongue without her conscious thought. "Somewhere south."

"Where it is warmer."

Allethaire shivered. "Much warmer."

Yes, that's what she'd do. Go south. Texas, maybe, with its millions of acres. Or *really* south to South America. No one would find her there, at least not easily, and she could use the time to find the answers she needed. To figure out what she'd done wrong.

But her eyes burned from a sudden sting of tears. And the glaring truth. She didn't want to go south at all.

"No husband, dear?" Margaret patted Allethaire's knee in sympathy. "Or children to keep you at home?"

Allethaire knew she meant well and likely interpreted Allethaire's weepiness for loneliness. Or maybe she only kept up her nosy chatter to pass the time until the train reached Helena.

Whatever her intentions, her query touched a spot inexplicably raw. Allethaire latched onto her composure. "I'm afraid I'm too busy to have need of a husband. I have greater—" she almost choked on the word "—aspirations for my life."

"Aspirations. Hmm." Margaret didn't seem to know what to make of it. "But what better way to share them than with a man who loves you?"

Allethaire blinked fast and fought an overwhelming feeling of loss. Frustration, too, and the unmistakable sensation of her life spiraling out of control.

She clutched her purse to her chest. Her fingers found the familiar shape of the slender bottle inside.

"Excuse me, Margaret," she said, rising un-steadily to her feet. "I—I must go to the lavatory."

But the train unexpectedly lurched and threw her off balance. She yelped in surprise and fell back into her seat.

Scree-eech. Hiss, Hiss, Hiss. Scree-eech.

The bespectacled gentleman across from her jerked his glance to the window and frowned. "We're slowing down."

Movement in the glass startled Allethaire. Blurred shapes of men riding alongside the tracks. In a flash, they were gone.

"Why are we stopping?" Margaret asked, bewildered.

"Have we reached Helena already?" Allethaire asked.

But that didn't seem possible. She could see nothing of the town. Not a hint of civilization. Only mountains and the endless Montana range.

Muffled shouts sounded from outside. Some-where toward the back. Male voices, their words indecipherable.

Clunk! Something—or someone—landed against the door.

Scree-eech. Hiss, Hiss, Hiss. Scree-eech.

Allethaire gripped her seat. Something was wrong, terribly wrong, for the Manitoba to stop now, in this desolate stretch of territory.

Pop!

A gunshot! Another *pop!* confirmed it, and oh, God, oh, God, what was happening out there?

Murmurs rippled through the passengers, each of them as alarmed as Allethaire. Heads twisted toward the rear. A few men stood, their stances revealing their intention to march past the row of seats and see for themselves what was transpiring.

But before any of them could, the door burst open.

The train's conductor stumbled forward with his arm twisted behind his back. Blood trickled down his left temple.

Collective gasps went up.

Allethaire couldn't breathe.

"What's the meaning of this?" someone shouted.

A red bandanna covered the face of the man holding the conductor captive. He kept his revolver pressed to the conductor's head and pushed him forward, past the stove, into the aisle.

"What do you want?" another man yelled.

"A woman," the outlaw gritted. His gaze raked over each passenger's face.

Until he found hers.

"Her name is Allethaire Gibson."

Chapter Two

Mick Vasco pounded the last staple into the fence post, gave the barbed wire a testing tug and called it a morning.

He'd been out riding fence since just after dawn, and the Montana cold had seeped into his bones but good. He'd already sent the rest of the fencing crew back to the line camp. By the time he joined them, they'd have the big enamel pot brewing with plenty of blistering hot coffee for all of them.

Mick hooked his hammer onto his saddle, but delayed mounting up. The air carried the smell of impending snow, a crisp scent that slid through his nostrils and reminded him that here in the valley, they'd yet to feel the brunt of a true Montana blizzard. Soon, he knew, they would, and a renewed anticipation to head back to camp swept through him.

Still, caught up in the peace and silence, he lingered beside his horse. His pensive gaze snagged on the Bear Tooth Mountains in the distance, their peaks already tipped with pristine white. At the foothills, thousands of acres of rangeland stretched in every direction. Beside him. Behind him. Around him.

It boggled his mind sometimes. All that rangeland. The fact that it was half his, especially.

The Wells Cattle Company. Split right down the middle with his half brother, Trey Wells. His heritage. His legacy. Hard-won after a lifetime of denial and deceit and hell, why was he thinking of all that now?

Mick's mouth tightened. Because he still hurt from his father's betrayal. Likely always would, too. Three years ago, upon finding out Sutton Wells had raped Mick's mother, a Basque woman, Mick had lashed out and made some stupid decisions. Before everything was said and done, an innocent woman had been kidnapped, a man had been killed and Mick had gone to jail for his sins.

Turning grim from his ruminating, he swung up into the saddle. But the mood dug in and wouldn't let go.

He'd paid the price for his stupidity, and Mick had no intention of making the same mistakes again. He'd gotten what he wanted. His rightful inheritance. His place in the Wells empire.

Times like now, though, when he was left alone to contemplate the immensity of the WCC, the self-doubt crept in. Like a flock of angry crows pecking away at his confidence and pride and exposing the raw flesh of...unworthiness.

If not for the unfortunate circumstances of his conception, Mick knew too well he'd never be able to claim a spread as fine as the WCC. He wouldn't own a horse as well-bred as this one, either. A golden palomino quick on his feet and trained for cattle. He'd done nothing to deserve the privilege of being a Wells. Not like Trey, who'd grown up working day in and day out alongside Sutton to build the ranch into the respected, powerful operation it was today.

Mick pulled the collar of his coat closer to his ears and pinned his gaze on the foothills. Therein laid his roots. A small Basque village where every sheepherder and his family struggled to survive. With the winter barreling into their lives, they'd struggle to stay warm, too, and find enough food to eat.

A tight sigh of worry slid through his teeth. Mick felt guilty for his comforts, all right. The birthright, which assured he'd have all the food and warmth he needed.

With more and more clarity, he'd begun to realize he had a responsibility to his Basque family. He had to find a way to help his people, to ensure them a future as stable, as promising as his own.

He didn't have an inkling of how, though. Or where to begin.

A distracted part of his brain registered the sound of a train clattering down the tracks behind him. Lured by his troubled thoughts, he nudged the palomino forward and contemplated that long line of fence instead. Funny how those wooden posts and barbed wire symbolized his new life. How he'd begun to earn his place in the WCC. By learning the ropes from the ground up. Digging posts and stringing barbed wire, like any lowly cowboy in the outfit. Without regard that he was half owner of the land the fence held in. Or that he was part Basque.

Suddenly a gunshot echoed throughout the valley, and Mick's head whipped toward the sound. A pair of riders approached the train—the St. Paul, Minneapolis & Manitoba on its regular run—and damned if the steam engine hadn't started to slow.

Scree-eech. Hiss, hiss, hiss. Scree-eech.

Mick reached for his Winchester. No reason for that train to stop out here. No reason but trouble.

He shot a quick glance behind him. He half hoped to see someone from the outfit coming out to check on him and give him a hand, but there was no one.

Except him.

Mick had no intention of letting that train get robbed on WCC land. He knew for a fact the Manitoba carried passengers west. Innocent folks who'd be powerless to defend themselves or their belongings against thievery.

Damn it to hell.

He spurred his horse after the train and braced himself for what laid ahead.

The outlaw's harsh gaze bored into Allethaire and chilled her blood, rocking her with the certainty she'd seen those eyes before.

"You're coming with us," he said.

She drew back in horror. "I'll do no such thing."

That voice, muffled behind his bandanna—she'd heard it before, too, but before she could identify it, put a place, a name to the man, Margaret clutched Allethaire's arm in a protective grip.

"Ach! What is the meaning of this, young man?" she demanded. "What do you want with her?"

"Please, Miss Gibson." The conductor ignored Margaret. He stood stock-still, clearly afraid to move with the revolver against his temple. He appealed to Allethaire with a panicked expression. "He wants to talk to you."

"About what?" she croaked.

"Get up and walk out of this car with us," the outlaw grated. "Or he dies."

Margaret's grip tightened. "Talk to her? What is going on here?" She faced the outlaw head-on. "Who are you? Why are you doing this?"

"Shut up!" His arm lifted as if he intended to backhand her. Fearing he would, Allethaire bolted to her feet.

"All right!" she gasped. "I'll go with you."

"But, Allie!" Margaret protested.

"I'll accompany her," said the scholarly passenger across the aisle. He rose. "She shouldn't go back there by herself."

His concern touched Allethaire. What had she done to deserve it?

"I'm not afraid, sir," she lied, her heart pounding from the knowledge that the outlaw wanted something from her. That he'd known she'd be on this train. In this car. He'd sought her out in this godforsaken country for reasons she couldn't yet fathom.

The shadowed eyes, so familiar, yet elusive, kept her riveted. A hard shade of green, cold and unforgiving.

He clasped her shoulder, yanked her away from her seat and into the aisle.

"Go on," he snarled.

Allethaire caught herself from stumbling to the floor.

"Don't touch me," she snapped.

"To the back. Move."

The revolver lifted just long enough to punctuate the command. Allethaire didn't dare refuse. She couldn't risk anyone getting hurt on her behalf, especially the terrified conductor, most at the outlaw's mercy.

She began to walk, haltingly at first, keenly aware of the stares of each passenger upon her. Of how they sat frozen in their seats, too afraid to help her or the wounded conductor and oh, God, did the outlaw intend to *kidnap* her? Hold her for ransom like Woodrow Baldwin did?

No. It couldn't be. Surely not.

Oh, God. Oh, God. Oh, God. Please not.

She kept walking, purposefully, one step at a time. A part of her noted how her gait was surprisingly steady. That the train had come to a complete stop, held captive by the ruthless outlaw and his accomplices who had ridden in out of nowhere to lay claim and find *her*, of all people....

The back door swung open, and another man wearing a bandanna appeared. He grasped her elbow and hustled her through, forcing her to step down onto the metal grate between the cars. The cold Montana air smacked into her, making her eyes water and her breath catch, and another quick step up took her through the opened door of the adjoining car.

The baggage car.

Trunks and valises of all shapes and sizes filled shelves on both sides of the compartment. In the corner, bound and gagged, a man sat with his knees pulled up. He appeared unharmed and was clearly helpless, though very much alert. By the badge he wore, he was some sort of security agent for the Manitoba, but he'd been no match for the outlaws who had overpowered him. A third man with a bandanna covering his face stood guard over him, and at Allethaire's arrival, he straightened sharply.

"You found her," he said.

"I told you she'd be here." The outlaw pulled the door closed with a resounding slam. He pushed the frightened conductor toward the captured agent. "Sit over there and keep your mouth shut. Or else."

The trainman didn't have to ask what "else" meant. He scurried toward the agent and cowered beside him, drawing his knees up, too.

The three masked men swiveled their stares onto Allethaire. She swiveled *hers* to the lone trunk on the dusty floor. The trunk set apart from all the others.

Her own.

She recognized the brass plate, monogrammed with her initials in elegant script, and the edges trimmed in rich brown leather. The trunk was a gift from her father on her last birthday.

Why was it sitting there?

"Open it," the outlaw said, his voice chilling through the red cotton fabric.

She faced him. Thought of all she'd brought with her. Ordinary things any woman would pack on a journey west. Unease filtered through her. "Why?"

"Because I told you to."

He could have opened the trunk himself. Any

one of his gang could. It'd take only a shot, a single one, to blow through the lock....

But they wanted her here. They wanted to prove something. They'd gone through a great deal of risk to bring her out here and force her to open her own trunk.

Why?

The gripping green eyes held her on the brink of recognition.

"Who are you?" she asked. Familiar, elusive, those eyes. A haunting glimpse of someone in her past. "Tell me your name."

"Shut up."

She reached out to yank the bandanna from his face, but too quick, his arm swung, connected with her wrist and she staggered sideways in a burst of pain.

She clutched the wounded limb to her chest and fought tears. She wasn't going to give him the satisfaction of seeing how much she hurt.

"Open the trunk," he ordered.

The outlaw seemed perilously close to losing his control, and Allethaire gave up the fight. She'd open her trunk. She'd show him she had nothing of interest to anyone. Certainly not to him and his gang of roughnecks.

She fumbled in her purse, found the key and knelt in front of the trunk. Her attempts proved awkward with her throbbing wrist, but she managed. The latch flipped up. She managed to unbuckle the leather straps, too, and they fell free. Finally she yanked up the trunk's lid.

And there, lying on top of her navy blue serge dress, was an envelope. One she had never seen before. A parcel, really, thick from the contents it held.

"Well, well, well," the outlaw crooned. "Look at that. A package. What d'you suppose is in it?"

He'd moved closer to Allethaire. So close the toes of his scuffed boots stood on the hem of her dress, pooled around her. She could smell the greed in him. The anticipation of the coming moments.

"I have no idea," she grated.

But she intended to find out. Someone had invaded the privacy of her personal belongings. Someone the outlaw knew about. He knew the parcel would be there, and she'd bet her father's fortune he knew what was inside, too.

Her fingers ripped at the envelope and yanked out a stack of green bills. *Thousands* of dollars, planted in her trunk.

A small fortune.

She dropped the bundle as if it'd suddenly caught fire.

The outlaw snatched the money back up again. He riffled through the stack, as if the greenbacks were playing cards, and cackled his glee.

"Tsk, tsk. Don't you know it's wrong to steal someone else's money, Miss Gibson?" he drawled. "Shame on you."

She rose to face him. A warring mix of confusion and alarm stirred inside her. "I haven't stolen anything. You know I haven't."

"Let's just say the Literary ladies aren't going to be very happy with you when they find out."

She blinked. "The Literary—what are you talking about?"

He stuffed the money into an inside pocket of his coat, but tossed aside the envelope. "Let's get out of here, boys."

A slip of paper fell out of the tattered envelope. A copy of a bank draft, marked as Paid. Drawn off the Ladies Literary Aid Society's bank account, and suddenly, a horrifying rush of dread clutched Allethaire by the throat, choking the air she tried to breathe.

The account contained the funds for the new

library she'd tried to build. Money raised from her hard work and so many others', too. Every dime intended for the City of Minneapolis to use.

The draft had been made in her name, but it was a payment she'd never asked for. Or authorized. Or knew about.

Horror rocked through her. Someone had set her up, making her look as if she'd stolen the money and fled to Montana. An embezzling scheme, with all the evidence pointing to *her,* and the Manitoba's conductor and security agent acting as witnesses.

Who was that someone?

Who was the outlaw working for?

"Who are you?" she cried, swinging out with her sore wrist to yank the red bandanna from his face.

This time, she succeeded. Recognition tore away the last three years of her life and threw her backward into time. Into the horror from being kidnapped and held for ransom. The men responsible. Woodrow Baldwin and one of his accomplices, a man she knew only as Reggie.

Reggie.

No longer in jail for the crime but here, in this rail car, setting her up for a crime she didn't commit.

He shoved her aside, against her trunk, in his

haste to escape. Her balance lost, she toppled to the floor with a cry, and the other two in his gang rushed past to flee with him.

But before they could, the railcar's door burst open. A man loomed, wielding a Winchester rifle. Black-eyed and dark-haired and erupting out of her past, too.

The last of Woodrow Baldwin's accomplices.

Mikolas Vasco.

His expression cunning and fierce, his glance sliced through the compartment. He cocked the rifle. The sound cracked through the stunned silence.

"Nobody move!" he ordered.

Chapter Three

In the span of a single heartbeat, Mick's brain registered trouble.

Big trouble.

The commotion he'd heard on the other side of the railcar's door had warned him as much, but he never expected to see a gang of armed and masked train robbers coming at him, on the brink of escape.

He figured the surprise of his arrival and the threat of a cocked Winchester gave him the advantage. At least for now.

But not for long.

"Hold it right there," he ordered.

The men froze in midstep.

"Put down your guns real slow," he commanded. "Then get your hands up."

"Well, I'll be damned," one of them said. "It's Mikolas Vasco."

Mick's gaze latched onto the man closest to him. The leader, considering he was the first in line to try to save his sorry ass. He hadn't bothered to obey Mick's orders, and neither had the other two, but Mick guessed being recognized was enough distraction for them to forget to shoot him—at least for the time being.

"It's me, Reggie," the outlaw said, his voice sounding carefully hopeful through his bandanna.

Mick hid his surprise. His unease. He'd never again expected to see the lowlife who had helped destroy his stepfather's flock of sheep three years ago. Along with Woodrow Baldwin, Reggie had been instrumental in helping Mick make the biggest mistake in his life, and did he think Mick owed him any favors for it?

Like letting him and his gang out of this railcar? Scot-free?

"Fancy meeting you here." Mick held the green eyes with his own. "Like this."

"Didn't know you were out of jail," Reggie said, nonplussed.

"Didn't know you were, either."

"I ain't going back. Just so you know that, too."

Mick understood the warning Reggie gave. The

three barrels leveled at his chest proved he meant every word.

"Depends on what just happened in here," Mick said evenly.

"He stole my money!"

Mick slashed a startled glance sideways to find a woman he hadn't even realized was there picking herself up off the floor. Nearby, two men sat huddled in the shadowed corner, clearly disarmed, roughed-up and made captive by Reggie and his men.

"Don't let him go," she pleaded.

She took a frantic step toward Mick, and if he'd never expected to see Reggie again, he sure as *hell* never expected to see Allethaire Gibson.

A thousand times never. Not here, on this train, victim once again of a crime leveled against her... and damned if she wasn't as beautiful as ever. More beautiful than even his lustiest fantasies.

Three rifle barrels swung toward her, and Mick's protective instincts kicked in. She didn't seem to notice she could be shot in a blaze of reckless fury, or if she did, she didn't much care, so great was her desperation.

"Give the money back, Reggie." She reached an

arm out, as if she intended to take it right off his person. "We all know you stole it. Give it back."

Mick hastily angled his body to keep her from getting closer, no easy task when he had to keep his eye on Reggie and the others and keep the door blocked, too, so they wouldn't all run out.

"It's in his coat, Mikolas," she said, straining to maneuver around him. "I have to get it."

"Let me handle this," he growled. His unease ballooned from the situation fast spiraling out of his control. He couldn't corral a fretting female and a gang of hoodlums desperate to escape at the same time.

"Get away from the door," Reggie said, his rifle abruptly swinging back to Mick.

"Can't do that just yet," he said. Every muscle inside him coiled.

"It's three rifles against your one."

"I can count."

"You want to get shot?" Reggie snarled. "Move!"

As if on some unspoken signal, one of the gang— Mick never saw who—rammed into Allethaire, like a billy goat against a fence post. She cried out and fell against Mick. At the same moment, Reggie hit Mick from the other side. Hard. So hard Mick catapulted into the racks crammed with baggage, and he went down in a tangle of petticoats and passenger bags, bringing Allethaire with him—and damn!

His rifle went off, finding its mark in the car's ceiling.

Reggie yelled. Boot heels clamored. Cold air swirled into the compartment. And Mick swore.

"They've gone!" Allethaire scrambled off him.

One-handed, he hurled a canvas satchel from his chest and bolted to his feet. His glance clawed through the open door to hear the crisp staccato of horses' hooves. A lone rider flashed by, tearing off into the distance.

Mick flung the door wider and glimpsed the other outlaws escaping, too, each in different directions.

His jaw clenched in frustration. They'd be hell to find scattered like they were, but he had to try. He swung toward Allethaire. "I'm going after them."

She'd already gotten up from the floor. "I'm going with you."

"You're not going anywhere, Miss Gibson."

They both whirled toward the conductor, who was no longer cowering in the corner with the security agent but hastening clumsily toward a revolver, likely kicked aside during his scuffle with the outlaws. He scooped up the gun and swung toward them, holding the gun high in a two-fisted grip.

"I'm afraid we have to detain you with regard to the funds found in your trunk," he said.

She drew back in alarm. "Detain me?"

Mick's challenging gaze lifted from the revolver. "What the hell is that supposed to mean?"

Behind them, the security agent wrestled with the ropes around his wrists. No longer gagged, thanks to the conductor who helped untie him, he jumped to his feet.

"There's been a large amount of money found in Miss Gibson's possession, sir, of which there's considerable question regarding its rightful ownership." Mick doubted the man was a day over twenty, but he took his duties as seriously as someone far more experienced. He straightened to his full height, clearly exerting his authority. "I intend to find the truth in where that money came from, even if it means I have to have her arrested to do so."

"Arrested?" Allethaire's fingers flew to her mouth in horror.

"Yes. You've been accused of stealing the money. The authorities will ascertain the truth."

"It's stolen, all right," Mick gritted.

And the longer he stood there, the farther away the money got, and the harder it would be to find Reggie and his gang, too.

But something kept Mick where he was, with his boots planted on the floor. Something in Allethaire's expression—genuine and vulnerable and terrified—that coiled in his chest and inspired in him a fierce need to shield her from all that made her hurt.

Right along with a healthy dose of guilt from how he'd failed her three years ago on account of his part alongside Woodrow Baldwin in holding her hostage, making her an innocent victim for his own selfish gain.

"The sheriff will attend to the robbery. It's his job," the agent said, giving Allethaire a stern look. "Mine is to protect this train and everything on it. I simply want to ask you a few questions."

"You have no right to accuse me," she said hoarsely. "I've done nothing wrong."

"I'm not accusing you of anything, miss," the agent said.

"The hell you're not," Mick growled.

The agent hurled him an imperious glance. "We

must know what that money was doing in her trunk. The draft says—"

"I don't know how that draft got there," she said.

"And yet the lock on your trunk is in perfect condition, with no sign of tampering."

"But—"

"And you alone have the key."

The blood drained from her cheeks. She trembled from the implication of the evidence mounting against her.

"She's staying, mister," the conductor said to Mick. "But we've got to notify the sheriff immediately."

"You do that," Mick drawled.

But his mind was working. Gauging the distance between Allethaire and the door he hadn't yet bothered to shut. The door opposite the one which the conductor inched toward…

Still holding the revolver high, the trainman slid a quick glance at the security agent. "Keep your eye on her, Richard. Here's your gun. Let's hope she'll cooperate, and you'll have no need of it."

Allethaire made a tiny sound in the back of her throat, revealing her dismay that they could think her dangerous enough to shoot. That they had no intention of letting her go anytime soon.

The little sound convinced Mick he had to act fast, and he took keen note of the seconds ticking by. Reggie was long gone by now. So was the money. And Mick had to get the hell off this train...

Behind him, through the open doorway, a woman's shocked cry jolted his thoughts. The deep rumble of male voices revealed growing outrage, and he realized the passengers in the adjoining car had surged together to see what was happening, where Allethaire had gone.

"There she is!"

"But where is the ruffian who took her?"

Mick didn't have to turn around to recognize the German-laced accent in Margaret Butterfield's voice. He wasn't surprised to learn she was on the train; most everyone in Great Falls knew she closed up her restaurant every year at Christmastime to visit her daughter in Cheyenne. In the few years since he'd become acquainted with her, he'd learned she always came back two days early, so she could cook up meals for those who needed them on Christmas Day.

"He's run off with his gang, Margaret," Mick said.

He heard her quick gasp. "Mick? Mick Vasco? Is that you? Why, whatever are—?"

"Regardless of what happens in the next few minutes, Margaret," he said, keeping a grim-eyed watch on the conductor and security guard. "Let Trey know what happened. You hear me?"

She hesitated, absorbing the information. "Yes, but—"

"Paris, too. Right away."

"Paris?"

Mick heard Margaret's shock. He *saw* it in Allethaire's face.

"No. Not my father. Don't say anything to him," she said. "Don't you dare, Margaret!"

"Paris? Gibson? The industrialist?" the conductor asked.

"You're his daughter?" The security agent gaped at her in stunned surprise.

Before she could respond, Mick took advantage of their distraction, stepped forward and hooked his arm around Allethaire's shoulders, hauling her against him, her back to his chest. With the other hand, he held the cocked Winchester leveled and steady. "That's right. She is. And I'm taking her with me."

On a swift inhalation of breath, she arched and writhed against him.

"I'm not going anywhere with you," she grated.

"It's for your own good."

Mick tightened his hold. He didn't know how he was going to get them both out the door without the security agent burning some powder on them. He hadn't forgotten the overanxious passengers behind him, either, hell-bent on preventing their escape.

But instinct told Mick he had to try. Allethaire was a wealthy woman in her own right, so why would she steal someone else's money? Besides, Mick knew how much she hated outlaws. Knew it firsthand from those days three years ago when he'd been involved in her kidnapping. Made no sense she'd want to become one herself.

He didn't understand the evidence against her, but he knew one thing—he didn't trust Reggie any farther than he could spit. Whatever scheme the man was involved in had put Allethaire in a hell of a fix, and leaving her to fend for herself against arrest would be a big mistake.

Mick owed it to her to act now and find answers later.

He *owed* her.

"You can't take her anywhere." The agent—Richard—narrowed his eyes. He held the revolver aimed straight-armed at Allethaire.

"The hell I can't."

"You're impeding justice if you do."

"The way I figure it, you lost your chance at justice when you let that gang run out of this car."

Richard stiffened. "I didn't just 'let' them!"

"Mick." Behind him, Margaret sounded worried. "Are you sure about what you are doing?"

Mick ignored her. Allethaire's breathing came in quick, panicky pants, but she'd quit wiggling, as if she readied herself for whatever happened next. Her fingers dug into his forearm and the shape of her body pressed into his, rigid, wary...but warm and slender, and damn it, he couldn't let himself be distracted by the feel of her.

Not now. Not like this.

He pivoted, bringing her with him with every backward step. Changing their direction, heading toward the opposite door, away from that bunch of wide-eyed passengers crowded outside and looking in.

The conductor and security agent turned with him. Allethaire's trunk stood between them and Mick. Their tense expressions revealed their unease.

Mick didn't trust that unease. Made for itchy trigger-fingers, for sure.

"Don't let them go, Richard," the conductor gritted. "She's beholden to her actions, and now, so is he."

The security agent's grip flexed over the revolver. Mick detected the faintest tremble in the way he held his weapon.

"Don't go any farther, mister. I'll shoot to stop you. Don't think I won't," the agent gritted.

That tremble told Mick the agent didn't make a practice of shooting people. Might be he never had to, given his young age, and Mick shifted his hold on the Winchester just long enough to reach behind him and open the door.

"You're going to have to fire your gun into her first to get to me, Richard. You know that, don't you? Then you'll be responsible for bringing both of us down." Cold air swirled against his backside. A swath of morning sunlight beamed inward, stretching wider the more he pushed at the door. "You sure you want to do that? Considering she could likely be innocent of everything you're accusing her of."

The agent swallowed.

"Don't listen to him, Richard," the conductor snapped. "Here. Give me that gun! We can't let them escape, y'hear me?"

"Oh, God." Allethaire sucked in a frightened breath as the trainman wrested the weapon from the agent.

"I won't let them hurt you," Mick muttered into her ear. "I swear I won't."

Movement near the door jerked his attention. Margaret's matronly shape reached for something propped in the corner.

A broom.

"Don't take another step, mister." Holding the revolver once again, the conductor speared them with a feral glance. "Not a single one."

Behind him, Margaret swung the broom and smacked him hard against the shoulder. The blow toppled him sideways into Richard, who yelped and fell into the rack of baggage. Both men scrambled for footing and whirled toward her in surprise and outrage, their concentration lost.

And Mick made his move—out the door into the biting cold, taking Allethaire with him.

Chapter Four

Allethaire's feet barely touched the narrow iron steps, so fast did Mikolas Vasco hustle her off the railcar and toward his horse, a golden palomino grazing on the winter-grass. The air stung her nostrils and slammed into her cheeks, but it was the horror of what was happening that catapulted her heart into her throat.

"Climb up, climb up," Mikolas ordered in a terse voice. He planted a hand against her back, pushing her toward the saddle. "Hurry!"

She veered away. "I'm not going with you. You're not going to kidnap me again, Mikolas. Damn you."

He gripped her elbow and spun her back toward his horse. "I'm not kidnapping you. I'm saving you from those fanatics in there. Get into the saddle."

"Do you want ransom money?" she demanded,

twisting away from him again. Fighting him with every ounce of resistance she had in her. "Is that why you're doing this?"

Several passengers peered around the corner of the railcar. "Hey, there they are! Hold on, you two! Stay right there! Don't move!"

Mikolas swore and brusquely grabbed her a second time, hefted her onto the palomino with pure brute strength and shoved her into the saddle with a rough hand to her fanny. He leaped up behind her and grabbed the reins.

"Trust me, Allethaire. Just trust me, all right?" he gritted.

Passengers spilled out of the railcar. The scholarly gentleman. The conductor, too. Margaret on the heels of Richard, the security agent.

Maybe one of them would listen to her. Just give her a chance to explain…

"Let me off this horse," she said. Mikolas' chest pressed heavy against her back. He clamped his arms tight around her waist, keeping her in the seat while his mount bolted into a run. "Let me *off!*"

She was fully prepared to throw herself out of the saddle to escape him, and she twisted and squirmed and tried to lift her leg over the palomino's neck. But the speed of the ride, the ground racing by, the jarring motion of a fast gallop…oh, God, she couldn't do it, after all.

Tears of frustration welled. She'd be crazy to hurl herself off the horse and be killed. *Crazy*. Not that Mikolas would allow it, but his grunts revealed she'd given him a good fight, and it galled her to give it up.

To let him win in this new round of kidnapping.

The biting wind cut through her hair. The cold sucked at her breath, and yet she hardly noticed. She didn't care. She was only aware of how far away they'd ridden, that the Montana range sprawled in endless desolation for as far as she could see, and how would she *ever* get back to that train?

Finally the palomino began to slow. Puffs of air billowed from his nostrils. The big horse couldn't run so fast for long, and especially not while doubly-burdened, but to slacken his pace now, out here in the middle of nowhere, filled her with a rush of apprehension from what Mikolas Vasco intended.

His gloved hand pulled on the reins. The palomino trotted to a stop, shuddered and blew noisily.

"Get down," Mikolas said.

He swung from the saddle. Without his body to

warm her, a chill slid through her coat. She didn't move and glared down at him from her seat.

"Why?" she asked.

He kept firm hold on the leathers lest she attempt an escape. Which Allethaire had no intention of doing. Not at the moment, at least. She'd learned Mikolas possessed quick reflexes and a deceiving amount of strength that gave him the advantage of an agility she could never match. He'd merely find a way to best her.

"We're going to talk," he said.

She bristled. "I have nothing to say to you."

His mouth hardened. "Allethaire."

"Except, of course, to wish you to hell for what you've done."

"Listen to me."

"And to insist that you take me back to the Manitoba. Now. This instant."

"So they can arrest you?" he shot back. "Then throw you in jail until they figure out what you did with that money?"

"I did nothing with it." There those tears came again. Frustration and hurt and worry, all welling up to sting her eyes. "I don't know how it got in my trunk. Or why."

And now all the money was gone. Every dime stolen, thanks to that no-good Reggie and his gang.

But more than anything, she hurt and worried for what the library had lost. So much hard work, and possibilities, and oh, the horrid scandal that would ensue once the news reached Minneapolis.

"I don't give a rat's ass about that money, Allethaire," Mikolas said softly.

Her chin kicked up. "Well, I do! And why should I believe you, anyway?"

"Get down from my horse."

"I don't want to."

She knew how churlish she sounded, but there was no help for it. She knew the kind of man Mikolas Vasco was. A criminal who'd set out to use her for his own selfish gain three years ago, so why would she do anything he said now?

She only wanted to go home. To be safe and happy again.

Except she had no home. Not even with her father, since he'd likely disown her once he heard of the mess she'd made of her life. She'd shamed him and the Gibson name, both in Minnesota and now in Montana Territory....

Mikolas cocked his hip. His stance signified he'd take all the time he needed until she complied. Yet she sensed the impatience in him. Saw it in the way his fist gripped the reins.

"We can stand here until we both turn blue from the cold," he said slowly. "Or you can do as I tell you and listen to what I have to say. Once you do, I'll take you where it's warm and safe."

Emotion pushed into her throat. *Warm and safe.* The words smacked of bribery, but they hammered down the last of her resistance. He sounded sincere enough, and she found herself pathetically desperate to believe him.

"Fine," she said.

Only then did she realize how hard she'd been gripping the saddle horn, her lifeline during their frenzied escape. She loosened her fingers. Carefully. The movement speared pain through her wrist, but she kept her reaction hidden. What if Mikolas tried to use her injury against her?

He made no attempt to help her dismount. Allethaire was glad. She didn't need or want his assistance, and once on the ground, she stood with her feet spread, positioned between him and his horse.

The heat from the palomino's muscular body enveloped her, but the brooding intensity in Mikolas' dark eyes left her chilled. She didn't know what he was thinking or what he intended to do with her in the coming moments.

"I'm not going to hurt you," he rumbled. "Let's get that straight between us right now."

She swallowed. She dared to pull her stare off him and peruse the horizon. They'd stopped in a valley, she realized. A very desolate valley without a hint of the Manitoba in the distance. Or even tracks. A small herd of cattle dotted a bluff, and a seemingly never-ending line of fence stretched beyond her range of vision, but besides that, there was nothing.

Nothing.

He could hurt her, or kill her, or do whatever he wanted with her, and no one would know. No one would hear. He'd taken her off the Manitoba and spirited her out here into nowhere.

Why? To prevent her arrest, as he claimed? Or would the unexpected opportunity of her abduction lend itself to something far worse? Would he see her as unfinished business from three years ago when he was a troubled sheepherder, driven to exact revenge against the wrongs dealt to him in his life? Only to end up in jail in payment for his crime?

Yet, strangely, she felt no fear. Not really. Even

when she was held as Woodrow Baldwin's captive, Mikolas had never harmed her, though he'd had plenty of chances. In fact, of the three of them— Woodrow, Reggie and Mikolas—it'd been Mikolas who had watched over her through Woodrow's bouts of wrath....

Allethaire swiveled her glance back to him. He stood dark and tall before her, and she tilted her head slightly to better see him beneath the brim of his hat.

"Where are we?" she asked.

"On the WCC."

"The Wells Cattle Company?" She wouldn't have thought so, this far from Great Falls. "Trey's land?"

"Mine, too."

"Yes," she murmured and accepted his curt correction. Her father had told her of how the two brothers now shared their father's legacy. "So I heard."

It would explain, she supposed, how he happened to be close enough to the Manitoba to try to thwart Reggie and his gang's robbery, and wasn't it just her luck that the money got away and Mikolas ended up with her instead?

"We have a line camp not far from here." Mikolas watched her, gauging her reaction to what he had to say. "Some of the outfit is there, waiting for me. That's where we're headed. Just so you know."

A line camp? She shook her head in growing dismay. "No. I want to go to my father's."

"It's too far. And snow's coming."

Her gaze jumped toward the sky. Sure enough, dingy gray clouds had begun their descent over the valley. The stillness in the air warned of more to come, and Allethaire had lived through enough Minnesota winters to recognize what that dingy gray meant—moisture building and building until the clouds opened up and spilled it all out, and in this cold, the moisture would certainly spill as snow. Lots of it.

Her dismay deepened into desperation. She had to get to her father's before the storm set in. She had to find a way.

"Don't even think about stealing my horse and escaping from me," Mikolas warned with appalling perception. "You don't know this part of the territory, and we both know what happened the last time you took off without knowing where you were going."

She didn't move, didn't react, but it was the scalding truth. In her mind, she relived the argument she'd had with his half brother, Trey, three years ago. They'd been engaged to marry then, and she'd expressed her refusal to live in his beloved Montana. His equally-stubborn unwillingness to live in her home in Minnesota clashed with her own selfish needs, and she'd left his ranch in a snit, intending to return to her hotel in Great Falls. In seemingly no time, she'd gotten herself good and lost, and soon after, Woodrow Baldwin found her.

She shut her mind down to the horrors of that terrible night. Allethaire had learned her lesson, all right. She had no intention of making the mistake again by running off by herself.

Yet.

"I'm not a fool, Mikolas," she said, eyes narrowed in her convictions. "Nor am I a meek little lamb who will allow herself to be led by the nose for whatever depraved game you have in mind."

"No game, Allethaire. Depraved or otherwise."

"I'll see you thrown back in jail forever if you betray me."

"I'm not going to."

"My father will see to it that your reputation is in shreds—again."

His jaw hardened, and she took triumph that the barb stung.

"Are you finished?" he demanded.

"We'll get the governor of the territory involved, too. And Trey. And—"

"Damn it, Allethaire. Why can't you just trust me?"

Her chin jerked up. "Why not, indeed?"

He blew out a breath, heavily laced with a frustrated oath, and straightened. "If you're done threatening me, then let's mount up. You got any gloves with you?"

Her glance dropped down to her bare hands, already reddened from the cold. Funny how she hadn't noticed until now.

"Yes," she said and awkwardly rummaged inside her purse, hanging from her uninjured wrist. She didn't find them, but latched onto her handkerchief, buried beneath her bottle of brandy.

Lord, but she craved a drink to get through the coming moments and hours. Whatever Mikolas intended.

Yet she had to leave the bottle right where it was. Hidden. Pulling out the handkerchief instead, she dried her nose, stuffed the delicate linen into her pockets and pulled out her gloves.

"They the best you can do?" he asked.

She ignored his frown and tugged them on, one

after the other. The thin, supple leather conformed to the shape of her fingers, and once in place, she pulled the chinchilla-trimmed edges over her coat sleeves.

"They're all I have," she said.

She refused to apologize. How was she to know she'd be whisked off a train and thrown into numbing cold? She'd fallen in love with the gloves in Paris last year. They were the epitome of high fashion and matched the chinchilla muff she'd left behind in Minneapolis, since she fled the city so quickly and hadn't thought to bring it. The muff would've been far warmer. So would her thick woolen mittens, lying neatly in her dresser drawer back in her bedroom at this very moment.

She blinked against a rush of disappointment. Of pathetic and unadulterated longing.

Well, what did it matter? Mikolas was right. The kid leather would fare poorly against the Montana weather, but they were better than nothing.

"You got a hat?" he asked next.

She held out her arms, palms up, and glared at him. What did he think she had? A whole other trunk of clothing hidden under her coat? And now that he'd asked, her ears began to burn. A breeze she hadn't realized blew stirred against her hair, chilling her all the more.

"Does it look like I have a hat?" she retorted.

She'd left that behind, too, thanks to him. On the train. Margaret would likely have found it by now, and would the woman even appreciate a more fashionable piece of millinery? A French creation of velvet and chinchilla and black ostrich tips?

"Wear this, then. You're going to need it." He tugged at the scarf wound around his neck. "It's long, so tie it around your head first."

He held out the scarf, knitted of thick black wool. Another time, she would have refused his offer. A *warmer* time. And under these deplorable circumstances, she should have.

But she didn't.

She couldn't.

Knowing her weakness and hating it, she took the muffler and laid the wool over her head and around her neck, as he'd done, then tucked the ends inside her coat's collar.

Immediate comfort soaked into her. Blissful warmth. His body heat and scent, too. Leather and tobacco. All of them together...and not unpleasing.

More disturbing and ridiculously confusing.

His dark head moved in a quick nod of satisfaction.

"All right," he said, still holding the reins. "Let's go."

She refused to meet his gaze. Refused to let him know how grateful she was that he'd shared his scarf when he could just have easily kept it for himself and let her freeze.

She turned and climbed into the saddle, freeing her foot from the stirrup so he could swing up behind her.

He settled in. Once again, his big body shielded hers from the cold. He spurred the palomino into an easy canter, and Allethaire set her sights on what lay ahead, taking a small measure of assurance that, if nothing else, whatever happened when they reached their destination, Mikolas wasn't going to hurt her along the way.

Chapter Five

The edges of a piece of paper tacked to the cabin's front door fluttered in the wind. Even before reading the note, Mick had a pretty good idea what it said.

Snow had begun to fall. Just a scattering of flakes, not enough to cover the ground, but soon, they'd thicken and heap. He had plenty to do until that happened. Because once it did, they weren't going anywhere anytime soon.

Things had taken a turn, for sure. That turn wasn't necessarily a good one, but then, that depended on Allethaire. He didn't know what he was going to do with her while they rode out the storm together, just the two of them cooped up in the cabin. For hours on end.

He suppressed a sigh. Who knew when he rolled out from beneath his blankets before dawn that his morning would end up like this?

Allethaire Gibson, back in his life.

Yeah, things had taken one hell of a surprising turn, but at least, some of the fight had gone out of her. She hadn't spoken during their ride, and neither had he. Safer that way. Easier, too.

But it didn't mean his thoughts hadn't gone all haywire over her in the meantime. Her body in front of his, mostly, while they shared his horse. Might be he'd gone too long without a woman, but she felt damn good sitting so close, letting him learn her shape, soak in her warmth. In that, the cold worked in his favor.

She looked small, huddled in her coat like she was. But she looked more relaxed, too. Like she trusted him to get her where they needed to go. Or maybe she'd just accepted the fact that with things being the way they were, he had to. Mick conceded she brought out a protective streak in him as wide as the Montana sky. And that got him to wondering how this whole thing was going to end.

He figured whichever way it happened, she had more at stake than he did. She stood to lose the most. Which meant she fired up a need in him to keep her from getting hurt, as best as he could.

"Where is everyone?" Allethaire asked.

His thoughts scattered with the stark reminder of

how he'd been sitting here, ruminating in front of the cabin like a preoccupied idiot, with neither of them getting any warmer in the falling snow.

"Looks like they headed out."

The place was deserted, all right. The corral, too, and no light shone through the cabin's window. But thin wisps of smoke curled from the chimney, impetus for Mick to dismount.

"But you said—"

"I know what I said."

That some of the outfit would be waiting for him, and he headed toward that piece of paper, the reason why they weren't.

But in midstride, only a few feet from the door, a thought occurred to him, and his heart jumped to his throat. He swore. And swung back around toward his horse.

Allethaire's eyes widened in surprise. "What's the matter?"

She could have hightailed it out of here the minute Mick's boots hit the ground. She could have torn off without him, leaving him stranded, with no means of going after her.

But she didn't.

She hadn't moved.

Hell, the idea had never even occurred to her.

A gully-washer of relief poured through him, weakening his knees. Leaving him feeling stupid for thinking she would.

"Nothing. I just—" He cleared his throat. "Nothing."

Before he made even more of a fool of himself, he pivoted toward the door and ripped the paper off its nail.

> Headed back to the ranch. See you there.
> Jack and Crew

Jack Hollister, one of the cowboys on the WCC, would know to leave with the rest of the fencing crew before the snow hit. He'd know, too, that Mick would've done the same thing and would be headed home, soon after his arrival at camp.

But he wouldn't know about Allethaire.

Might be he'd put two and two together once the news reached the ranch, but that could take a few days, depending on the snow's severity. And who knew where things would stand by then?

"What does it say?"

Allethaire's tone held a mix of curiosity and impatience. He turned back to her.

"The outfit took off for home," he said. "They didn't want to get snowed in out here."

She went still, absorbing the news. "But we will be."

"Yep." He strode toward her.

"Just the two of us?"

He heard her horror. "You got it figured right." He halted in front of her and clasped his mount's bridle. Firmly. "Get down."

"If we keep riding, we could make it to the ranch, too."

"The hell we could."

She had no concept of the distance. Snowflakes had already begun to gather on the top of her head, sprinkling his black scarf with flecks of white. Her cheeks and nose had turned rosy, her eyes bright, and he knew she had to be as cold as he was. Colder, most likely, since he, at least, wore a full set of fleece-lined underwear beneath his clothes.

"There's coffee inside, Allethaire." He gentled his voice to coax her. "Won't take me long to build up the fire, either."

Her teeth worried her lower lip, but finally she nodded and slipped her foot into the stirrup to dismount. Yet her soft groan warned him of the stiffness that gripped her limbs, her inability to move as easily as she thought, and his arms lifted to catch her when she all but fell out of the saddle.

He stumbled back a step beneath her weight, but his embrace held her fast against him. For a moment, she didn't move. Didn't make a sound. As if she needed some time, just a little time, to absorb his warmth.

Her face pressed into his coat. She stood with her shoulders hunched and her arms folded together. She shivered.

"I'm sorry." Her words sounded breathless. Oddly intimate. "I'm…purely…frozen."

The admission cut through him. He blamed himself, but staying on the train hadn't been an option for either of them.

"Let's get you into the cabin," he said.

He eased her away and would've kept his arm around her shoulders, just to make sure she didn't fall, but she took an awkward step back.

"Mikolas, if you so much as—I swear I'll—"

"You want to stand out here and keep threatening me, Allethaire?" Impatience sharpened his tone. "Fine. I'll stand out here, too, for as long as it takes you to get it through that stubborn head of yours that I'm not going to hurt you."

Her chin kicked up.

"Because if I was going to, I would have done it by now," he continued before she could snap back a response. "And I sure wouldn't have brought you all the way out *here* to hurt you, because it's going to snow and I could have gotten myself home a hell of a lot faster if I just would've hurt you *sooner* and gotten it over with."

Her mouth opened.

Then closed.

She sniffed and swung away from him in a huff, swirling her skirt hems. She strode toward the cabin. At the door, she waited with her shoulders and back stiff until Mick decided she intended to cooperate. Finally he strode to the cabin, too, reached around her and opened the door.

She went inside, not looking to see if he followed. Which he did, firmly latching the door behind them, shutting out the wind and cold and affording them blessed respite.

Silence hovered in the small quarters. Jack and the rest of the fencing crew had left the place stocked and clean. WCC rules, and something Mick and Trey strictly enforced as a courtesy for the next group of cowboys riding in.

Times like these, for Allethaire's sake, Mick was glad for the courtesy. His glance found the fireplace; the fire had been banked, but not long ago, and embers still glowed hot. With plenty of wood stacked and ready to burn, he removed his gloves and made quick work of building the fire up again. Soon, flames roared in the block.

He straightened and found Allethaire watching him.

"You're all but unaffected by this, aren't you?" she asked.

"By what?"

Strangely he heard no accusation in her tone. Instead, fatigue. Puzzlement. Curiosity, too.

"This." Her glance touched on the window, their surroundings, both inside and out. "Everything here."

"The cold? This camp?" He moved closer.

"Yes."

The snow had melted on his scarf, still wrapped around her head. The droplets glistened in the fire-light.

"You forgot I was born a sheepherder's son," he said. Though Sutton Wells had fathered him, Mick would always consider Gabirel Vasco, the man who had loved him and raised him, as his true father. "I grew up herding sheep all year-round. I'm used to the cold."

She made a little sound, clucking her tongue against her teeth. "And I don't think I shall ever be warm again."

If she intended her complaint to invoke his sympathy, well, hell, it worked.

She hadn't moved since she came into the cabin. She kept her arms crossed against her chest, holding in what little of her body's heat she could catch. Mick knew what it felt like to be so cold, muscles refused to move and skin hurt.

He dared to reach out and rub her arms, from her shoulders down to her elbows and back up again.

"Mikolas, don't," she said.

He expected her resistance, and his grasp tightened to keep her from twisting away. "You need to get the blood moving, Allethaire. You'll feel better when it does."

"I'll be fine in a minute."

Yet, despite her protests, she remained still, keeping her gaze pinned to his coat. Might be she was thinking of how he'd never touched her like this. Freely. Not once and certainly not when they'd been with Woodrow Baldwin.

Her gaze lifted to meet his. He sensed her unease, but she didn't act on it. In the golden firelight, her eyes were a shadowy blue beneath lashes long and elegant. With her skin rosy, her cheekbones high and delicately curved, her mouth full and tremulous…she was a beautiful woman, all right.

A thousand nights, he'd thought of her. Worried over what he'd done to her. If she could ever forgive him—and why would she?

It was too much to hope for, her forgiveness. He didn't deserve any of it, but God knew that didn't stop him from wanting her. And that want was barreling through him like a locomotive, gathering steam the longer he stood here, touching her. Filling his head with ideas of ways to warm her faster and more pleasurable than the way he was doing it now.

He swallowed an oath and pulled his hands off her. He had to get out of the cabin, or he'd do something he'd regret later.

"I have chores to do outside," he muttered. "I'd best do them before the snow gets heavier."

And with that, he left.

Allethaire's startled gaze stayed on the closed door. She wasn't sure what had just happened between them, but there was one thing of which she was certain.

Something had.

The air sizzled with a strange little charge when Mikolas stood so close in front of her, rubbing his hands along her arms. The way he looked down at her, as if he could see into her very soul, those black eyes of his somber and brooding....

Of their own accord, her feet took her toward the window. She searched through the pane and found him, stringing rope between the cabin and a small barn.

That was how she remembered him most. Brooding.

But he was different now, she mused, watching him work. Stronger. More confident. No longer hurt and angry for what Sutton Wells had done. For most of his life, Mikolas had been denied his heritage and the Wells side of his family, but he'd seemed to put all that behind him now. Thanks to Trey and the Wells Cattle Company, his life had taken a new direction.

But Allethaire couldn't forget he was still an outlaw. An ex-convict. He was still capable of kidnapping. Hadn't he done that very thing just this morning, at the Manitoba?

Nor could she forget how defenseless she was against him out here in this godforsaken country. With the two of them inside this tiny cabin, no one knowing of their whereabouts, and the night stretching out ahead of them.

She would have to remain on her guard at all times and not turn her back on him for a single instant. Who knew what he would do when he caught her unawares?

An apprehensive tremble went through her, wrought further from an overwhelming sense of confusion and uncertainty. Should she be afraid of Mikolas Vasco?

Or could she trust him?

And what about the troubles she'd left behind in Minneapolis? Or the money that had mysteriously ended up in her trunk? How did Reggie know the envelope would be there? Where had he fled with his gang? Would she ever see him—or the money—again?

Her head pounded with the questions that seemed destined to have no answers, and a familiar craving welled in her blood. A need to forget. To feel nothing.

Allethaire turned from the window with a gallant resolve to ignore the bottle of brandy in her purse. A brown and white speckled cowhide covered the floor in front of the fireplace. She knelt and removed her gloves, then held her hands toward the flames, enduring the tingly sensation of cold giving way to the heat. It wasn't long before she warmed enough to take off the black scarf and then her coat.

With the thawing of her bones, she began to feel human again. Wind whistled through the rafters, and she noted how the day had darkened, how snowflakes swirled and thickened. She noted, too, how for the first time since her journey west, she was someplace warm and protected from the elements.

In a twisted sort of way, she had Mikolas to thank for it, she supposed. But being here only delayed the purpose of her trip—meeting with her father to explain the circumstances of her failure with the library project.

Her pulse pounded with dread at the prospect. He'd be furious. Appalled and scandalized. But mostly, he'd be disappointed in his only child, who could no more succeed at an endeavor she attempted than he could *not* succeed in one he did.

Paris Gibson was just that way. Born with the golden touch. Capable of vision and foresight and endowed with the courage to pursue his dreams, for his own good and that of the rest of the world.

Allethaire was none of those things, it seemed.

Not that she hadn't tried. And despite her attempts at working hard to be just like him, she'd failed.

Miserably.

Blinking fast and furious, she turned toward her coat and rummaged within its folds for her purse, her movements growing quick and desperate until she found what she was looking for. She flung off the cap with one hand, lifted the bottle to her lips with the other and took a starved swallow of the brandy, then closed her eyes with a faint grimace while the liquor streamed down her throat and into her belly.

She relished the fire. The taste. The way the pain of her thoughts faded, little by little. Numbing her blood. So much so that she gulped another swallow. And then another. Shuddering through them without a care to her weakness, her insufferable addiction...

A slow, jagged sigh of satisfaction escaped her. Her eyes opened, and the bottle sagged down to her lap. She stared into the flames with her brain cured of its torment and emptied of conscious thought...until the strange sensation of swirling cold jarred her senses.

Her glance jumped toward the door. Daylight

streamed inward on the tails of the wind, and oh, God.

Looking furious, Mikolas stood in the doorway.

Chapter Six

The sight of her with that damned bottle tore right through him. He'd all but forgotten her penchant for brandy when he was holed up with her and Woodrow's gang. Until now. But the memory sailed back with crystal clarity—and a good deal of consternation besides.

Mick took it as a personal affront. Did she think she needed to drown her troubles the minute his back was turned? Didn't she trust him enough to take care of her?

Or maybe she couldn't bear to be with him, after what he'd done three years ago.

Whatever the reason, he intended to set her straight, once and for all, and not when her brain was fogged from spirits. She had to accept her predicament and face it head-on.

Starting now.

He pulled off his gloves and tossed them aside. Walked toward her, step after purposeful step.

She watched him come with eyes wide and a wagonload of guilt in her expression. She snatched the bottle off her lap to hide it behind her. As if he was stupid enough not to see it.

He extended his hand.

"Give it to me," he said softly.

Her throat moved. "No."

He waggled his fingers. "Give it to me now."

"I won't drink anymore." From her knees on the speckled cowhide, she cocked her head back, keeping him in her sights.

He towered over her and fought impatience. "Allethaire."

"I promise I won't."

How many times had she made the avowal, to herself or someone else? How many times had she broken it?

He bent and caught her wrist, not caring that she cried out. He yanked the bottle from her grip, strode toward the door and hurled the container as far as he could throw it. Brandy streamed in midair; the bottle turned end over end and landed with a dull thud out of sight.

By the time morning rolled in, evidence of her compulsion would be buried in snow.

Mick slammed the door closed and glared at her. He warred between compassion for her weakness and anger from her inability to overcome it.

"I wouldn't have thought you'd still have your liking for brandy, Allethaire. Guess I was wrong."

She stood. Awkwardly, he noted. And she held her wrist against her, as if it pained her.

"I've been under a great deal of stress lately, Mikolas," she said. Her eyes glittered in the firelight. She struggled with composure. "I don't expect you to understand, but please keep your judgments to yourself. You know almost nothing about me."

"What's the matter with your wrist?"

A growing realization that he could be responsible, compounded by a good dose of regret, spurred him to take a closer look. He folded back the cuff on her sleeve and examined the smooth skin, the slender bones beneath. She allowed him his inspection, and in the cabin's lengthening shadows, the joint did indeed show a faint swelling.

"I fell on it during a scuffle on the train," she said stiffly. "It hurts but it's not broken."

"It's sprained. Come here." He took her by the elbow and led her to the table. "Sit down."

She complied, amazingly enough. He found a clean washcloth on a shelf, immersed it in a bucket of icy cold water and wrung out the excess. Taking the injured limb carefully, he wrapped the cloth around it.

"Move it as little as possible so the swelling can go down," he ordered gruffly and removed his coat. "I'll make coffee, and then you're going to tell me everything. From the beginning."

"Why should I?" He could feel her gaze on him while he filled the black enamel coffeepot with water from the bucket. "My problems are my own."

"Not anymore they're not." He hefted the pot onto the stove.

"I just need to talk to my father."

Her voice wavered on the last word. Father. One glance at her face, and Mick could tell she was all but terrified at the prospect.

"That bad?" he asked.

She managed a jerky nod. "That bad."

He lit the wood that would heat the burners and turned toward her. "I've always known Paris to be as proud of you as a father can be."

"Really?" Her brow arched with skepticism; her

chin quivered in dismay. "Well, he won't be anymore."

"Always known him to be fair, too. He'll do what
he can to help you through this."

"How could you possibly know him well enough
to predict his reaction, Mikolas?" Her tone snapped
with challenge. "I'm his daughter. I know far better
than you how he'll feel about—about what I've
done."

Mick regarded her. His scarf had matted her hair
against her head, but a few golden tendrils coiled
along her temple. A longing to loosen her pins and
fluff the silken mass to its usual fullness swept
through him with an intensity that compelled him
to curl his fingers into fists in resistance.

She didn't know how Paris had eventually found
forgiveness in his heart for Mick's crime, and how
Mick's inquiries into her well-being every chance
he could get had instilled a knowing gleam in
Paris' expression. It had got to the point where
the man started volunteering any news she'd sent
him in her correspondence. Mick always soaked
in every word and had sworn Paris into a solemn
vow not to give Allethaire an inkling of Mick's
interest.

Because she detested him for ganging up with

Woodrow Baldwin. She hated Montana for all her memories of it; besides, what kind of life could Mick expect to have with her?

None. Whatsoever.

Likely she didn't know what a good friend Mick considered Paris to be. Or that Trey did, too. A friendship that went beyond their business dealings around the hydro-electric plant the industrialist was building on Wells land.

She needed to know, though, that Mick had a pretty good idea what he was talking about.

"This thing you say you've done has something to do with the Ladies Literary Aid Society, doesn't it?" he asked.

Startled, she drew back. "How did you know about that?"

"I know about the library you wanted to build, too."

"You do?"

"I told you. Your father is proud of you." The water in the enamel pot began to boil. He added coffee grounds and noted the time. "He talks about you and your community service work often."

"He does? To you?"

As if he was the lowest of the low and undeserving of her father's time and effort? Mick scowled. "And anyone else who will listen."

She groaned and covered her lips with her fingertips. "Oh, no."

He expected her to take some comfort from his response, not be horrified from it—which meant things must be worse than he thought.

He took a box of crackers from the shelf and added a jar of blackberry preserves that Zurina, his sister, had made, and put both on the table.

"You had breakfast this morning?" he asked, going for a knife and a couple of plates.

"No, but I'm not hungry."

"Well, I am." He slathered a few crackers and slid a plate toward her. The snack would tide them over until he could fix them both a more substantial meal later. He turned his chair, straddled it and rested both arms along the back. "So start talking."

"About what?"

"Where that money in your trunk came from, for starters."

"I have no idea where it came from."

His gaze remained steady. "None?"

"If you intend to badger me until you think I'll say what you want to hear, then let's just end this conversation right now."

He held up a hand. She was as touchy as a plucked jaybird. "Easy, Allethaire. I'm not accusing you."

Though he conceded, the phrasing of his question sounded like he was. And that made him no better than the Manitoba's suspicious conductor and Richard, the security agent.

Mick went for a different angle in hopes she'd be more willing to cooperate. An angle that put him on her side, working with her to find the answers that would keep her from getting arrested.

"The trainman claims no one jimmied the lock." His mind clawed through the blur of tense moments before he'd whisked her off the train. "From what I could tell, no one had."

"No." Her expression turned pensive. Deeply troubled. "Which means someone planted the money when my trunk was already open."

"Someone you know?"

She bit her lip. "Once I locked it and left my house, I went straight to the train station. My key never left my purse. I never had occasion to open the trunk until this morning."

She avoided looking at him and had yet to answer his question.

"Who would have put the money in your trunk, Allethaire?"

Finally her gaze latched onto his. "*Would* have? Or *could* have? There's a difference."

He inclined his head, giving her the point. "Both."

"I don't know who would have or why—but… Jenny could have."

"Who's Jenny?"

"She's been with me since my mother died. Before I even started school. I packed my belongings myself, but then I left to arrange for a driver, and—" Allethaire heaved a worried sigh "—she closed up the trunk. By the time I returned, it was sitting by the door, ready to go. I was in a terrible rush and left soon after for the station."

Mick made a mental note to mention the woman to George Huys, the police chief in Great Falls.

"I know what you're thinking," Allethaire said, her tone quickly defensive. "But she's like a mother to me. She would never hurt me. Or—or frame me with an envelope full of stolen money."

Reminded by the scent of brewed coffee that the pot was fresh and ready, Mick rose to pour them both a cup. Steam swirled from the black liquid.

Allethaire curled her fingers around the tin but didn't drink.

"Sometimes the lure of money turns people into someone they aren't," he said quietly. No one knew better than he did the truth in those words. There was a time when he was like a stranger in his own skin. "But if you don't think Jenny had anything to do with that envelope, then I believe you."

"Do you?"

"Yes."

It was easy enough to believe. Didn't make sense for a woman who'd raised Allethaire like her own daughter to turn against her after all those years. Why would she, when she enjoyed the Gibson wealth as much as Allethaire did?

"Thank you," Allethaire whispered and lifted her cup to sip.

Mick guessed his trust in her meant something. Relief, if nothing else. But they were a long way from finding out who was behind setting her up for a crime she didn't commit.

He turned his chair around to more comfortably face her. He bit into a cracker and kept thinking.

"Tell me about the Ladies Literary Aid Society," he said. "Did everyone get along? Any problems?"

"None. The ladies were very dedicated and

worked hard to bring the library plans to fruition. I consider them all my friends."

"Then you must have worked with someone from the City of Minneapolis."

"Yes. Charles Renner. He was on the City Council."

"And?"

She lifted a shoulder. "He was a former business partner of my father's. When one of their mutual interests failed, they parted ways."

"On good terms?"

"Of course. Paris Gibson has no enemies. He's a remarkable man, and everyone loves him."

Mick nodded. That much was true. But he filed the politician's name away in his memory as one more person for George to investigate.

"So what went wrong, Allethaire?" he asked softly. "If no one you know has a vendetta against you, why are you running away to Montana?"

"Because someone *does* have a vendetta against me. A great sum of money is missing from the library account. An audit revealed there were multiple drafts signed by me, effectively stealing the funds we worked so hard to raise."

Forged signatures? Damn.

"And you're sure you didn't sign them?" he asked. "In the normal course of business?"

"You mean, by accident?"

Hearing her say the words made the idea sound far-fetched, for sure. But stranger things had happened, and he had to ask.

"Of course not," she said firmly. Easy to see she was offended that he *had* asked. "Why would I write any of those checks to myself? I had no need of those funds. Not one dime."

"No."

Again, Mick believed her. He couldn't figure why someone went through so much trouble to destroy her. Damned shame he—or she—had, too. He rubbed his jaw and let her talk.

"I was unable to trace the money, of course, and without the funds, we were forced to scrap our plans. The police had to be called, and once the news reporters caught wind of it—"

She covered her face with her hands. The cloth he'd wrapped around her wrist slipped onto the table, but she didn't seem to notice.

"I couldn't bear to see the story hit the papers." Stricken by the agony that consumed her, Mick strained to hear the muffled admission. "Everyone already hated me for what they believed I'd done. They said it was because I'd become a fallen woman when I was kidnapped and living with out-laws. The scandal was awful, my reputation was in shreds and it was only going to get worse. I couldn't stay in Minneapolis. I just couldn't." Her shoulders shuddered on a sob. "God, I'm such a coward."

Mick hardly knew the moment when his arms took her against him. It seemed that it just hap-pened, that she was there, leaning into him, bun-dled tight within his embrace. Her torment reached inside his chest and scraped him raw with guilt from knowing he was partially responsible, even as it kicked in a fervent vow to make the bastard who'd done this to her pay.

With every breath, every fiber of his being.

"All of this will ruin my father's good name." She sniffled. "He's done nothing to deserve it, and it's my fault. My fault."

Mick slid his hand up her spine and down again. Long, soothing strokes that let her know he was there, listening, consumed by a need to make her life right again.

"Can't see why you think you're to blame if you don't even understand how all this happened," he said. His cheek pressed into her hair, the golden strands like satin against his skin.

"I was determined to prove myself to him." Her voice was an agonized whisper, full of pain and self-recrimination. "If I wasn't so vain, so selfish of my own reputation, then none of this would have happened."

"Nothing wrong with wanting to prove yourself in this world."

God knew it was important to him, too. Allethaire had her father's respected name to live up to, but Mick had Trey's. And in the territory, there wasn't a finer cattleman than his half brother. Mick had had his hands full with getting folks to accept him. Being part-Basque, a sheepherder and a jailbird all rolled into one hadn't made the job easy, but most days, Mick figured he'd done well enough. Took some time, but folks had come around, and in the past couple of years, he'd made plenty of friends. Good friends.

"This whole thing is bigger than you think it is," Mick said grimly. In light of her fragile mental state, he refused to use the term "conspiracy," but it was there. In the back of his mind. "Don't forget Reggie's involved somehow, which means it's gone beyond your plans for a library."

A mournful moan spilled into his shirt. "Oh, God. *Reggie*."

Mick guessed the outlaw's part in stealing her money had yet to sink into her thinking. He had to admit she had plenty to comprehend as it was, and none of it easy.

Gently he eased her back. Her tears had thickened her lashes and streaked her face, but her wide, mournful eyes had never been more clear, more beautiful, than they were now, peering up at him.

Gone was the distrust and fear. Instead an unexpected kinship had sprung between them. A warmth. With the baring of her troubles came a tenuous trust, one that Mick valued beyond measure.

A trust he never expected to get.

Longings he'd banked for too many months, for long hopeless years, surfaced in his blood. An ages-old yearning that a man felt for a woman who meant something to him.

Yearnings he couldn't have. At least, not yet, but he had now, this moment, and he wasn't going to let it go without making the most of what it could be.

He eased the pins from her hair and relished the luxury of that glorious mane falling over his hands and onto her shoulders. Taken aback by his boldness, she drew back slightly with a hushed inhalation of surprise, but he cupped his hand behind her neck, keeping her close, with her face only inches from his.

"I'm going with you when you talk to Paris," he said quietly.

That surprised her, too. "It's not necessary, Mikolas. I—I feel better about all of this now, and—"

"Call me 'Mick.'"

She blinked. "What?"

"Everyone calls me 'Mick.'"

The WCC cowboys had been quick to shorten his name when he joined the outfit. It'd been like a rite of passage, stepping from the sheepherder's life into a cattleman's, but Mick hadn't really minded. Acceptance by them had been too important. Besides, deep in his heart, where it really mattered, he was still Mikolas, Gabirel Vasco's son.

"All right," she said, soft and careful.

"If you don't mind, from now on, I'm going to call you 'Allie.'"

She cocked her head, and a little smile touched her lips. "Why?"

He didn't explain that he felt like it was a rite of passage for them, too. A new beginning. And he sure as hell didn't explain that 'Allethaire' smacked of high-society and formality and big city ways— or that here in Montana Territory, folks lived simpler, less pretentious lives.

"Because I like it," he said instead.

Slowly she nodded. "My father used to call me that quite often."

"There. You see?" He smiled, too.

She'd yet to pull away, he noticed, and the air changed. Hummed along his skin. Crackled, almost, with an awareness that warmed his blood and stirred his loins. She wasn't moving, but her breathing quickened, and he knew she felt it, too.

The deepening firelight brushed her cheeks with a sultry glow. Accented her hair with lustrous gold. Painted her lips with a delectable ruby fullness, and how could any man keep from helping himself to a long, leisurely taste?

Yearning fired up in him, but good. A yearning too long banked.

His head lowered. He expected her to move away and shatter the moment, but instead, her lashes drifted downward. Her head tilted slightly to better fit her mouth to his, and when their lips touched, when he experienced the intoxicating softness, he tasted lust, and an incredible sensation rocked through him.

A hunger.

A need he could no more deny than his own lifeblood, and his embrace tightened on a groan. Her arms circled his neck. He crushed her to him, his enfolding embrace pressing her breasts into his chest, inciting a whole new kind of sensation. A whole new hunger and aching need.

A need that was fast spiraling out of control. For both of them. But mostly for him, for she was still too fragile, too vulnerable, and if he went too fast, if he went too far, he would only break her in the end.

He loved her too much not to give her the time she needed. That they both needed. Dredging up all his will, every ounce of his power and strength, he reluctantly drew back.

And wondered how he was going to get through the night without making very slow, very sweet love to her.

Chapter Seven

The morning dawned calm, clear and eye-wateringly cold. The snow had moved on, leaving drifts so white, so incredibly pure that Allethaire could've stood on the cabin's front step and just soaked the sight of them in, for hours on end.

But of everything, it was the peace that struck her most. The serenity. She'd never felt the beauty of Montana the way she felt it now. Quiet, rustic and proud. And so very different than the constant bustle of Minneapolis.

Perhaps the serenity had something to do with her own. After sharing her troubles with Mikolas—Mick, she corrected—she didn't feel as alone anymore. Not nearly as afraid. She'd never expected his loyalty and strength, but he gave both freely, with fierce resolve to make everything right again, using any means within his power.

And oh, those kisses. Her fingers lifted to her

lips, and she relived the feel of his hard mouth on hers. His hunger had been tightly-leashed. Barely under control. Mick Vasco was a breath-stealing specimen of masculinity, corded muscle and darkly rugged looks, and what woman could resist him?

She almost hadn't.

She didn't want to think of what would have happened if he hadn't pulled away, giving them the restraint they both needed. She couldn't let herself be involved with a man like Mick, who was deeply rooted here in Montana. Besides, why would he want a woman with a future as bleak and uncertain as hers? A woman on the run from her problems?

Big problems.

"Ready to head out, Allie?"

Her thoughts scattered, regrouped and centered over him. She had to admit she liked how he'd taken it upon himself to shorten her given name, just because he preferred it. As if he had every right. She liked how he said it, too. Easily. Smoothly. Making her feel less pretentious. Less compelled to put on airs. And funny how "Allie" helped lighten the burden that came with bearing her father's name—and became more her own.

Her gaze stayed on Mick while he approached. With his Stetson pulled low against the brilliance of the snow, he led the palomino hitched to a sleigh. Earlier, while she cleaned up after breakfast, he'd swept a path across the small yard, and he halted at the end of it.

"I'll get the blankets," she said.

She hurried inside toward the woolen pair folded in front of the fireplace. The flames were already banked but still contained enough heat in the embers to warm the coverings for the ride out to the Wells ranch. Bending, she scooped them up and turned to head back outside, but her glance snagged on the bunks lining the wall.

Her belly fluttered. Last night, she'd taken the bottom one, Mick the top. Both of them had spent their share of time tossing and turning with the memory of their kisses heavy on their minds. Mick had been as aware of her nearness as she'd been of his, and with a certain amount of female satisfaction, it pleased her that she was the reason for his restlessness.

Aware Mick waited, she hastened outside, taking care to firmly latch the door behind her. In moments, they were both settled on the seat and headed toward the WCC.

"Going to be a pretty Christmas if the weather holds," Mick said, his narrowed eye scanning the mountains on the horizon, then lifting to the blue, blue sky. "Seeing's tomorrow is Christmas Day, looks like it will."

"These past weeks, I've hardly thought of the season."

In light of her troubles with the library project, neither she nor Jenny had been of a mind to put up a tree or unpack their decorations. Now that Christmas had nearly arrived, the knowledge saddened Allethaire all the more. The festive holiday had always been her favorite.

"Zurina is looking forward to it."

Mick's younger sister. Trey's wife. At the time of her kidnapping, Allethaire had been betrothed to Trey. It wasn't long until they both realized a union between them was never meant to be. Their differences, their wants and needs, were too insurmountable to overcome.

But as soon as Trey had met Zurina, he'd fallen deeply in love, and she with him. They were destined to be together for the rest of their lives.

"How is she, Mick?" she asked.

His chiseled profile showed his pleasure. "Happy. Very happy."

"Good," she said, meaning it.

"They have a little girl now."

"Do they?" Her smile faltered on a twinge of envy. With the mess her life had become, having a child of her own, a husband, a home, seemed elusive. "That's wonderful."

"A spitfire just learning to walk. She's named Catalin, and she's queen of the ranch, let me tell you."

Allethaire laughed softly. "I'll bet."

Mick fell silent. She sensed a pensive shift in his mood. After long moments, his dark glance settled over her.

"Warm enough?" he asked.

"Yes," she said, glad she had his black scarf to wind around her head and neck again. "Today isn't as cold as yesterday."

"Sit closer to me anyway."

He slid his arm around her shoulders and pulled her against him, hip to hip. Beneath the blankets on their laps, he sat with his knees spread and feet planted against the sleigh's jostling. Sharing the heat of his big body, feeling safe and comfortable, she almost purred.

Yet the brooding silence that had come over him reminded her of the man Mikolas Vasco had been when she'd first known him.

"What about you, Mick?" she dared to ask. "Are you happy these days?"

"Most times."

"And the others?"

A muscle moved beneath his cheek. He hadn't bothered to shave this morning, and the beard shadowed his features, giving him a rugged, primitive look that curled her toes.

"I feel guilty," he said.

Even though the answer surprised her, she understood. She'd known plenty of guilt in her life, too, but none more so than in the past three years.

"Because of what you've been given."

"Yes." He contemplated her. "How did you know?"

She swiveled her gaze toward the horizon and was struck again by the territory's breathtaking beauty. Its tranquility. As if the rest of the world was a million miles away.

If only her troubles could be that far away, too.

"I've always had my father's wealth, even when his business dealings weren't successful. But as I've grown older, it's become important to me to make my own successes. Follow my own dreams."

The Ladies Literary Aid Society and the Minneapolis library project had been her first real attempt to do both, and yet she'd failed terribly.

"To rest on your own laurels, and not Paris'," Mick said.

"That's right." Her gaze lifted to his. "Do you feel that way about Trey?"

Mick appeared to choose his words carefully. "He's given me a very different life with him at the WCC. A very privileged one."

"Your heritage," she said quietly, thinking of how hard his father, Sutton, worked to make the Wells Cattle Company as powerful an operation as it was today. Wells blood ran in Mick's veins. He was entitled.

"My heritage, yes. But my heritage is Basque, too." He sighed heavily. Clearly the situation troubled him. "I feel guilty that I have so much. More than I need, for sure, and yet my Basque family has very little."

They were simple people, Allethaire knew, guided by the sheep they constantly tended. Most barely survived, and they led difficult, lonely lives.

"You're only one man, Mick," she said. "And sheepherding has been a part of the Basque people for generations."

"I know."

"What can you do to change that?"

"Change must begin with the young."

"Yes," she said.

"They must be given hope, and the ability to make their futures more promising than their fathers' and grandfathers' had been. With or without the sheep."

"Yes," she said again, marveling. Hadn't she had a similar vision with her library? Improving lives through books, culture, education? "Of course, you're exactly right."

He grunted. "And what have I done about it, besides nothing?"

"It's an honorable dream, Mick, and I have no doubt you'll achieve it somehow." Impulsively she leaned toward him and kissed his stubbled cheek. "I admire you for it, you know. Very much."

"Yeah?" His gloved hand took her chin, holding her still. "Show me how much, then."

His head lowered, and he helped himself to another longer, more languid kiss. The bristle above his lip awakened a new sensation, a primitive and exciting one, and it wasn't long before their cold mouths warmed in wet, heated pleasure.

Mick drew back. His black eyes glittered over her, and she held her breath at what he was about to do. What he was about to say—

A horse blowing nearby jogged the silence. Mick

swore and jerked his head toward the sound. Alarm shot through Allethaire, an instant fear that Reggie and his gang, or *worse*, the police, had finally found her.

A couple of riders approached, snow billowing in little clouds beneath their mounts' hooves. Rifles filled their scabbards, but neither man reached for the weapons.

"That you, Mick?" one of them called out.

Mick's hand fell away from Allethaire's chin, and he turned full toward them. "Jack?"

"Got Nubby here with me."

With their hats pulled low and their knitted scarves high around their necks, Allethaire couldn't see their shadowed faces well, but as they drew closer, she recognized Nubby Thomas, the WCC's foreman. Once a longtime friend of Sutton's, he was, she knew, one of the most loyal cowboys on the ranch's payroll.

"That Miss Gibson with you, Mick?" he asked.

"It is."

"Hello, Nubby." She straightened, discreetly putting distance between herself and Mick. What must the two cowboys think, seeing Mick and her sitting as close as lovers on the sleigh's seat? And just coming off a kiss, no less? "It's been a few years, hasn't it?"

"Yes, ma'am." He touched a finger to his hat brim, though his shrewd, grizzled gaze took her in. "You two all right?"

"Just fine," Mick said.

"Got worried when you didn't show up at the ranch yesterday," Jack said.

"Thought we'd ride out and see if we could figure out why," Nubby added.

"Ran into some trouble, that's all."

Somber, Jack nodded. "So we heard."

Both fell into step beside the sleigh, a horse on each side. Allethaire took comfort in their presence.

"I'd like to introduce you to Jack Hollister, Allie," Mick said.

"I'm pleased to meet you," she said and would've extended her hand if she could've reached him.

"Likewise, ma'am." Hair the color of buckskin hung down past his coat collar to his broad shoulders. A scar slashed his cheek, but his smile came easy.

"He showed up at the ranch about the same time I did," Mick added.

"And you two have been double-trouble ever

since," Nubby muttered, but the twinkle in his eye belied the grumble in his tone.

"Yeah, well, he might be Trey's kid brother, but I'm better-lookin'," Jack retorted.

She laughed, knowing he poked fun at the disfiguring scar on his cheek, and she found herself liking him immediately. "How much farther until we get to the ranch?"

"Won't be but a few minutes," he said.

"Just ahead, in fact." Nubby pointed.

In the distance, rising up out of the snow, a wooden beam inscribed Wells Cattle Company announced to visitors they'd arrived at the most prominent spread for miles around. Beyond that, down a long tree-lined lane, stood the ranch's headquarters. A stately two-story house trimmed in deep blue and graced with a winding porch. The structure was as fine as any Allethaire had seen in the city.

"Looks like there's a hell of a greeting party up there." Mick frowned.

Indeed, assorted rigs crowded the expansive yard, and dismay skittered down her spine. She didn't know who had arrived at the WCC, or why, but she wasn't of a mind to see *anyone*.

Not yet. Maybe never. And what if the police waited inside?

"Bad news always travels fast, don't it?" Jack commented.

Mick sighed his annoyance. "Lightning hangs fire by comparison."

Several dogs ran toward them, barking their exuberance. Somewhere beyond the house, a rooster crowed. Cowboys spilled out from the barns and corrals, and by the time the sleigh slid to a stop in front of the house, the front door had already been flung open wide.

And there stood her father. The almighty Paris Gibson, dressed in his usual expensive dark suit and crisp white shirt, wearing a frown on his face and bearing thunder in his eyes.

Allethaire swallowed hard. The time to face him had come.

"Would you like cream or sugar, Allie?"

Zurina Wells handed her a cup and saucer painted with delicate pink flowers. Fresh coffee steamed above the cup's rim, and Allethaire accepted the china with a grateful smile.

"Black is fine, thank you," she murmured.

Though she preferred something much more

bracing to sip. Like the liberal amount of whiskey Trey poured in Mick's crystal tumbler, in the spirit of warming his belly after their cold ride in from the line camp.

But, of course, she kept her craving to herself. She'd just have to get through her humiliating confession alone, without liquid courage.

She lifted the cup to her lips with her hand trembling. At least Mick was here, gathered in the Wells' parlor with everyone else. From the frequent glances he slid her way, she knew he wasn't leaving anytime soon. He stood with Jack and Nubby in front of the fireplace, and his stance appeared relaxed. But from the moment Zurina had kindly invited her to take a seat on the velvet couch, he'd hardly moved. As if he refused to let her out of his sight.

Once they alighted from the sleigh, she had thought to beg a private moment with her father, but in the end, thought better of it. The simple fact of her presence here at the WCC entitled everyone to know of her purpose in coming to Montana for the first time in three years, without announcement of her intentions. She could only hope the ugly news of the embezzled library funds hadn't yet clawed its way from Minnesota.

Allethaire wanted them all to hear the truth from her own lips. She figured everyone in the room had a vested interest in the circumstances, one way or another.

Unfortunately.

She took another sip of the black brew and discreetly watched Zurina hand Margaret Butterfield her own pink-flowered china cup. As darkly beautiful as her brother was handsome, Zurina had grown into the role as the matriarch of the Wells dynasty with enviable grace and confidence.

Of course, it'd been Margaret who had driven out to the ranch as soon as the snow let up to inform Trey and Zurina about the train robbery, and that Mick had whisked Allethaire off the train to avoid arrest. Her father had arrived soon after, accompanied by the local police chief, George Huys.

Both men stood with Trey, who worked one-armed while filling crystal glasses with whiskey. His curly-haired daughter slept peacefully on his shoulder, and though a small crib occupied a far corner of the room, he clearly preferred to hold her instead. Fatherhood, Allethaire could tell, suited him.

A good dose of self-pity welled up inside her. He'd found a happy life with Zurina and their baby.

Family, friends, respect, prosperity—and roots firmly planted right here on the ranch.

A home to be envied.

Allethaire had nothing of the sort. Nothing to embrace and cherish and work to keep for the rest of her life.

Instead she faced a future rife with scandal. All her attempts to succeed in her own way had somersaulted into disaster. She could never go back to Minnesota, could never have the life she dreamed of having there.

And soon, when her father heard of what she had done, how she'd failed, his disappointment and frustration would be more than she could bear.

Thrashing waves of hopelessness tore through her, filling her with sadness, with fear, and blinking fast, she lifted her cup yet again in a pitiable attempt to hide her pain.

By the time she swallowed and carefully returned the china to its saucer, she realized the parlor had grown silent. That everyone had found a seat. That they'd turned their attention toward her. And waited.

Everyone, except one.

Her father moved with the authority and power of a prized stallion. He paused only long enough to unbutton his jacket before he settled in the chair across from her. Handsome and distinguished as always, his white hair and moustache impeccably trimmed, he leaned back and crossed his ankle on his knee.

His troubled gaze hooked with hers.

"All right, Allie," he said quietly. "Start from the beginning."

Chapter Eight

Like an old faucet spewing water in fits and spurts, the words came.

They kept coming, too. Growing stronger the more Allethaire talked. Her thoughts turned logical and organized into sequence. Her brain cleared. By the time she'd finished, her heart had lifted, her pain was gone and she came to one startling and unwavering conclusion.

She'd done nothing wrong.

Nothing, nothing.

Maybe it was just being forced to bring the entire chain of events out into the open, with every detail explained so that her father would understand. Or maybe it was the lack of rancor in his questions and in his expression that helped convince her she wasn't the failure she thought she was. Whatever the reason, she had nothing left inside her. No more secrets to keep.

But the silence that fell afterward had her swallowing hard—and bracing for the worst.

Until, in the span of another heartbeat, the room erupted into a cacophony of voices, a startling and unexpected mix of support, dismay and outrage. Vehement expressions of a need to help. To fight. And though she expected it, searched and looked for it, no one uttered a single accusation. Not a word of criticism.

Not a single, solitary *hint* of one.

"Ach, you poor, poor dear," Margaret said in her German accent, her round face full of sympathy. "What a terrible thing for you to go through."

"Yes, how awful for you, Allie." Zurina added her own heartfelt commiseration. "How could those people think you'd embezzle one dime from them?"

"We'll do everything we can to find Reggie and his gang." Trey's vow rang firm.

"Just say the word, George." Jack's grim glance slid toward the police chief. "We'll start right now."

Nubby gave a quick nod. "You just about got yourself a full-blown posse, right here in this room."

Their loyalty moved Allethaire, and emotion pushed up into her throat.

"Not so fast, boys." Mick set his glass down and moved toward her. His hand clasped her shoulder, and the warmth of his touch, his strength, soaked into her. "There's a few things we have to keep in mind."

Her father steepled his fingers under his chin. His silence commanded Mick to continue.

"Reggie's smart," Mick said. "He'll know we won't be able to track him. He's got the snow in his favor."

"Mick's right," the police chief said. "Hell of a lot of territory to cover, and it's plenty cold, besides. We can't just go charging out of here until we have more to go on."

"He's working with somebody in Minnesota." Mick nodded his conviction. "That's how he knew Allie would be on the Manitoba and that the money was in her trunk."

George consulted his notes. "So far, our best suspects are Jenny and—"

"No, not Jenny," Allethaire and her father interrupted in unison, both shaking their heads in finality. Allethaire would go to her grave believing the woman who had been like a mother to her was innocent of any wrongdoing. Ever.

The police chief swung his glance between both

of them, jotted a notation, then checked his notes again. "Which leaves the Ladies Literary Aid Society...and Charles Renner."

"Damn him!"

Allethaire jumped at her father's explosive outburst. He bolted from his chair and jabbed a finger at George.

"It'd be just like Charles to do something like this to me. Wire the Minneapolis police chief immediately and have him investigated. He's your man, I'll warrant!"

"But—"

"He's got connections to the bank where the Ladies Literary Aid Society kept their funds. He's just devious enough to use my daughter against me!"

"But—"

"Revenge, George! Revenge!" Her father fairly shook with impatience and frustration. "Why didn't I see it before now?"

Allethaire leaned forward in alarm. "Are you sure, Daddy? He was always the perfect gentleman to me. He was very enthusiastic about my library idea, too, and—"

"I'll just bet he was." Her father's lip curled with contempt. "He was merely a wolf in sheep's clothing, Allie. I've know him years longer than you have, so you can trust me on that."

She blinked and sat back. Handsome, charming Charles? Always efficient, full of ideas and quick to help? A wolf, driven for revenge?

She didn't know what to make of it. It didn't seem possible, and yet…her father was almost never wrong, and she *did* trust him. Trusted him more than she trusted herself.

"Well?" He swung back to the police chief. "What are you standing there for, George? Get moving!"

"Yes, sir. Certainly, sir."

Everyone in the room knew that when Paris Gibson barked an order, obedience was the best recourse. It was all part of his power, his influence and ability to accomplish great things.

Clearly the Great Falls police chief was no different. Flustered, he stuffed the notepad into an inside pocket of his jacket and headed for the hallway.

"On second thought, I'll ride into town with you," her father said suddenly. "I'm going to hire a private detective. Charles won't get away with any of this!" He headed for the hall, too, and the coat tree heavy with their wraps. On an apparent afterthought, he swung back toward Allethaire. "You're coming with us, aren't you, honey?"

"I'd like her to stay here, at the ranch." Mick spoke before Allethaire could. That he dared to defy the almighty Paris Gibson left her taken aback.

"You would?" she asked.

"Yes, I quite agree." Zurina exchanged a quick glance with Mick and hastened forward. "Really, Paris. She's hardly had a chance to thaw out from her ride in from the line camp. After what she's been through, she needs a hot bath and a good long nap."

A bath? A nap? Allethaire pressed her fingers to her lips to hold in a squeak of longing.

Mick's fingers curled around the back of her neck in a possessive gesture that revealed he had no intention of letting her leave. "Plans are to go out today and find a tree to decorate. Allie hasn't had much of a chance to enjoy Christmas so far, and I'm hoping she'll want to help."

Her heart fairly sang with an anticipation she hadn't felt in so very long. She barely kept from jumping up from the couch and throwing her arms around Mick's neck.

"I would love to help decorate," she said quietly instead.

"Well, that settles it." Margaret hefted her bulk from the couch. "George, I will follow you into town. I have too much work to do at the restaurant." She patted Allethaire's arm and winked. "I have brought your trunk, dear. The Manitoba's conductor asked that I make sure you get it. It is so heavy, I think you have brought plenty of your belongings and can stay a long time."

A long time. Here, in Montana, at the WCC.

Allethaire didn't know what to make of that, either. But, oh, it was almost too much to hope for.

"I expect you to come visit me in town." Margaret winked. "Folks around here love your pa so much, and they will want to get to know and love you, too."

"Thank you," she said, touched by the offer. By the kindness of her words, especially. "I'd like to do that."

Looking pleased, Margaret headed toward the coat tree, too.

"Well, Allie?" Her father waited, his thick brow arched. "You're sure you don't mind staying?"

She thought of his apartment, of how it'd be well-appointed yet fashionably austere and would possess none of the warmth and friendliness of the Wells' home.

But most of all, his apartment wouldn't have Mick.

"I'm sure." She stood and hugged her father. "If Trey and Zurina will have me, I'd like to stay here."

"Of course, they'll have you," Mick growled. "Or else."

His sister laughed, and so did his half brother, and before Allethaire knew it, everyone left.

Leaving her to bask in the strangely pleasurable sensation of being left behind.

By midafternoon, the sun shone high and warmed the air to just the right temperature, making a ride out to the nearby bluffs a pleasant excursion.

Mick slid a covert glance toward the beautiful woman on the horse beside him and amended the thought.

Having Allie with him hiked a "pleasant excursion" up to a downright *perfect* one.

He couldn't believe his good fortune. He'd spent the rest of the morning and part of the afternoon doing chores to give her time to have that bath Zurina promised and whatever else a woman did to while away a good portion of the day. But when Allie emerged from the house, dressed in her chinchilla-trimmed hat and coat, looking refreshed and relaxed and so gut-wrenchingly elegant, well, Mick figured the wait was worth every minute.

Not once in all the weeks and months that she'd been on his mind did he think he'd ever have the privilege of being with her like this. The freedom. That she'd even agreed to stay at the ranch and not with Paris was a big surprise. That she wanted to ride with him, just the two of them, to pick out a Christmas tree for Zurina proved to be the biggest surprise of all.

"It's all so majestic, isn't it?" she said in an awed voice.

His ruminating fell apart. "What is?"

"Being out here."

She sat in the saddle with ease, and her body rocked gently with the horse's gait. Mick's staring wouldn't stop. A woman with her grace and bearing, with the Bear Tooth Mountains and the pristine snow as a backdrop…she made a fetching sight a man couldn't forget.

"Not sure 'majestic' is the word I'd use," he murmured, thinking more along the lines of what he'd like to do with her while they were all alone out here on this majestic range of his. Lusty things like finding someplace warm and private and making long, slow love to her. Giving them both a Christmas gift neither would forget...

As if she knew the way of his thoughts, her mouth softened in amusement. "It's very majestic, Mick. Being out here is like having our own winter scene for Currier & Ives."

"For who?" The unfamiliar names distracted his fantasy.

"Currier and Ives." She blinked in surprise. "Haven't you heard of them?"

His defenses marched into place. The question struck a raw spot that had been growing more inflamed of late.

"Never," he said, hating to admit it. "Should I have?"

"Their work is all the rage."

"I wouldn't know."

A moment passed. He could feel her watching him.

"I understand. Well, they're printmakers, Mick. Their colored lithographs are quite lovely and increasingly popular with the American public."

But not with a Basque cowboy who had never in his life set foot outside the territory to see one.

Nor had most of his people, his Basque family, who had grown up living poor with very narrow, very uncultured lives.

With no hope of changing. As long as sheep-herding dominated their survival and consumed their hope, their lives wouldn't get better. They'd never experience or enjoy the finer things in life that those who were wealthier and more well-bred took for granted.

Like Currier and Ives lithographs—or whatever the hell they were called.

His mood darkened from another onslaught of guilt. He'd been given a whole slew of privileges on account of the Wells bloodline he'd inherited, a wealth he had yet to truly earn, and he had a responsibility, an increasingly fierce *need*, to share. To give some of those privileges back to the people who'd made him the man he was.

And the need in him wasn't going away anytime soon.

"I'll show you one sometime," Allie said. "If you'd like."

They approached low-lying foothills. Beyond them, higher up, his people lived their unassuming existence, the core of which would include staying warm and having enough food to get them through the harsh winter.

He knew those things, of course, since he'd once lived in those hills, having grown up with Zurina in a small Basque community hidden behind the pines, too far away to see.

But it was there. An entire community with no future.

"Mick? Is everything all right?"

Allie's question reminded him he'd yet to respond to her offer to see one of those pictures she liked so much, but what did it matter? How would it help?

He scowled and reined in. "Yeah. Everything's just fine."

Looking skeptical, she reined in, too. She opened her mouth, then closed it again. Swiveled her glance toward the foothills. And swiveled it back toward him.

"All right," she said carefully, as if she understood what haunted him but didn't quite know what to do about it.

Mick dismounted and went for a change of subject. "We'd best get started on finding a tree. It'll get dark fast out here."

She dismounted, too. "Zurina wants a big, fat one."

He squinted an eye over the dark green expanse of junipers, firs and pines spread out for miles around them and above them. All shapes and sizes, too many to count.

"Shouldn't be a problem," he drawled, going for his ax.

Snow crunched beneath her fur-trimmed boots. She stopped in front of a Douglas fir, stepped back and set her hands on her hips, giving the thing some serious consideration.

"How about this one?" she called back to him.

A corner of his mouth lifted. It was fat, all right. And twice as tall as she was. She had an eye for pretty trees, but no comprehension of the logistics.

"Too heavy for my horse to pull," he said. "And way too big to get through the front door." His gloved fingers worked at unhooking a coil of rope from his saddle. He didn't even mention not having an ax big enough to cut through the trunk. "Keep looking."

Snow crunched again. She disappeared from sight, but he could hear her moving around.

"Come take a look at this one, Mick," she called

again, her voice faintly muffled through the branches. "Oh, never mind. It's too big, too."

"Don't go out far, Allie. I'll join you in a minute."

He left her to her devoted search. Obviously she took great pride in the honor of choosing a tree in Zurina's place. With Trey busy with ranch chores, Zurina hadn't wanted to take her baby into the cold and had opted to stay home and unpack Christmas decorations until Mick and Allie returned with the perfect tree in tow.

Mick hobbled their horses, hefted the coiled rope onto his shoulder and grabbed his ax. Allie's footprints in the fresh snow would make finding her easy, and he took his time in perusing the pines along the way. He didn't much blame her in being fussy in her choosing, but he had to make sure the job got done in plenty of time to get back to the ranch before dark.

Spurred by the thought, he shoved a glance through the needle-heavy branches behind him and glimpsed the ranch in the distance. He tilted his head and studied the sky, gauging how long before the sun would set.

Not long. He'd have to prod Allie to make her decision soon. He hadn't seen or heard from her, in awhile, and an unexpected ripple of unease tumbled down his spine.

Might be he was overreacting, but suddenly, he needed to see her. Know that she was safe. It'd be just like her to get so wrapped up in her tree-choosing that she'd wander off farther than she intended.

And damned if he hadn't left his Winchester strapped to his saddle.

He debated going back for it, just in case, but discarded the idea as soon as it took shape. Retracing his steps would take too much time and would only delay his finding her. Besides, he likely wouldn't need it anyway.

He kept telling himself he wouldn't.

But his steps quickened through the snow. Suddenly, from somewhere high above him, a hawk noisily flapped his wings and took flight, jogging branches and leaving behind a soft dusting of snow in his wake. Mick didn't know if he'd startled the bird, or if something else did, but when another hawk flew off, too, his unease sharpened.

Something was out here, in the woodlands. Maybe it was Allie, or a bear, or something smaller, like a wolf, but something had disturbed the hawks.

In the next moment, a sharp gunshot confirmed it.

Chapter Nine

Allie's heart jumped into her throat.

Oh, God. *Mick!*

Had he fired the shot? Or had someone shot at him? Was he hurt? Dying? Already dead?

She whirled toward the sound, but the echo rippling through the pines proved confusing. Had the shot come from farther out—or right here in the woodlands? In truth, it seemed to come from behind her, or was it more toward her left? Was someone watching her? Was Mick looking for her?

The questions slammed back and forth inside her brain. Though her frantic gaze clawed through the branches, she couldn't see anything. Couldn't hear anything. And without thought to the wisdom of what she was doing, without a care to her own safety, she picked up her skirt hems and ran through the snow back to their horses, her terror building at what she'd find when she got there.

* * *

Mick pressed his body against the trunk of a ponderosa pine. With the tree's high crown of branches that kept him covered in shadows, his vantage afforded him an unobstructed view of the two men mounted on horses not ten yards in front of him.

A gray-feathered grouse had dropped from the sky and landed dead in the snow. Supper, evidently, for Reggie and his gang. Which meant they were holed up somewhere nearby.

"I told you not to fire," Reggie snapped, though he was the first to holster his revolver and slide out of his saddle. "You forget how close we are to the Wells' spread? Someone could've heard."

"The bird just flew up in front of me, Reg. I had to shoot."

Sighing his disgust, Reggie stood over the fowl. "You have any idea how to cook one of these?"

"Carl will know."

Mick digested the information. Seemed the three-man gang was still together, with one of them—Carl—left behind. To likely guard the money they stole while Reggie and this one ventured out.

He studied Reggie's accomplice. He had some Indian in him, but he wore the clothes of a white man. Mick committed him to memory. The police chief would need to know as many details as possible to help with his investigation.

Reggie grasped the grouse by the legs and straightened. "Let's get out of here."

"Hold on. I'll tie the bird to my saddle. He's too heavy to carry."

"Hurry it up."

Reggie stood facing the other man's horse, his back to Mick. Mick knew he had to do something, and do it fast. He couldn't just let the two ride out. They had to account for their crimes, for stealing Allie's library money, especially, and who knew how long it'd be before the law would catch up to them?

But Mick was keenly aware he wasn't armed, and the outlaws were. Second after valuable second passed while Mick debated the two simple weapons he did have....

Using more guts than brains, he stepped out from behind the ponderosa with the lariat swinging in his hand. He'd learned how to rope plenty of ornery calves during the past few years, and throwing the hemp around a man standing stock-still and unaware only a few yards away was going to be as easy as pie.

The loop found its mark, and Mick jerked the rope hard; the noose tightened around Reggie's torso, pinned his arms to his sides and knocked him flat on his back in the snow. He yelled out an enraged oath. Mick held the rope taut with his boot clamped against the slack.

The other outlaw went for his revolver, just like Mick expected.

"Drop the gun, or you'll have an ax in your chest by the time you take your next breath," he snarled. "And it'll be your last."

The outlaw froze. His eyes locked on the lethal tool Mick held up, aimed and ready to throw.

"Do it, Boone," Reggie said, his glance jumping between them. "Drop the gun like he says."

"The hell I will," Boone said, but he looked as nervous as a prostitute in church.

"We got to figure he's not alone." Reggie's voice hissed. "Even if he is, you fire that gun again, and this place'll be crawlin' with WCC cowboys in no time."

Boone licked his lips. But still he didn't move.

"I got a deal to make with him," Reggie added, sounding more desperate than he did before. "And I can't hardly talk when I'm all laid out like this, can I? So do what I'm tellin' you, Boone, and do it *now*."

Mick took plenty of comfort in knowing Reggie didn't have an inkling of Allie being out here, too. Mick prayed she had the sense to stay away, even though she would've heard the gunshot, same as he did....

The weapon dropped into the snow, and Boone's expression revealed he wasn't too happy in letting it go. Mick didn't like he was still on his horse, but Reggie had started clawing at the rope around him, and Mick had his hands full keeping him tied up and under control.

"Stand up, Reggie. Real easy. Then take that holster off and throw it, as far as you can." Mick took a step toward Boone's half-buried revolver, the urge running strong in him to be armed. "I'm not interested in any kind of a deal, so save your breath and just do what I tell you."

The outlaw managed to get to his feet, carefully unbuckling his holster. "Listen, Mick. You and me, we got cheated out of that ransom money three years ago. Remember? With Woodrow?"

Mick's lip curled at the ugly memory of their combined stupidity. "I remember."

"The Gibson woman, she got lucky, that's all.

The posse got to her before we could get our money."

"I remember that, too." The law, saving Mick and Reggie from themselves.

"Yeah, well, we could do it again, you know," the outlaw said. His holster dangled from his fingers, then fell to the ground. "We can do it right, just the two of us."

Mick narrowed an eye. "You asking me to gang up with you on another heist, Reggie?"

"Something like that."

Boone stiffened. "What the hell are you talkin' about?"

"Shut up!" Reggie snapped, shooting him a look that would melt coal.

"Seems to me you got plenty of her money the other day, Reg," Mick said coolly. "When you stole it from her on the Manitoba."

A slow grin curved Reggie's mouth. "And there's plenty more where that came from. If you're interested."

Interested?

Mick was interested, all right. For reasons Reggie was too brainless, too greedy, to fathom. Before Mick could peel any more information from him, movement from the trees stopped him.

Allie stepped into the clearing, looking like she'd come to life right out of the pages of some high-fashion magazine. Only the rifle against her shoulder destroyed the illusion; the steadiness of her grip and the determination in her expression revealed she hated Reggie enough to use it.

"You're going to give that money back to me, Reggie," she said with a calm that raised the hairs on the back of Mick's neck. "You're going to tell us who you're working with, too."

The outlaw paled, but recovered fast from his surprise. "I ain't tellin' you nothing."

"Then you'll die right here."

She issued the warning with cold-blooded intent. Knowing it, hearing it, scared the hell out of Mick.

Wasn't right a woman should have to avenge the wrongs done against her like this. That she planned to do so with his own rifle while he stood by and watched stuck in his craw even more.

"Come over here, Allie," he said softly. "Give me my gun."

"I can do this," she said, not taking her eyes off Reggie. "Your job is to not let them get away."

Therein lay the trouble. Mick couldn't keep Reggie hog-tied with Boone still on his horse, ready to bolt any minute, and it didn't matter neither of them wore their shooting irons. What mattered was that Mick was at more of a disadvantage than they were.

Worse, Allie couldn't shoot both outlaws at the same time. If it came to that. And it likely would, any second now.

A fierce need to feel a weapon in his hand surged strong within him, and he dared another step toward Boone's, still half-buried only a few feet away.

Reggie's attention followed him.

Understanding flickered in his venomous eyes.

Then…like twin bolts of lightning, they both dove for the guns—Mick for Boone's, Reggie for his own. The rope fell loose. Reggie twisted and kicked out, making a vicious connection with Mick's jaw. Pain exploded like liquid fire through his bones; his head snapped back, and he rolled backward in the snow.

From the feathery fringes of consciousness, through the flames of pain, a gunshot registered in Mick's brain. Hoofbeats rumbled across the earth…and then, everything fell silent.

He didn't know how long he laid there, all sprawled out in the snow, but when he came to, Allie's face swam into focus.

"I think we should call Doc Shehan," she said, sounding worried.

She laid a hand against his cheek; the cool leather from her gloves soothed the throbbing in his jaw. He wanted to tell her he was fine and not to bother the good doctor. After all, it was Christmas Eve.

But the blurred shape of someone else's face distracted him. All around him, low voices rumbled.

"He's coming to." Trey. He was here, with Allie?

"Looks like he'll live."

Damned right he was going to live. Mick groaned and tried to sit up. Jack slid an arm around his shoulders and saved him the trouble of doing it himself.

"Take it easy, Mick. Is your jaw broke?" he demanded.

Mick opened his mouth to find out. Closed it. Wiggled it. Did everything all over again, only faster. He hurt like the dickens, but the jaw seemed to work the way it should.

"He'll live," Trey repeated, but he sounded more relieved this time.

"Oh, thank God."

Mick swiveled toward Allie's soft voice. He wondered how long she'd been kneeling beside him, hanging onto his hand in a death grip. For the time it took the WCC outfit to come running?

His arms ached to take her against him, but a few matters needed clarifying first.

"Where's Reggie?" he asked, sounding hoarse.

"Dead." She gave him a solemn nod of assurance. "Over there."

Mick turned. The body lay within reaching distance; blood stained the snow crimson.

"I killed him," she said, matter-of-fact.

He frowned. "I figured."

"But the other one got away." Allie shifted her glance toward the horizon and sighed in obvious regret.

"Boone," Mick recalled.

"Yes." She turned back. "Boone."

Mick marveled at what she'd done. The courage she'd shown. The strength. "Couldn't be helped, Allie."

Her mouth curved downward. "We still don't know where the money's at, though, and that's what I wanted most. The money back."

"The police will find them." Mick was convinced of it. "They'll get the answers we need. The money, too."

And whoever set her up, Mick added silently.

If it was the last thing he ever did, he intended to find the mastermind behind the theft.

"I hope you're right." But she looked unconvinced.

"I am. Come on. Let's go home."

He stood, shakily, bringing her with him.

She bit her lip. "What about Reggie?"

Trey rose, too. "Jack and I will take care of him."

She appeared relieved. Then, she cocked her head toward Mick. "But we can't leave yet."

He frowned. "Why not?"

"We still have to find a tree. Remember?"

Damn. He hadn't.

"I've found the perfect one," she said. "I know right where it is."

How could he deny her? It was Christmas, after all.

Twining her fingers with his, she led him out of the clearing and deeper into the pines.

Chapter Ten

Later That Night

Wrapped in the golden glow of a single lamp, Allie sat nestled in the corner of the parlor's velvet couch with her knees pulled up and her hands curled around a cup of warm mulled cider. A thick woolen afghan covered her lap. Her belly was still full from the festive dinner Zurina had served earlier: roasted lamb—*cordero asado*, she'd learned—with potatoes and all the trimmings, followed by a delightful Basque almond candy called *turron* for dessert.

It had been a Christmas Eve she would always remember. The exotically different foods, the laughter, the exuberant songs—all were Basque traditions that had given her special insight into Mick's life. They'd helped shape him into the man he'd become.

Afterward, when the table was cleared, they decorated the tree, and the fragrant scent of fresh-cut pine still lingered throughout the room. Ribbons and strung popcorn draped the stately branches; strands of cranberries glistened like rich jewels in the lamplight. She couldn't recall ever seeing a tree more beautiful.

Now, the Wells' household had retired for the night, but Allie couldn't sleep. Not after such a glorious and tumultuous day.

Who would've guessed she'd ever kill a man in her lifetime? Who could've known?

But pull the trigger she had, and with few regrets. Reggie would've killed Mick if she hadn't kept him from it. He might have killed her, too….

But oh, when word of what she'd done sailed across the miles to Minneapolis, her already shredded reputation would never be the same. The gossips would smack their lips, rub their hands together and the scandal would catch fire all over again.

Allie Gibson, outlaw killer.

Allie. Not Allethaire.

She stared down into her cooling cider. Funny how she'd come to think of herself as a new person. A stronger one. Tonight, the wine flowed freely, but she'd had no desire for its numbing effects.

She'd had no pain to chase away. No fears to bury, if only for a little while.

She had Mick to thank for that. She had only to look into his dark eyes and feel his power, his strength. Somehow, knowing he was near, his strength became hers, too.

Even more important, though, never once had he considered her guilty of stealing the Ladies Literary Aid Society's money. Instead he'd protected her and vowed to find the truth, and she trusted he would—one day soon. He showed her what a safe and happy life in Montana Territory could be like. The friends that could be made. She'd seen, too, the closeness he enjoyed with his family. The loyalty the entire WCC outfit paid him and Trey.

He'd built a simple but powerful life, without the pretenses of the big city. And, at some point during the time she'd been with him, a longing had bloomed inside her to share his happiness with him.

Yet what right did she have to want such a thing? Because her life in Minneapolis was over?

Or because she'd fallen in love with him?

At some point, that had happened, too. The realization filled her heart with hope and warmed her blood, leaving her not at all sure what to do about it.

The cheerful chimes from the clock on the mantel struck once, twice, announcing Christmas Day was already two hours old, and what had she done to prepare for it? She had no gifts for anyone. Not her father. Not Zurina or Trey. Not even Mick.

Especially Mick, who had given her so much. Tenderness and caring and kisses that filled her with a hunger the likes of which she'd never before experienced.

Therein lay her restlessness. A disturbing and frightening uncertainty of where to go from here.

If not for the hard work she'd spent formulating her plans for a beautiful new library, she had nothing to show for her accomplishments the past several years. Nothing to share, to give to the people who deserved it most....

Her heart skipped a beat.

Her eyes widened.

Slowly she put aside her cider and sat up.

Or did she?

The library was her greatest effort. Her pride and joy. When before had she been able to give a finer gift?

To those who deserved it most!

Filled with a sudden rush of excitement, of renewed anticipation for Christmas, she flung back the afghan, scrambled off the couch and fled upstairs to her room.

Mick frowned at the light peeking out from beneath Allie's door. The dawn of Christmas Day would crest along the horizon soon. Time for his usual routine of morning chores, but he couldn't fathom why she'd be up at this early hour.

Curious, he nudged her door open and found her seated cross-legged and barefoot on the bed, looking feminine and appealing in her pink nightgown and robe. Her blond hair flowed loose and easy down her back. Papers covered the quilt in a neat crescent in front of her, and she wielded her pencil with an intense concentration that kept her from noticing he was there.

He could no more stay away from her than not breathe, and he stepped inside, carefully latching the door closed. The muted click pricked her attention, and her startled glance lifted.

"Mick!" she gasped.

He put a finger to his lips. "Shh. You'll wake Catalin."

She held up a hand in mute command to keep him from getting closer.

"Go away," she said in a loud whisper, but something about the light in her eyes belied the words.

"Why?" His curiosity raged. He kept coming.

"I don't want you to see what I'm doing yet."

He halted at the side of her bed. "When then?"

She splayed her fingers over the papers, hiding them from view. "Soon. I'm just not ready to show you *yet*."

Gently, firmly, he removed her hands. "Show me what?"

He deciphered sketches of something. A building. He tilted his head to see it better. A very intriguing looking building, three stories high and cathedral-like.

She swept her hair behind one ear. Tapped her pencil in obvious procrastination to keep from answering.

"Your Christmas gift," she said finally.

He blinked down at her in stunned surprise.

"Come. Sit beside me. I'll show you." She patted the mattress, her excitement clearly growing.

He sat, and the bed dipped from their combined weight. Allie lifted a set of blueprints from beneath the pile of sketches.

"This is the library that the Ladies Literary Aid Society intended to build before—all the trouble began."

So *this* was the project that meant so much to her, he marveled. Damned shame she couldn't see the job done. His gaze soaked in the details of the structure. Handsome details, professionally drawn.

"And this—" she lifted a single sheet "—is an idea I had. To honor my father."

Mick studied that drawing, too. Noted the similarities to the blueprint. Saw her talent, the beauty of her vision.

"For Paris?" he asked, amazed, knowing the man couldn't help but be honored.

"Yes. I've modified the Minneapolis design, just quick changes, really. I know how much he's respected here in the territory for his work with the hydro-electric plant and all. Because of him, Great Falls is growing, but there's no school for higher learning here, and I thought that—that the town could use one. Named after him."

"It's a damned good idea, Allie." He meant it. Paris Gibson was fast proving himself an icon in the territory. Folks would fall over themselves in their haste to revere him in such a way.

She lifted another paper. And gently laid it on his lap.

"And this is for you," she said softly.

For a moment, Mick didn't move. "Me?"

"And the Basque people."

He stared at the penciled outline. A striking four-sided clock tower, incorporated into the school's design.

"The tower will be a symbol that will reach out across the territory for all to see. It will be a part of the school, a reminder that all are welcome. It will represent the time has come for Montana to prosper. My father's hydro-electric plant will be instrumental in that."

Emotion lodged in his chest. He stared and stared.

"Do you remember when you told me that change begins with the young?" she asked.

"Yes," he croaked.

"This design, my school, will be an opportunity to bring education to those who don't have the opportunities that others have. The Basque children, and so many others, will have a promising future inspired by knowledge."

Her generosity, her brilliance, humbled him. Filled him with a love and hunger that burned his throat and robbed him of words.

"It will take some doing, of course." She kept talking. Because he couldn't. "The towns-people will have to approve the venture. Funds will need to be raised. It could take months, probably a couple of years, before everything is said and done, but—"

An unsettling wave of unworthiness roared into him. He'd never be able to repay her. He'd never make her feel as happy, as complete, as she was making him feel right now. How could he, when he was only a sheepherder's son? A cattleman's bastard son? A cowboy, deep in his heart?

"Allie." He swallowed. "I can't—I'm not sure—I could never—"

"What's the matter, Mick?" She cocked her head. Though a small smile curved her lips, uncertainty dimmed the glitter of excitement in her eyes. "You don't like my idea?"

His brain scrambled for assurances, but their differences stifled them. Would they always?

"I know my reputation is in a shambles right now," she said, the admission coming in a fractured rush. "But I'll—"

"To hell with your reputation, shambles or otherwise," he growled, grasping her shoulders, desperate to make her believe.

"I'll find the truth in who stole the library's money, I swear."

"I swear it, too." His grasp tightened. "We all will."

"Then what is it, Mick?"

Still, he hesitated, his heart torn that she was high-society, and he was cattle and sheep. She knew only big city living. He'd never live anywhere else but on this wild, unforgiving land. She was born and bred culture, and nothing could change that. He was born and bred Basque and cowboy, and nothing would ever change *that*, and—

"I love you, Mick."

His worries screeched to a blazing halt.

She kept her gaze direct on his, and he almost fell into the pools of blue, darkening with a little desperation of her own. She knew his worries, his fears. Read them as plain as words on a page.

Because they matched her own?

His reservations crumbled.

"Allie. Sweet, sweet Allie. I love you. I'll always love you."

His arms took her against him; his mouth captured hers in a fervent declaration of all she made him feel. Love, happiness, exhilaration. Relief, too, that the burden of his responsibilities, his need to give back to his beloved Basque people, was lifted and shared by this incredible woman.

How had she known her dream could be so perfect? How could she have guessed she'd given him the most perfect of gifts?

How could she have *doubted?*

After long, delicious moments, his head lifted, and his finger traced the swollen wetness of her mouth. He intended to spend the rest of his life making sure she never doubted again.

"Guess that means you'll have to live in Montana for a spell," he murmured.

"I don't want to leave," she admitted in earnest. "Not for a single minute."

"Then live here as my wife, Allie. Make your home with me forever."

Her breath caught. "Your wife?" On the wings of an elated cry, she gifted him with a new plethora of kisses that assured him of forever. "Oh, Mick! Yes!"

He fell back with her against the pillows. With his heart filled with love, he showed her just how glad he was that she'd found her way home to him.

To live a lifetime of Christmases together.

* * * * *